I0534670

Baltimore, Maryland 1970. Nicole Redman found herself lost in an unforgiving world of outlaws whom she had grown to love, respect, and understand. Morally bankrupt by the rules of society, the outlaw bikers lived by one rule - an eye for an eye. The brotherhood ran deep, and Nicole 'Peaches' Redman was proud to call the Argots her family. In her wildest dreams, she had never imagined herself becoming a prostitute, a dancer, a biker chick, a murderer, or a reputed drug dealer. When life handed her lemons, she made lemonade.

The Wee Hours II: Peaches

PEACHES

THE WEE HOURS II

W.D. BURNS

Bad Ass Outlaw Publications

BAD ASS OUTLAW PUBLICATIONS
4216 Riverview Lane
Lorian, OH 44055
www.badassoutlawpublications.com

This book is an original publication of Bad Ass Outlaw Publications.

William Daniel Burns
PEACHES: THE WEE HOURS II
Library of Congress
Copyright 2010
TXu001889306
revised 2015

Editing, typesetting and cover design by J.D. Williams
(www.behance.net/jdwilliams)

ISBN: 978-0-9962651-9-5

Printed in The United States of America

10 9 8 7 6 5 4 3 2 1

PEACHES: THE WEE HOURS II

INDEX

Dedication

In loving memory of my best friend, Robert 'Bobby' Jenkins. We met when I was only sixteen, married, and employed at Wilson's Amoco on Mountain Road in Pasadena, Maryland. Bobby, his wife, and three children, two girls and a boy, lived at 587 Riverside Drive. Throughout his life, Bobby referred to me as his "other son." He loved his family dearly, and he led by example.

I would also like to dedicate this book to my former mother-in-law, Joyce O' Rourke Whitson. She thought it was so unfair to her when her daughter and I divorced. Joyce once told me that she didn't carry me beneath her heart, but that I grew in it.

Acknowledgements

Special thanks to Colleen Brown, for without her assistance this book would not have been possible. Props to my Editor in Cheif and friend, Ronnie Jones.

CHAPTER ONE
SNITCH ROAST

"The next time I tell you to steal a van, steal something worth stealing," Bulldog complained to Jammer. Bulldog was six-two, a solid two hundred and fifty pounds, with long brown hair and a full beard. His right hand man Jammer was an inch shorter with piercing blue eyes, long blonde hair and a thick beard. Five years earlier, when Bulldog was elected Sergeant of Arms for the Argot motorcycle club, the first member of Bulldog's crew was Jammer. He next picked Rooster, Cupcake, Kapote, and Tiny to help him run security and protection for the outlaw club. Recently, J.D. became their newest Prospect.

"It's rusty, but trusty," Jammer cracked.

The Ford van was white, rusty, leaking oil badly, and blowing clouds of smoke out of the exhaust. There was no time to argue, they were already at their destination. It was 4 a.m. and they had unfinished business to take care of.

Bulldog parked the van a few doors down from the red brick row-house, located at 20 West Pratt street, grateful the six cylinder engine was at least quiet. They were less than ten blocks from the harbor, making the blowing wind bone chilling cold. As the crew quickly filed out of the van, crystals of snow danced around a street lamp at the corner. Turning their collars up to protect them from the bitter cold, they each grabbed their toboggan masks, and followed behind Tiny to the front door. While Bulldog looked up and down the street, the other men watched for any movement on the quiet street. A car, a person, a curtain suddenly opening, or a light coming on in a neighboring house. It took Tiny less than one minute to pick the lock on the front door of the row-house, and even less time than that for them all to crowd silently inside, where they all covered their faces. A stairway to their right led to the upstairs bedrooms. Bulldog took the lead, creeping up the stairs, careful not to make any noise. The first bedroom was empty, but in the second Roger Pickett was curled up in a fetal position covered in a blanket. He was alone so they removed their masks. Cupcake, Tina, and Rooster stood on one side of the bed, while Kapote, Jammer, and J.D. stood on the other side of the bed.

"Good morning!" Bulldog announced loudly, flipping a light switch to light up the room. Bulldog stood at the foot of the bed as a startled Roger Pickett popped up like a jack in the box. He looked around at the sight of the men surrounding the bed and his eyes went wide in terror. In a modest gesture he snatched up the blanket to cover himself. It was a pathetic sight, a reaction someone would anticipate coming from a girl.

"What do you want?" He screeched in a high voice.

"You're not in a position to be asking questions. Don't talk, just listen. Follow my instructions and I promise that when we leave, which will be in about five minutes, you will be alive and unharmed. Nod if you understand?" Bulldog grinned.

Roger nodded, his eyes tearing.

"Lay down and stretch your arms out to the side of the bed." Roger complied. The Prospect handed Jammer a rope from inside his jacket, and Bulldog instructed Jammer and Tiny to run the rope beneath the bed. Bulldog tied Roger's hands and feet tightly to the bed,

"I've got six hundred dollars in my wallet," Roger yelled.

Bulldog grabbed the pants draped across the back of a chair next to the bed, removed the wallet, and took the six hundred dollars. "Why thank you, Roger."

The men around the bed laughed. J.D. stepped forward, looked at the pathetic sight of Roger Pickett, and said, "Open wide!" As Roger opened his mouth J.D. jammed an apple in it, then wrapped binding tape around his head to hold the apple in place.

Bulldog took a knife from his pocket, bared two wires and connected them. He placed a chair next to the bed, set a timer for five minutes, then placed the bare wires in a pile of gunpowder. When the timer went off, it would create a huge spark.

"Do you remember your old friend, Charlie? Charlie Redman, the guy you grew up with, The two of you went to grade school together. The guy who sold you cocaine, and the guy you set up for the police. Well my friend, we are here to insure that it doesn't happen a second time. Charlie has such a forgiving nature. Unfortunately for you, I don't. And when you fuck over one of us, you fuck over all of us. However, I always keep my promises. I promised that when we left you would be alive and unharmed." After saying this, Bulldog doused Roger from head to toe with a gallon of camper fuel. "We're leaving now," Bulldog whispered with a smile.

Roger was already crying and struggling to free himself from his bonds, muffled sounds escaping from around the apple in his mouth. The crew locked the door behind them as they exited the row-house. They sat in the van with the engine running. Bulldog rolled a joint, lit it, and passed it around. When they saw flames coming from the upstairs bedroom, Bulldog drove away.

They parked the stolen van in front of a store on East Broadway, then walked to the corner of Fleet Street and turned left. The Wee Hours was less than a block down the street on the left. Ramrod, the club president, was inside the after-hour club waiting for them. Bulldog grinned broadly as he walked through the door with his crew. Ramrod was bellied up to the bar talking with the club owner, Gus Valakos. It was illegal for the club to sell alcohol, so it was sold to members only and served in clear plastic cups. Seeing his brothers entering the club, Ramrod grinned and took a sip from his cup. Gus glanced in the direction of the door and watched as the bikers filed in, one after another.

Bulldog and his crew were happy to get inside out of the bitter cold. Ramrod pulled Bulldog to the side and asked if everything had gone according to plan.

"We had ourselves a nice little snitch roast," Bulldog bragged.

Fifteen minutes later the crew piled into Ramrod's emerald green 1970 Chevrolet Caprice Classic and drove away, returning to the cabin in Pennsylvania. The cabin sat on a hundred acres just outside of Harrisburg.

* * *

The fire was reported at four twenty-two in the morning. When the fire department responded, the entire upstairs was engulfed in flames. Neighbors were evacuated from their homes and forced to stand outside in the bitter cold. They wrapped themselves in blankets, stood on the sidewalk, teeth chattering.

At that moment, Roger's upstairs bedroom window blew outward.

"I hope we can get this fire under control before it spreads to the adjacent row-houses," one of the fire-fighters shouted.

"Is there anyone inside?" The Fire Chief questioned the onlookers.

An elderly lady stepped forward. "As far as I know, there's only one tenant. A young man, who, I believe, is an unemployed carpenter."

"That's his black Ford Bronco parked across the street," another neighbor added.

A foul stench passed through the upstairs bedroom window. The stench was nauseating and unmistakable. It was the smell of burnt flesh.

As the fire subsided the row-house became a crime scene, the police cordoning off the front of the building with yellow tape. A call was placed to the Baltimore City Homicide Division.

Betty Crawford was the first detective to arrive on the scene, trailed a few minutes later by Detective Marks, who parked his white Cadillac Coupe Deville in the middle of the street. The entire street was packed bumper to bumper with emergency service vehicles. Marks stepped out of his car, turned up the collar of his long tan overcoat, stopping to stick a cigar in his mouth and lighting it.

"Damn, it's cold!" He announced as he approached Betty. In the summer, he had affectionately referred to her as 'Twinkle Toes' because of her exposed polished toe-nails. Today her toes were covered with insulated thermal boots. Everyone at the station thought Detective Marks strongly resembled the movie star, Jackie Gleason. Betty was easy on the eyes, and she could out think, out wit, and probably out fight most of the men in the department. She held a third degree black belt in karate. Despite all this, Detective Marks still felt a woman's place was in the home.

"What do we have here?" Marks asked.

"I just arrived myself." Betty Crawford reported, then added. "But there's obviously a burnt body inside. The neighbors said a single white male lives in the residence. That's his black Ford Bronco parked across the street.

A fire-fighter exited the still smoking structure and made a bee-line directly for the two detectives. "The Chief asked me to let you know that there's a crispy critter in one of the second floor bedrooms. The bedroom is on the left."

The Fire Chief joined them a few minutes later. "By the time the Fire Inspector arrives the fire should have cool down enough for you to enter. It should be no more than another twenty minutes."

It was closer to a half an hour before the Fire Inspector arrived from investigating another fire across town. Due to the freezing cold the spectators had long since escaped inside the warmth of their homes.

"Is this your first burnt body?" Detective Marks asked Betty as they made their way inside the row-house.

"Yes." She frowned, wondering for the first time why she had not chosen another profession a long time ago.

"Do you think you can stomach it? It's a gruesome sight."

"I'll do my best, Sir."

At the sight of the charred body, Betty took two steps backwards and puked to the side. The sight and smell was horrific.

"Step outside and get some fresh air. There's not much we can do here. I'll make a report of how the body was discovered. You can call forensics. Hopefully, they will be able to discover something."

"Yes, Sir." She replied, pinching her nose with two fingers and rushing towards the open door,

"Release the body to the coroner for an autopsy." Detective Marks ordered before he departed the building.

Betty Crawford was glad she had dressed warmly. She wore a heavy wool multicolored winter jacket with a detachable hood, covered her hands in soft latex leather gloves, and securely wrapped a white knitted scarf around her neck. Even with the precaution taken, she felt the icy cold cutting into her, causing her to shiver.

"Go home! I'll see you at the office in the morning." Detective Marks suggested as he walked past her in the direction of his car. He stopped long enough to unlock the car door, stuck a cigar in his mouth, lit it, and said to himself, "This is one Hell of a way to start a New Year." It was January 2, 1970.

* * *

Nicole's ex-husband, Charlie Redman, had served time for possession of marijuana and while incarcerated at the Maryland House of Correction, he met Brad Bernhagen. Brad's nickname was 'Juice' and he was well known for making homemade wine. Prisoners called it 'hooch', military personal labeling it 'spud juice'. By any name it served its intended purpose. It got guys drunk.

During their time in prison Brad told Charlie stories about his life in Florida as a drug dealer. Charlie doubted the stories of his selling large quantities of marijuana and cocaine, especially when Brad never received money the entire time he was in prison. But when Juice was released on parole, he sent Charlie photos of girls on the beach, wearing string bikinis, and most important of all a hundred dollar money order each month.

When Charlie was released from prison, Brad sent him a kilo of cocaine with a note telling him to get on his feet. With the proceeds from the sell of the drugs, Charlie's first purchase was a blue 1965

Corvette Stingray.

Before he knew it, Charlie found himself working as a drug smuggler alongside Brad. Once a month he would fly into Naples, Florida, and they would use Brad's Donzi speed boat to meet a freighter or shrimp boat twelve miles out to sea, where they would off load the packages of cocaine. For helping to smuggle the drugs under the cover of darkness, each month Charlie was sent a kilo of cocaine through the United States Postal Service. Charlie's loyalty led to an introduction to drug kingpin, John Leder. With his friend Brad's support, Charlie was offered the opportunity to sell unlimited amounts of cocaine. Unsure of his ability to move large amounts, he was given fifty kilos of cocaine to get him started.

Using the resources of his ex-wife, Charlie was soon moving ten kilos at a time to the Argots biker gang. He felt extremely blessed for these past events and especially for the aid of Nicole. He could still recall the circumstances surrounding the initial sell of the drugs. Charlie's cost was $18,000 per kilo, his original selling price set at $28,000 for each kilo. Acting on her own, Nicole agreed to sell kilo's to the outlaw biker club for $25,000 a piece. When she informed him of the arrangements, he had been highly upset.

"I've made a deal to sell ten kilos of cocaine." She had spoken quietly, due to the fact they had been sitting in a Truck Stop.

"What's the deal?" He could recall his wide grin at the prospect of selling ten kilos.

"I'm selling ten kilos tomorrow for twenty-five thousand dollars each. I'm taking two thousand dollars a kilo for myself for putting the deal together and taking all the risks. Is that alright with you?"

"What happened to the twenty-eight thousand dollars a kilo. Do you think I'm nuts? Do you think I'm going to settle for a measly five thousand dollars a kilo for myself?"

Nicole's own angry words still rang in his head. "Do I think you're nuts? You stupid asshole!" She had leaned forward to hiss at him. "I'm making you fifty thousand dollars cash. By the end of a month, that's two hundred thousand dollars. In five months you will be a fuckin' millionaire. You tell me if you're nuts, Charlie. You are an ungrateful arrogant asshole."

While Nicole was making her deals, he was still very busy servicing his long time customers. One of those customers had been his childhood friend, Roger Pickett. Charlie had known Roger since the fourth grade. Roger was a small time hustler, whose hustle was cashing printed or stolen checks. Roger had impressed Charlie with his technique of faking fingerprints.

The larger grocery stores in the Baltimore area earned a nice profit through cashing checks, but they required a thumb print on the back of each check. Roger had developed a sure fire way of getting around this system. Roger would place clear fingernail polish on his right thumb, then spray it with Aquanet hair spray, leaving it tacky and ready for a quick imprint. Roger would then press his thumb to his big toe, his thumb print becoming the imprint of his big toe, the grocery stores in the area never knowing the difference between the two. Their life long friendship led Charlie to fronting him a eighth of an ounce of cocaine.

After leaving Charlie's house, Roger had gone to the grocery store, where he was busted for shop-lifting. While being searched the cocaine was discovered in his pants pocket. To avoid his being charged, Roger agreed to set up Charlie, neglecting to tell the police that he still owed Charlie for the drugs. The police gave Roger marked money and he agreed to wear a wire when he made the buy from Charlie.

Roger drove to Charlie's house, knocked on the front door and Charlie welcomed his friend inside. Roger handed Charlie two one hundred dollar bills and asked to purchase an eighth of an ounce of cocaine. After excepting the money, Charlie replied, "I don't have any, but I'm keeping this for the money you owe me."

Minutes after Roger left, the police stormed the house and confiscated the marked money from Charlie's pocket, then arrested him for trafficking in narcotics. The search of the house netted a scale, but no drugs.

Charlie called Nicole from the police station, informing her of the situation. She called Ramrod, the president of the Argots and he called Harold Glazer, the clubs attorney. Harold rushed to the jail and advised Charlie not to answer any questions.

"Always invoke your Fifth Amendment right to remain silent and refer the detectives to me," Harold said, before contacting the bails bondsman Fifi London to post bail.

The search warrant proved to be invalid because of an incorrect address, but it made no difference because no drugs had been found. When Harold reviewed Charlie's alleged recorded confession, he laughed heartily. In the recording Charlie could clearly be heard saying he had no drugs, and that he was keeping the money for a prior debt Roger owed him. There was no mention of drugs being sold or the debt involving the purchase of cocaine.

Harold Glazer's fee for representing Charlie was ten thousand dollars. The case was dismissed.

"That was pretty stupid of me," Charlie admitted to Nicole. "You were lucky, Charlie." She told him.

When Harold Glazer told Ramrod what happened to Charlie, they were able to put two and two together and learn the identity of their supplier. Someone had threatened the source of a large part of their business, and it was dealt with appropriately.

CHAPTER TWO
FIRECRACKER

Charlie awoke from an early night at 7 a.m., showered, dressed, and made himself a large breakfast of steak and eggs.

Since his arrest, he had been careful to watch his every move in case the police were watching him. He was sitting at the kitchen table reading the morning newspaper and sipping on a cup of coffee, when he heard the local news reporting on a suspicious fire on Pratt Street, leaving one man dead. The identity, though not yet confirmed, was believed to be the resident of the home, Roger Joseph Pickett.

Moments later, Charlie picked up the phone receiver and dialed Nicole's number. She answered on the fifth ring, "Hello?" He could hear her yawn into the phone.

"Have you seen the news?" he asked.

"No! I'm still in bed, Charlie. When I got off work last night, I went to Hector's, and I didn't leave until four-thirty this morning. What time is it?"

"Eight o'clock. Roger Pickett died in a suspicious fire last night," Charlie explained in one quick breath.

"Roger who?" Came the groggy reply.

"The same fucking Roger I've known all my life and that was at our wedding. The news reported that he died in a suspicious fire."

"Fuck that snitch!" She cursed, her voice clear for the first time. "I really don't give a shit. Why are you calling me?"

"Because suspicious circumstances spells murder, and the police will more than likely be knocking on my door. What am I supposed to do?"

"Don't answer the door. Invite them in for coffee and donuts. Or, lawyer up. Refer them to your attorney. What do you want from me, Charlie?"

"I don't know."

"Look. Do you still have Harold Glazer's phone number?"

"Yeah."

"Okay, good. If you're worried about it, call him. I'm sure he's going to advise you not to answer any questions or talk to the police. You can always refer the police to him."

"You're right." Charlie replied, sounding relieved.

"Goodbye Charlie." Nicole yawned, and hung up the phone.

Nicole laid in her warm bed, thinking about how much of an idiot Charlie could be. She snuggled into the comfort of the bed, grateful for having purchased the most comfortable mattress on the market. She wrapped her arms around an extra soft king-sized pillow, and snuggled some more.

Thirty minutes later, she was dozing into a deep sleep when the phone rang for a second time. It rang a dozen times before she answered, thinking that it was probably Charlie calling again. She guessed he wanted to tell her what the lawyer had said.

"Bitch, it's about time you picked up the fuckin' phone!" Bulldog growled.

"I thought you were Charlie calling back," she yawned,

"What does he want now?"

"After he watched the news this morning he called to tell me that the guy who set him up died in a suspicious fire last night. He was worried the police will want to question him. I told him if he was all that concerned, he should be calling Harold Glazer, not me."

"Good advice, baby. Don't forget this is the club's third anniversary. It's the party of the year, and it's mandatory that all the club members attend. That includes you."

"I'll be there," Nicole yawned, then as a second thought asked. "What are you doing calling this early?"

"I haven't been to bed yet. I stopped by the Wee Hours last night hoping to see you, but you never stopped by."

"Damn it! Wouldn't you know it. Last night after work I went to Hector's. And I've been wanting some dick for two days."

"Well, when are you going to be here so I can give you what you want?"

"When you least expect me." She told him with a light laugh.

"Friday or Saturday, right?" He asked, trying to get her to be more specific.

"Friday afternoon. And I better not catch you in bed with any of those skanks." Bulldog laughed, then hung up the phone.

Nicole turned over to go back to sleep, thinking that if she got up by two o'clock, it would give her just enough time to shower before meeting Marsha at her house. They would leave from Marsha's around three to go spend time with Manny. It was something they did every week. Manny had started out as nothing more than a trick for the two women, but now he was family and the time they spent together was very important to them all.

When Nicole opened her eyes she looked over at the alarm clock on the nightstand, it read 1:45 in the afternoon. She sat upright on the edge of the bed, then stood to walk to the bedroom window. She pulled back the curtain with her left hand. The vehicles in the parking lot below were covered with a blanket of snow, and a light flurry was still falling.

"I hate winter," she said to herself aloud. She dreaded the mere thought of venturing outside.

Nicole showered, dressed warm, then walked to the kitchen. She made herself two slices of toast with butter and marmalade jelly. She opened the dishwasher in search of a clean glass, next going to the refrigerator to pour herself a glass of orange juice from an open carton.

After breakfast, she laid out two lines of cocaine, carefully rolled up a dollar bill and sniffed a line into each nostril. It was an instant high. Throwing on a winter coat, she grabbed her purse and exited the apartment. Walking to the elevator she pressed the down button, patiently waiting for the elevator to chime to a stop on her floor. When it opened she stepped inside, pressed the bottom button on the shiny metal panel for the basement and underground parking garage. The button on the panel lit-up as the elevator effortlessly moved from one floor to the next, the ride both quiet and smooth. She giggled to herself as a vision of fucking Bulldog in the elevator passed through her mind. Damn, she could not believe how fucking horny she felt. The elevator stopped on a chime and the door slid open. Her silver Mercedes convertible was directly in front of her beneath its protective cover. Parked next to it was her beloved yellow Volkswagen. It held many fond memories for her. She had driven her daughter Charlotte to her first day of school in the little Bug. The Bug was her safe haven when she wept for the loss of Charlotte and Stormy, who were murdered at the hands of Domonic Coroza.

While other vehicles may have difficulty traveling in the rain, sleet, and snow of the Baltimore winters, the little Bug was relentless in pushing through the bad weather.

Thirty-minutes later Nicole parked the Bug in Marsha's driveway, walked to the front door, not bothering to knock before entering.

"Marsha?" She called out.

"Make yourself at home. I just got out of the shower, and I'm getting dressed."

Marsha's house was an immaculately clean red brick ranch home in a nice, quiet neighborhood. With five kids living in the house, Nicole was amazed to always find the house so well maintained.

"Should I call Manny to let him know that we're going to be a few minutes late?" Nicole shouted.

"Naw, he's not going anywhere, and he will be delighted to see us. How have you been?" Marsha smiled as she walked out of the bathroom.

"Okay." Nicole replied with a smile. It felt good to see Marsha, and she was looking especially stunning today. "Your hair is different." Nicole noted.

"I had it cut, frosted, and permed. Do you like it?" Marsha spun around, showing off her hair and her lush curves in tight, cream colored, dress slacks.

"You look absolutely amazing."

"Well, let's not keep Manny waiting too long."

As usual, they left the house in Marsha's Mustang convertible. "I love this car in the summer, and I hate it in the winter," she declared. The seats were ice cold, the windshield fogged over, and they drove for five miles before they felt any warmth from the heater.

Manny stood at the sliding glass doors which led out to the balcony, looking down on to the cloud of falling snow. He watched the arrival of the Mustang, saw it creep into a parking space, then the girls' quick exit from the car, losing sight of them only as they entered the building. He went to wait for them at the door of his apartment, a big smile lighting his face.

"May I take your coats?" he offered, as they stepped into the plush apartment suite. They took a moment to remove their shoes.

"Thank you Manny," the girls answered simultaneously. Manny was such a gentlemen. It was no wonder they loved him so much.

"Would you care for something to drink? Perhaps some Sherry, Champagne, or a mixed cocktail?"

"Do you have any hot chocolate?" Nicole asked.

Manny chuckled. "I'm not sure, but if I don't, I will send out for some."

They all went to the large kitchen to check the cupboards.

"We're in luck. N-E-S-T-L-E-S. Nestles makes the very best chocolate," she announced with a giggle.

"Are there any marshmallows?" Nicole asked, smiling. "I don't see any."

"I will send out for some." Manny offered.

"No, that's okay." Nicole smiled at him. "A cup of hot chocolate will be fine."

They sat in the living-room making idle conversation. Manny rested comfortably in his favored brown recliner, just enjoying the sound of the feminine voices. Marsha and Nicole sat next to each other on a plush, soft brown, leather couch. The carpet beneath their feet was beige, with a white bear skin rug thrown before a large blazing fireplace. A glass coffee table sat before the couch, while matching end tables with chrome designer lamps were thoughtfully placed on each side of the couch. A huge oil painting of wild geese taking flight from a pond was centered on a wall in a gold frame. The tall golden reeds in the painting accented the many pieces of furniture place around the room. Long rectangular mirrors in silver frames, adorning other parts of the wall. The apartment suite was luxurious, speaking the fact that Manny always bought the very best.

"I was wondering if you'd like to trade your Mercedes in for a newer model?" Manny asked Nicole.

"Oh no. A deal is a deal. And I love my Mercedes."

"Well, if you should ever want to trade it in on a newer model, just let me know and I'll take care of it."

"Thanks, Manny." Nicole stood to go over and give him a loving hug.

"So what's new with you, Manny?" Marsha asked.

"Absolutely nothing. I went to the doctor yesterday for my annual check-up and he gave me a clean bill of health."

"Annual?" Nicole repeated, then asked. "When is your birthday?"

"December fourteenth," Manny laughed. "Don't ask me the year." Nicole sighed, feeling a sense of guilt.

"Why didn't you tell us you had a birthday last month? We would have thrown you a party."

"When you get to be my age, you stop looking forward to them."

"Your age? Just how old would that be?" Marsha inquired.

"If you two must know, I'm sixty-eight."

"No, you're not. He's lying." Nicole giggled.

"Yes, I am." Manny countered.

"If you are, then you are in remarkably good shape." Marsha observed.

Manny was in excellent physical condition. He was five-ten, a hundred eighty pounds, with noticeably white hair cut perfectly to hang neatly above the collar of his dress shirt. He had a hairy chest and around his neck he wore a gold chain with a Saint Christopher medallion.

"What's your full name?" Nicole asked.

"Why?" he grinned.

"Because I want to know." Nicole replied, then thoughtfully explained. "When Stormy was murdered, I didn't know that it was her because I never knew her last name. I don't ever want that to happen with you or to me ever again."

"My full name is Manual Luther Biden. Anything else you girls want to know?" Manny grinned.

Marsha and Nicole looked at each other and burst into laughter.

"Not at this moment."

Manny stood up, beckoning them with a little smile as he started for the bedroom. He excused himself for a moment to go into the adjoining bathroom, returning in a short time wearing a white bath robe. The girls knew what time it was. Marsha took Nicole by the hand, leading her over to the enormous round bed, where working together they turned down the white satin sheets. They laid down on the huge bed, kissed and fondled each other through their clothes as Manny settled into a cushioned chair beside the bed.

He watched Nicole run her hand up Marsha's leg, caressing her warm mound. Nicole unsnapped her slacks, but impatiently Marsha sat up to push them down her hips until she could toss them on the floor at Manny's feet. Nicole laughed her delight. Marsha was wearing sheer black bikini underwear. Nicole pulled Marsha's top over her head, exposing her firm breast encased in a sheer bra.

Next Marsha began undressing Nicole, unsnapping her snug jeans, and easing her back on the bed to tug on the bottom of her pants legs to remove them. Nicole arched her back trying to help her along.

"Damn girl, what did you do, pour yourself into these jeans?" Nicole and Manny both laughed. It was a struggle but the jeans finally came off. Marsha quickly lifted the sweater over her head, leaving Nicole naked from head to toe. Nicole never wore underwear, hating the feeling of the material against her skin. The round bed had a red velvet headboard, and the white satin sheets felt soothing against her bare skin. Using two fingers, Nicole slid Marsha's underwear off her body and to the floor. Suddenly they were kissing passionately, their hands rubbing and touching one another in demanding caresses. With Manny heating up at the sight of the two beautiful naked women, they positioned themselves so they could please one another at the same time using tongues and lips. Nicole was the first to reach an orgasm, while Marsha was not far behind, and her orgasm much more intense. Nicole climbed from the bed and hurried over to Manny. She fell to her knees and took his still hard manhood into her mouth. Within minutes, he cummed, groaning and moaning in sheer ecstasy.

They laid in bed with Manny, hugging him in between their warm bodies until they dozed off to sleep. They slept for a brief hour before Nicole and Marsha woke up to get dressed.

Marsha excused herself, going to the bathroom. It was an opportunity for Nicole to ask Manny about a personal question that had been troubling her for quite some time.

"Manny," she asked. "Why don't you ever have sex with us? Do you see us as dirty or worry about catching a disease?"

"Oh no! God no!" Manny's eyes teared as he explained. "My wife, Alexis, bless her soul, passed away twelve years ago this May. She was only forty-two when cancer ate her to the bone. I've remained loyal as much as I've been able to. I loved her dearly and not a day goes by that I don't think of her!"

"Does Marsha know?"

"No. It's not something I normally talk about."

"Well, I'm glad you don't think of us as being nasty."

"Never! God forbid that such a thought should ever cross your mind. If it wasn't for you and Marsha, I wouldn't have anything to live for. I love you both dearly and there's nothing I wouldn't do for you. I mean it. You are my family."

"I love you so much!" Nicole hugged him to her, kissing him

softly on the lips.

On the way out the door, Manny hugged Marsha, slipping five hundred dollars into her coat pocket, offering what she would no longer willingly take from him. She was the single mother of five children, and he knew she could use the money. He did not try the same thing with Nicole. She would never accept his money, and would only end up returning it in the long run. He had agreed to buy her a car of her choice instead of giving her money, and to her a deal was a deal. He lived up to his part and she was living up to hers.

Manny stood at the sliding doors of the balcony and waved goodbye to the girls, watching them walk to the Mustang and drive out of the parking lot.

He relaxed in his recliner, grabbed the remote control and switched the television on. As he flipped through the channels, his thoughts drifted to his wife, Alexis. He wondered if she would approve of his relationship with the girls. Knowing her as well as he did, she was probably laughing at his old ass, all because he had failed to have sex with such gorgeous women. Manny and Alexis had been childhood sweethearts, and he had often told her he had loved her the moment he laid eyes on her. Remembering all they had once shared together brought a smile to his face and tears to his eyes.

* * *

The Two O'clock Club was 'poppin', as Nicole called it, when she arrived for work shortly before 9 p.m.

"Am I glad to see you, Peaches!" Blaze exclaimed wearing a happy smile. "It's been a tough crowd, and none of these girls have given a performance to get these guys moving."

"Sounds to me like it's time for me to break out the fireman's outfit," Peaches laughed.

"Can you fill in for Sasha tomorrow night? She's down with the flu."

"No can do. The club is planning a party and I'm expected to be there. If I don't show up, my boyfriend and his whole crew will come looking for me."

"The sign at the door reads 'No Club Colors'. You know I run a respectable club."

"They have respected that. But if I don't show up I think we both know it will probably create a problem."

"Enjoy the weekend." Blaze said, and frowned. There were other girls that could fill in for Sasha but nobody brought in a crowd like Peaches.

Peaches loved being the center of attention, hearing the guys cheer as she removed her clothes, taunting them with the perfectness of her tight little body. She loved performing burlesque. It was fun and getting paid for doing what she loved made it all the better.

Peaches walked onto the stage wearing a red fireman's hat with a shiny badge in the center, a yellow raincoat, plastic yellow coveralls, and black rubber boots. In her right hand she carried a small fire-extinguisher filled with water. Peaches dropped the yellow coat to the floor, slowly unbuttoning her coveralls, while moving her hips to the tempo of the music. She dropped the coveralls on the floor, working the stage from one end to the other, leisurely strutting her stuff. She slid her black shorts down past her knees, stepped out of them, and kicked them to the side of the stage exposing her red g-string. Her ass was bare and nicely rounded on a petite frame. Grabbing her blouse with both hands, she popped the snaps, tossing the blouse to the side and exposing her small, but firm, breasts. Red tassels covered her nipples.

"Take it all off, you slut!" a drunken sailor yelled.

Peaches worked her way to the inebriated sailor, pointed the hose of the fire-extinguisher in his direction, and pulled the trigger, dousing him with cold water. The crowd clapped and roared with laughter.

"She's a natural." Blaze smiled, then laughed.

Returning to the dressing room Nicole felt a wet spot between her legs. "Oh shit!" She cursed, then asked if any of the girls had an extra tampon. Fortunately for her, one of the girls did.

"It happened to me once," the girl smiled.

* * *

By Friday morning, the snow outside was melting. Still she refused to take any chances. The Mercedes-Benz would be staying under its protective cover. She would drive the Bug to the cabin in Pennsylvania.

Bulldog heard the Little Bug as it drove up to the cabin and he stepped outside to greet her. They hugged. Then he ran his hand down her pants, smiled and said. "I hope you're still horny?" No sooner had he said the words before he felt the string from the tampon. "What's that?" he demanded.

"We've got company." She giggled.

"A firecracker? This is a fuckin' party. There's going to be drinking, fighting, and fucking all weekend. What in the fuck am I supposed to do, play with myself?" Bulldog growled, clearly angry.

"You selfish bastard. What in the fuck am I suppose to do? Deal with the real world, where bitches have periods!" She got right back in his face.

Ramrod heard the commotion from inside the cabin, attracted by all of the yelling and screaming. As he stepped out of the cabin Bulldog turned to him. "The bitch has got a firecracker stuck between her fuckin' legs."

"So, turn her over," Ramrod suggested chuckling.

If looks could kill, Ramrod would be dead. Peaches said not a word, her glare speaking volumes.

"Maybe Peaches will bless you with a blow job?" Ramrod grinned, then added. "Either way, like she said, deal with it."

CHAPTER THREE
WINGS OF AN ANGEL

Inside the log cabin, there were several bedrooms with connecting bathrooms, a large cooking area, and a huge stone fireplace in a spacious living-room. The only thing separating the living-room from the kitchen was a large counter with stools. The cabin had been completely refurbished with a hot water heater and electricity. The kitchen had an electric stove, a porcelain sink, and a old white refrigerator that opened with a handle. There were few modern conveniences to speak of. On the left side of the cabin were four grills made from two fifty gallon drums cut in half. It was a beautiful rustic setting.

Bulldog looked at Peaches, grinned, downed a long necked bottle of Budweiser, and said. "You're going to polish the old knob tonight."

"What's in it for me?" she laughed.

"Do what? You're the one sporting the firecracker, not me!" He growled. "Besides, you're my property."

"Property?" she laughed. "You've got life really fucked up if you think you're my boss."

"I can show you better than I can tell you. If you're not careful I'll pass you around like a bad case of the flu."

"Is that right? Well, before you do that perhaps you should ask Ramrod how he would feel about you costing the club money?"

"She makes a valid point." Ramrod butted in, grinning.

"Fuckin' bitch!" Bulldog snarled, opening another bottle of beer.

As night fell, the entire biker gang was chasing brews, snorting lines of crystal meth, and talking about the weather. The forecast was for early sunny skies, but with a late afternoon chill. The party was going to be awesome. The new Prospect J.D. was in charge of the ice and beer runs, and it was his responsibility to keep the tin wash tubs filled with ice cold bottles of beer.

When J.D. was twenty-two, he met the Argots at a local bar in town. He had been homeless and living out of his car. Ramrod took a liking to him, taking him under his wing, getting him to sell his car and purchase a Harley. The bike was not much more than a frame with a title. One of the club members stole a Harley, tore it apart, and built the Prospect a motorcycle that he would be proud to own. Jake Boyd was his birth name but he had a thirst for Jack Daniels, with or without Coca-Cola. That's how the club members arrived at the nickname of 'J.D.' It seemed fitting.

"I'm going to take a shower and go to bed," Peaches announced around midnight.

"Go ahead." Bulldog replied as if he was giving her his permission. Peaches ignored him, knowing that he was trying to show off for his club members. Those same members seated around the living room of the cabin, hid their snickers behind turned heads.

"I've got an idea," Ramrod suddenly said. "Didn't Peaches ask what was in it for her when you said she was going to polish your knob tonight?"

"Yeah, so?"

"Tell her that if she gives you a blow job tonight you will eat her pussy tomorrow."

"Fuck that!"

There was loud laughter around the room.

"It's time that you earn your red wings, bro." Ramrod said grinning broadly.

Encouraging hoots and catcalls filled the cabin. To earn silver wings, a biker has to have sex with a girl while his brothers watched. To earn his red wings, he had to eat a girl's pussy while she was on her period and the brothers watched. "By noon tomorrow I'll probably be so wasted that I'd eat the corn out of her shit. What the Hell, I'll do it!" Loud cheers went up from both the men and women.

A couple hours later, when Bulldog crawled into bed. Peaches threw her arm over his chest and curled up next to him. He ran his hand down her inner thigh, and her eyes popped wide open. She felt as if someone was trying to rob the vault while she slept. He kissed her neck, and whispered in the ear, "If you give me a blow job I'll eat your pussy tomorrow."

"That's nasty!" Peaches snapped. "You don't have to do that," she protested.

She decided to shut him up by going down on him. Peaches gave great head, the best he ever had. After he nutted, he held her tight and whispered in her ear. "A deal is a deal, baby."

She threw her leg over his and fell back to sleep.

The crow of a rooster woke her early.

"Cock-a-doodle doo," she whispered in Bulldog's ear. He let out a grunt, and rolled over in the opposite direction. She wrapped herself in his biker jacket, walked to the bathroom, washed her face, brushed her teeth, then sat down on the toilet to pee. "Damn it!" She yelled, jumping up from the wet seat. "What a bunch of inconsiderate bastards," she said to herself. What did she expect from a bunch of wild, crazy ass, drunken bikers. They were all one percenters who did not fit in with normal society. Every single one of them enjoyed living outside of the law. She was even beginning to wonder what was normal for herself.

Bulldog and Ramrod awoke to the smell of the fresh coffee Nicole brewed. There was plenty of food in the cabinets, pots and pans on the kitchen counter, but Betty Crocker in the kitchen she was not. More often than not, she burned the toast.

As Peaches sipped a cup of black coffee, she crossed one leg under the other, making herself more comfortable on the wooden stool. In her mind she went back over the past year of her life. starting with Charlie's exit from prison and her decision to raise their daughter Charlotte away from a life of crime and drugs. For years she had followed blindly behind Charlie, trusting that he would make everything perfect and right for their little family. She learned the hard way that reality could sometimes be a hard pill to swallow. The death of her baby girl had shocked her in ways she had never dreamed possible. Under cloudy circumstance she had met Marsha, whom she now loved with all her heart, their sexual relationship opening her to a world she had never known before. The times they engaged in sex were important to her only in a sense that it would bring Manny pleasure. Thinking of Manny made her feel good, knowing that he was the one man in her life that would be there for her in her time of need. Stormy had been her hanging out buddy and she missed the other woman for her happy laughter and easy smile. Then there was Bulldog and the Argots. They needed her to supply them with drugs and for that reason she knew she had their protection, but she was not foolish enough to think they loved her above a club member. At that moment Bulldog and Ramrod came out to join her. She looked directly over at Bulldog.

"What is your birth name?" she asked.

The question caught him by surprise. He took a second two grab a couple mugs out of a cupboard. Ramrod stood their grinning. "I know your name." Peaches announced, looking at Ramrod with a grin.

"You do, huh?" Ramrod chuckled, seriously doubting that she did.

"Yep. It's Johnny Rowe."

"How in the Hell do you know that?" Ramrod stared hard at Peaches, then looked over at Bulldog.

"Don't look at me, bro. I didn't fucking tell her." Bulldog swore.

"You must have a crystal ball." Ramrod snapped.

"Nope. The first time Harold Glazer came to my apartment to drop off money, he said that he was there on behalf of Johnny Rowe." She explained, making a reference to the club's attorney. "It was obvious I didn't know who he was talking about, so he added that I might know you better as Ramrod. He was right.

"Bulldog, the only reason I'm asking your name is because when Stormy was murdered, I didn't know her last name. It was a horrible feeling when I found out, and I don't ever want to relive that moment."

"If I tell you my real name, then you're my scooter tramp, and you will have to do whatever I say all day tomorrow."

"You're not going to try and pass me around?"

"Nope."

"No tricks?"

"Nope."

"Okay, it's a deal."

"My birth name is Richard Allen Doyle."

"When's your birthday?"

"Oh no. That's not a part of the deal. You're going to have to save that question for another day," he smiled.

"Shit!" Peaches cursed. In hindsight she wished she had made a better deal.

Bulldog and Ramrod stepped outside and leaned against a wooden handrail surrounding the tin roofed porch. It was almost nine o'clock. Bulldog lit a stick of marijuana, took a deep puff and passed it to Ramrod. The air was crisp and cold without a touch of wind, the sun overhead slowly warming things up, leading them to believe that it was going to be a fantastic day for a party.

By eleven, bikers were rolling in by the dozens, elbow to elbow in leather and greased Harleys. By now every biker knew Peaches on sight and they greeted her affectionately. She had earned their respect by kicking the shit out of two biker tramps on her very first visit to the cabin. Her interactions with Bulldog was earning her a reputation amongst the brothers as a kick ass, no nonsense, first class old lady. And on a scale of one to ten, her good looks tipped the scale.

At three, a horn blew, announcing that it was time for the games to begin. Two bikers riding Harleys, posted-up at opposite ends of a wide field. One of the biker's wore a welder's helmet, and a metal trash can lid tied to his chest for body armor. The opposing biker wore a deep sea diver's helmet, and a Teflon bullet proof vest. Each held an eight foot plastic pole. At the sound of a gun shot from a.45 held in Ramrod's right hand, they charged each other like knights on horses. The rules were simple; the first one to hit the ground losses. The brothers placed bets, then stood along the sides of the field cheering their chosen knight to victory. In less than thirty seconds a huge dent appeared in the lid of the trash can and the biker behind the shield went flying. The winner was declared with a rousing cheer.

Then there was a cock fight, a dog fight, and a wet T-shirt contest. Followed by a barrel race, motor-cross, and bikers on Harleys doing stunts. It was non-stop action. At the approach of night, they built an enormous bonfire and the traditional burning of a Japanese motorcycle commenced. The year before they burned a stolen red Kawasaki. This year the chosen motorcycle a blue 125cc Honda. The brothers claimed the imported piece of garbage was not worth the time it took to steal it.

By three o'clock Bulldog was wasted, and feeling no pain. He looked at Peaches, grinning broadly.

"Well, baby, last night I said I would eat your pussy today." He made this announcement in the midst of at least thirty other bikers, drawing forth hoots and cheers.

"Oh no you're not!" Peaches laughed, preparing herself to run. The bikers booed her words.

"Let me remind you, you promised to do whatever I said all day. Now bitch, lets see what you're made of. It's time for daddy to earn his red wings. That means I have to eat your pussy while you're on the rag, in front of my brothers."

"Oh no!" Peaches stared at him in anger.

"Oh yes! You don't want me messing with no other chicks."

"Is he for real?" Peaches looked to Ramrod for help.

"He's as serious as a heart attack." Ramrod assured her, returning her frown with a big smile. He could hardly wait to see what was going to happen next.

Peaches made her move, trying to dart in between two burley bikers. She was a few seconds too slow before Bulldog snatched her up and tossed her over his right shoulder. There was a roar of approval from the bikers. She turned into a wildcat in his arms, kicking and pounding him across his broad back. He carried her over to a picnic table, ignoring her screams and demands that he put her down. With her still draped over his shoulder, he grabbed the seat of her jeans and pulled until her tight little ass was exposed to the laughing crowd. He quickly flipped her around laying her on her back on top of the picnic table. Peaches found herself helpless against his brutal strength, finally deciding to go along with him because she had no choice. Seeing that she was willing to stop fighting him, he lay his black leather jacket over the table so she did not freeze her little ass off. He unbuttoned her half lowered blue jeans and slid them off. She wore black panties, which quickly came off beneath his large hands. He sat her ass on the jacket, pushing her backwards to spread her legs. Sticking his bearded head between her legs and using his teeth, he grabbed the firecracker and jerked it from her pussy.

The brothers and female bikers around the picnic table cheered him on. It was quite a show. One they would never forget. They began chanting, "Bulldog! Bulldog! Bulldog!"

Peaches looked down at Bulldog's face buried between her legs. He reminded her of Grizzly Adams. She closed her eyes so she would not have to see the faces of the cheering bikers, and felt his thick bushy beard rubbing against her thighs as his tongue circled her clit. Her pussy immediately lit up with pleasure. Bulldog parted the lips of her pussy with his thumbs, licking her clit back and forth, going faster and faster.

A new chant was picked up by the bikers. "Eat that red pussy! Eat that red pussy!"

Peaches had never experienced anything like this. She had never thought of herself as being an exhibitionist. Surprisingly, she was not embarrassed by the brothers watching Bulldog eat her pussy. She was the center of attention, and maybe that was all that mattered. This new experience came with a bonus, a breath taking climax. One like she had never before experienced. When Bulldog tried to come up for air, she pushed his head back down, bucking wildly against his mouth.

"Peaches! Peaches! Peaches!" The rowdy bikers changed their

chant.

When she climaxed a second time, Bulldog pulled back a beard mixed with a sticky cream and red tint. She looked at him, shook her head, and laughed. Bulldog unzipped his pants, dropped them to his knees, and thrust his rock hard eight inch dick deep inside her tight pussy. He fucked her hard, and within minutes they were both breathing heavily as they exploded together.

"Who's the boss now, bitch?" Bulldog grinned.

Deciding to let him have his moment, she smiled. "You are." The brothers chanted, "Prospect! Prospect!" Wanting the Prospect to earn his red wings.

Laughing, Peaches jumped up from the picnic table. "Show's over guys." Grabbing her blue jeans she ran off to the cabin bare ass naked.

The brothers chanted, "Encore! Encore! Encore!" as she opened the door to the cabin and disappeared inside.

Nicole went directly to the bedroom she shared with Bulldog. Once inside she entered the bathroom to climb into a hot shower. It felt good, a huge smile crossing her face as she thought about what had just happened.

After the shower she inserted a new tampon, dressed, and ventured outside to join the party.

The Prospect grabbed an ice cold long neck bottle of Budweiser, twisted off the cap, and offered it to Peaches.

"Thanks." J.D. said, happy she had rescued him.

"You owe me," Peaches giggled. She put the bottle to her lips, tilted her head back, guzzling the entire beer. For good measure she deep throated the bottle. The brothers cheered. She looked at Ramrod.

"That ought to give the boys something to talk about," she smiled.

"I think you've already given them something to talk about for years to come," he grinned. "Fire up the grills," he told the Prospect.

To celebrate the clubs third anniversary the evening meal was steak and lobster. The lobsters were flown in live from Bar Harbor, Maine. This was their first lobster roast and Cupcake was in charge of cooking the lobsters. He was the only one among them with any experience preparing the delicious feast. The fire was now mostly hot coals, the coals topped with seaweed, the live lobster tossed on top, then covered with fish net so they could not escape. Corn wrapped in aluminum foil was placed on top of the netting. The Prospect was put in charge of preparing the steaks.

Three years earlier, when Ramrod returned from Vietnam, he felt he no longer fit in with the people whose freedom he had fought to preserve. He was a man who had devoted his life to secure the freedom of others. Many of his Army brothers died in combat, some he held in his arms as they drew their last breath. Returning stateside, there was no heroes welcome, the airplane landing on an airstrip filled with protestors. Longing for the feeling of brotherhood he had once enjoyed in the military, he tried joining other clubs, but he was not accepted. So, three years ago, he, along with two other Vietnam Veterans, formed their own motorcycle club. On that day, the Argots were born. It was months after they accepted Tiny as a member that they began to expand. Tiny brought with him the recipe and experience of manufacturing crystal meth. Two years later, the club purchased the cabin and the land it set on. Ramrod dug a hole in front of the cabin, poured in concrete, and installed a flag pole. He proudly flew the flag of the United States of America. Below that he flew the flag to remember and honor the missing P.O.W.'s.

The original three that started the Argot motorcycle club were Johnny 'Ramrod' Rowe, Paul 'Rocky' Staubs, and Rodney 'Rod' Anderson. Rocky brought back some incurable disease from his tour in Vietnam, and died three years later. Rod married, had two kids, and moved to Alaska. He retained his patch, and remained loyal to his brother's and the club.

"Cupcake, you're the man," Ramrod said, feasting on a lobster. "This lobster tail is fit for a King!" On second thought, he added. "And the steaks are cooked and seasoned to perfection."

J.D. appreciated the compliment, but he was overjoyed that he had not been made to lick Peaches pussy clean. Especially after Bulldog fucked her.

CHAPTER FOUR
NO DEFENSE

Ramrod was six feet, one hundred and ninety pounds, with brown hair and piercing brown eyes. A brush or comb never touched his long hair, his method for managing the long unruly locks was to run his fingers through his hair. Women thought he was ruggedly handsome and reserved in that strong but silent way some men had.

He was a man that loved his club brothers so much that he would fight to the death for any one of them. He led the club with a iron fist, his number one rule being you never broke your word to another club member. His time in the military had trained him well in the arts of self-defense and war. If provoked, he was as deadly as a rattlesnake.

Hanging around the Argots, Peaches learned to hold her liquor and party for hours on end. Her willingness to challenge anyone to any contest earned her their love, trust, and respect. She became the club's little sister and officially recognized as Bulldog's old lady.

* * *

It was good to be home, Peaches thought as she parked the little Bug next to her Mercedes-Benz. She looked in both directions before getting out of the car and locking the doors. Her watchful nature came from having been kidnapped by Domonic 'Crowbar' Coroza in the same underground parking garage. He had taken her to his home with plans of first raping her, then killing her. Thinking quickly she convinced him to return to her apartment in hopes of retrieving a large sum of money. He never made it past his Cadillac parked in front of his house. Moments before the Argots delivered a car bomb that managed to blow him into a million pieces. By the grace of God, her life was spared, but she would have preferred he suffer a long, painful, and agonizing death. He deserved it. In a movie, she remembered watching Chinese gangsters strip a guy to his waist, stake him to the ground, and hold a huge rat on his stomach by the tail. Using a metal bucket, they trapped the rat against his belly. The next step was for them to light a torch, holding the heat to the metal until it turned red hot, the only escape for the rat was to eat through the man's stomach.

In another movie, a shiny metal plate was shoved into a guy's mouth, to hold it open while a poisonous snake was shoved down his throat. A fate such as that would have been more fitting for Domonic Coroza. He had deserved this and so much more. Dying in a car explosion was just too quick and her hardened heart would have liked to have observed his prolonged agony.

After taking the elevator to the sixth floor, she unlocked the door of her apartment and heard the phone ringing.

She hurried to the phone and answered. "Hello?"

"Hi Peaches. How have you been?"

"Who is this?"

"Marvin! I must say that I'm a little disappointed that you didn't recognize my voice."

"I'm sorry, Marvin," Nicole smiled to herself. "You sound different."

"I'm just getting over a mild cold. The reason I'm calling is to ask how your schedule looks this week?"

"I'm free Tuesday and Wednesday night." Nicole said, then quickly changed her mind. "On second thought, can we make it next Tuesday at 5 p.m.?" For a brief second, she had forgotten that it was her time of the month.

"Then, it's a date. Same place, the Hilton Hotel. Room seven-fifteen."

"Sounds great. Would you like for me to bring another girl?"

"That's interesting."

"For five hundred dollars each, you can watch or participate."

"On a scale of one to ten, how would you rate the other girl?"

"Off the charts. She's drop dead gorgeous."

"How can I say no to that?"

Nicole thought that one good deed deserves another. When

the police found her tied to Domonic's bed, she called Marvin and the police released her thirty minutes later. Just being his friend empowered her. She liked the feeling of being connected to such a prominent figure. Besides, he was good looking and great in the sack.

"I'll see you then." Marvin replied.

Nicole called Marsha right away, and told her to keep her schedule open for next Tuesday night. "I'll pick you up at four p.m. and there's five hundred dollars in it for you, compliments of the governor."

"Marvin Mandell?" Marsha said, sounding shocked.

"The one and only."

"Shit! I'd do him for free," Marsha laughed.

They spent the next ten minutes discussing the activities of Marsha's five children. At the end of the call, Nicole opened her purse, pulling out a baggy of cocaine to snort a couple lines.

Her weekly routine had began. Monday night, she closed the club, then stopped by one of the after hour joints, normally the Wee Hours. Tuesday, at 2:00 a.m. Charlie stopped by the apartment carrying a gray gym bag. Inside the bag were ten kilos of cocaine, individually wrapped in brown paper, and sealed tight with brown plastic tape. Wednesday afternoon Harold Glazer stopped by the apartment carrying a briefcase.

Nicole would never forget the first time she met him. She looked through the peephole of the door in her apartment expecting to see a biker. Instead, she saw a man dressed in a three-piece gray pin-striped suit. He had brown wavy hair, rosy red cheeks, and he was fifty pounds overweight. Probably an insurance salesman, she immediately thought. When she unlocked and opened the door, Harold introduced himself.

Now, months later he stood in her kitchen with another briefcase filled with money. Two hundred and fifty thousand dollars, all hundred dollar bills wrapped in five thousand dollar wrappers. Payment for ten kilos fronted to the Argots. Harold neatly stacked the money on the kitchen table. Nicole placed the money in a brown paper grocery bag, then put it in the hall closet. After Harold left the apartment she hung around the place cleaning up. At 2 p.m. she drove to Marsha's house, the two of them would go together to see Manny. Thursday afternoon, she delivered the money to Charlie, then drove to work.

Monday afternoon, Nicole completed the task of paying all of her bills, and taking both of her cars to the local carwash for detailing. It was still early when she finished, and she did not have to start performing at the Two O'clock Club until 9 p.m. Nicole picked up the phone, deciding to give Charlie a call.

"Hello." He answered on the second ring. "What are you doing?"

"I was watching the last of the snow melt in the backyard and wondering how long it would be before I was mowing again."

"Bored, huh?" She laughed.

"Pretty much."

"Would you like to meet me at the Truck Stop in Dundalk for lunch? I'm buying."

"When?"

"Is forty-five minutes good for you?"

"I'll see you there," Charlie promised.

When Nicole arrived, his 1965 Corvette Stingray was parked near the front door. Charlie was sitting in a booth inside the restaurant looking out of a window. He watched as she parked the yellow Bug next to his Corvette.

Nicole walked into the restaurant. Spotting Charlie, she quickly took a seat in the booth across from him.

"How have you been?" she asked.

"I'm good." Charlie replied with a half smile.

"Have you heard anything more about Roger Pickett?" "Not a single word," he frowned.

"Charlie, I'm sure you're not the only person he fucked over. You didn't kill him, so I wouldn't give it anymore thought. It makes no sense to worry about it."

"I'm thinking about moving back to Anne Arundel County.

There's a house in Millersville I'm hoping to buy."

"How much is it?"

"Two hundred fifty thousand. It's a red brick home. Four bedrooms, a modern kitchen, two and a half baths, and a two and a half car garage. There's a formal dining room, a great room, a club like basement with the bar and special lighting. It has a private tennis court and a heated swimming pool. Great for entertaining."

"My concern is how you're going to pay for it."

"May I take your order?" A waitress interrupted them.

"I'll have a hot roast beef sandwich with fries. Gravy on the fries, please." Nicole ordered.

"Anything to drink?"

"Just coffee."

"And you, Sir?"

"I'll have the Club sandwich with a side order of fries and a large Coca-Cola to drink."

"Would that be all?"

"Yes, thank you." Charlie smiled.

The waitress was friendly, and she had a beautiful smile. But she was extremely skinny with no tits or ass. Definitely not Charlie's type, but he checked her out anyway. Charlie checked out every woman. It was just natural for him to do so. As the waitress left with their order, Charlie leaned over to whisper.

"I've got over a million dollars saved. Two hundred and fifty thousand isn't going to hurt me."

"Charlie, any purchase over ten thousand dollars is reported to the internal Revenue Service."

"I didn't know that," he frowned.

"My suggestion is to call Harold. Maybe he can set up a Trust Fund, and you can buy the house through the Trust. The home wouldn't belong to you. It would belong to the Trust Fund."

"But it would still be mine, right?"

"Yes, the Trust Fund would be managed by you."

"I'll call Harold as soon as I get home. It seems like he's good for all kinds of things."

"I guess he is," she smiled.

"By the way, what's up? Why did you call me? Is it my good looks, my irresistible charm, or are you just plain horny?"

"None of the above. I just thought that it would be nice to have lunch and talk."

The waitress returned with their orders. She sat their plates in front of them, then asked. "Can I get you anything else?"

"No thanks," Nicole answered smiling.

"Enjoy your lunch." The waitress returned her smile, then left them alone to eat their lunch.

They both attacked the food, remaining silent for a long moment, each of them lost in their own thoughts.

"I had a bench placed next to Charlotte's grave in case you ever felt like sitting there," Charlie finally broke the silence.

Nicole felt her eyes immediately grow moist.

"What a really thoughtful thing to do, Charlie." Nicole said, wiping a tear from her eyes.

"I've made some pretty colossal mistakes in my life, but marrying you, or our having Charlotte wasn't one of them."

"Charlie, I only divorced you to give our daughter a better life." Nicole admitted.

"I know." He replied, looking out of the restaurant window.

"I may as well tell you, I perform burlesque at the Two O'clock Club. It's downtown on Baltimore street."

"You're a stripper?" Charlie beamed.

"No, I'm an entertainer." She corrected him.

"If I stop in sometime, will you introduce me to some of the other girls?"

"I knew that I shouldn't have told you!" Nicole spat, regretting she had opened her mouth.

"It's okay." Charlie grinned. "If I do stop by, I will act like I don't even know you. I'll just enjoy the show."

"Don't get me fired, Charlie!" Nicole said sharply.

Charlie and Nicole enjoyed the rest of their lunch in silence. It was three o' clock when Charlie left a tip on the table, paid the check, and they walked outside. After saying their goodbyes they drove off in opposite directions.

Returning to her apartment, Nicole did two lines of cocaine before turning the television on. The news reported that at 11:00 p. m., police and paramedics rushed to the White Horse motel in Essex to the scene of a shooting which was apparently the result of a love triangle. The manager of Kay's nightclub, Tommy Brown, was found lying on the floor of his motel room in a pool of blood having been shot five times. Billy King, his girlfriend of three years, was being charged with first degree murder. Her arraignment was scheduled for 9 a.m., the following morning.

Kay's was less than a block from the Two O' clock Club on the opposite side of Baltimore Street. Nicole was sure she had met Tommy Brown, but she could not remember his face.

Blaze stopped Nicole at the door when she arrived at work.

"If the police ask you any questions, don't talk to them."

"What are you talking about?" Peaches asked, wondering if it had something to do with Roger Pickett, Charlie, or Bulldog.

"Didn't you hear what happened?"

"I'm not sure what you're talking about." Nicole replied.

"Natasha found her boyfriend, Tommy Brown, with another girl and she shot him five times at point blank range."

"That was Natasha on the news? I didn't know her name was Billy King. And, I didn't know that her boyfriend owned Kay's."

"He doesn't. Tommy was the doorman and manager. Or, should I say was." Blaze corrected herself.

"By the sound of it, Natasha's in a lot of trouble." Peaches frowned.

"I've already called an attorney, Harold Glazer. He raced over to the Baltimore City jail. Harold promised that he would stop by later to give me an update."

Nicole did not bother telling Blaze that she already knew the lawyer. Nicole was on the stage performing when Harold arrived at the club a few hours later. He looked up at the stage, and for a brief moment, he wore a look of shock, only to break into a huge grin a few seconds later. Peaches returned his smile, making a gun with her fingers, and shot him dead. Harold laughed heartily.

Blaze watched Peaches and Harold's interaction with a small smile. When he joined her at the bar she ordered them both a drink. She knew the only drink he ordered when he came to the club was Crown Royal on the rocks. He seated himself on a stool next to Blaze at the horseshoe bar, and asked. "Did you watch the evening news?"

"No, I've been sitting here all night," she explained.

He found it difficult to converse with Blaze, her beauty could be very distracting. Her red hair fell below her shoulders, her blue eyes alive and sparkling. She always wore low cut blouses that accented her 44 double-D breasts. His eyes explored her from her head to her chest, as he began to speak. "Billy was read her Miranda Rights and while she was being escorted to jail she told a reporter that the no good two-timing bastard got exactly what he deserved, and if she had more bullets she would have reloaded and shot him five more times. It was all filmed on camera."

Harold swirled the ice in the glass, took a sip of whiskey, then continued. "She shot him three times in the chest. When he hit the floor she stood over him, and as he begged for his life she shot him two more times in the head. She has no defense. There's not a jury in the world that's not going to convict her. She shows no remorse. In her mind it was justified. Billy doesn't need a lawyer, she needs a miracle."

"Shit!" Blaze cursed. "The girl's got a screw loose."

"She won't consider an insanity defense. She firmly believes that a jury is going to find her actions justifiable. I'm sorry, but I can't help you with this one."

CHAPTER FIVE
MAMA

Billy King was arranged at 9 a.m. The small courtroom was filled to capacity with friends, family, and newspaper reporters. Blaze and Nicole seated themselves on a wooden bench in the front row. As Natasha was escorted into the courtroom by two Deputies, she looked over to Blaze and Peaches with a bright smile on her face. She was a slender woman in her mid twenties, with long black hair and a shapely body. Within minutes a thin elderly, gray haired Judge in a black robe entered the courtroom.

"All rise!" The Bailiff shouted. "The Honorable Judge Thomas Shelby presiding." Once the Judge was seated, he continued. "You may be seated. Court is now in session."

The Judge quickly appointed Natasha an attorney, set bond at one million dollars, and adjourned Court.

As Natasha was led from the courthouse in handcuffs, she glanced over her shoulder, held her hands up and waved goodbye with her fingers.

"You really do love her, don't you Blaze?" Peaches asked.

"She's one of my girls." Blaze sighed, wiping a tear from her eye. "What can I say? She's stupid, but we're family. Natasha will always be one of my girls."

Blaze's reference to family instantly made Peaches think of Manny and Marsha. Then, her thoughts wandered to the family she had left behind in Georgia eight years ago. The thought immediately left her with a heavy heart.

Several months earlier Nicole met the governor at the Two O' Clock Club, also at the time she had been shocked to discover that Blaze and Manny had been friends for over twenty years. It seemed like everyone either knew Blaze or had heard of her. Throughout the rest of the day, Nicole only thought of two things: her family, and Bulldog. Whenever she thought of her father who had passed away, she started to cry, so she tried not to think of him too often. But it was hard not to, for there were so many fond memories of his taking her hunting and fishing. She was a daddy's girl, for sure.

* * *

Wednesday morning, Detective Marks parked his white Cadillac Coupe DeVille in the employee parking lot of the Baltimore City Police Department, reaching inside his suit jacket, he removed a round plastic container from his shirt pocket, twisted the cap, and pulled out a dark Cuban cigar.

"Only the finest from Havana," he said to himself with a smile.

He clipped the tip, flipped the top off of a silver Zippo lighter, flicked the flint with his right thumb, and lit the cigar, all in one motion. He looked at the watch on his left wrist, noting that the time was 7:55 a.m. The clock on the dashboard read 7:56. He wondered which was correct? As he did every morning, he waited to hear the morning news before going into his office. There was a three alarm fire in Baltimore County at Imperial Packaging, a shooting at a neighborhood bar in Anne Arundel County, the Wooden Nickel. A pre-dawn raid netted five pounds of marijuana in Baltimore County. Yesterday's results from Billy King's court appearance were repeated. She was appointed an attorney and bond was set at one million dollars. Even though the shooting occurred in Essex, the trial was held in Baltimore City. It was not his problem, and he was thankful for it. He had enough of a caseload to deal with already. Today was sunny and cold, but the weatherman reported the possibility of light snow in the 7 day forecast.

The big man grabbed his off-white London Fog topcoat, which was draped neatly across the front seat, slipping it on as he stepped from the shelter of the car. He slipped the matching hat on top of his head, turning the brim down slightly, using one finger and the thumb of his right hand, He looked up at the third floor window of his office, and he began to head inside, it was time to start the day.

Once inside, he made himself a cup of piping hot coffee. Betty Crawford was sitting at her desk shuffling through papers. She turned to say good morning, but Detective Marks spoke first. "I want everyone in the conference room in fifteen minutes."

Detectives Wyatt and Ronnie sat on the left side of the long mahogany conference table. Betty Crawford and Greg, and both junior detectives, sat on the right side. Detective Marks sat at the head of the table, already sipping on a cup of coffee. He rolled the now unlit cigar in his mouth.

"Where are we on the Pickett murder investigation?" He wanted to know.

"The report from the Fire Investigator ruled it murder by arson, sir." Detective Wyatt reported.

"Roger Pickett has two minor arrests. Check fraud and possession of cocaine." Detective Ronnie added.

"I sure hope someone has something more substantial." Detective Marks growled.

"Well sir, when Pickett was arrested on the possession of cocaine charge he made a deal to cooperate against his childhood friend, Charlie Redman. He agreed to wear a wire. The charges filed against Redman were later dismissed because of problems with the evidence." Detective Greg replied.

"Bingo! Now we have motive and a prime suspect. Good work! Do you have anything to add to that, Twinkle Toes?" he asked Betty Crawford.

"Yes. Forensics found strands of rope still tied to his hands, parts of an apple stuck in his mouth, and evidence of tape wrapped around his head." She explained.

"It sounds like a revenge killing or a hit," Detective Marks concluded. "Boys and girls, we've got ourselves a murder investigation, the first one of the year. Let's get busy."

* * *

Around noon, Peaches called the cabin for Bulldog. The phone rang, rang, and rang. Until finally the Prospect J.D. answered.

"Hello?"

"This is Peaches. Is Bulldog there? I need to talk to him." She said, then wished she had expressed more urgency.

"He's still asleep." She heard a yawn over the phone and what sounded like rain in the background falling heavily on the rusted tin roof.

"Wake his ass up!"

"Not me. I can't afford to get on his bad side."

"Golly gee. I wonder which would be worse. You waking him up and telling him it's urgent, or my telling him you walked into the bathroom while I was taking a shower, and tried to put the moves on me?"

"I didn't do that."

Peaches laughed.

"You're one devious bitch!" the Prospect declared.

"Yes, I am." Peaches giggled. "It's a tough world kid, but I'm sure you'll make the right decision."

"This had better be good." Bulldog growled, wiping the sleep from his eyes.

"I need to see you tonight. Meet me at my apartment. I'll come straight home from work."

"Is it important?"

"To me it is. And, it's personal. Plan on spending the night."

"Can I go back to bed now?"

"Yes. And tell the Prospect that I said he's a chicken shit." she laughed.

Bulldog slammed the phone down. He walked by the Prospect and said. "Peaches said to tell you you're a chicken shit." As an after thought he asked. "What the fuck was that about?"

The Prospect was sitting on the floor with a blanket wrapped around him. He shrugged his shoulders, moved closer to the fireplace, and replied. "I don't know!"

Bulldog stomped off back to his room to fling himself onto the mattress and was quickly fast asleep.

At three-thirty, Charlie knocked on the door of Nicole's apartment. In his right hand he carried a blue gym bag containing ten kilos of cocaine. He sat down at the glass topped dining room table, dug into his pocket pulling out his personal stash of cocaine, opened the baggy and asked Nicole if she wanted to snort a couple of lines.

"Of course," she said.

Charlie used his driver's license to lay out four lines of cocaine, each an inch long. "Ladies first," he offered, handling Nicole a cut down straw.

Nicole quickly scooped the four piles into one, made two lines three inches, and snorted a line into each nostril. She looked at Charlie with a broad smile. "Didn't you want any?"

Charlie laughed, shaking his head at her stealing his lines. He laid out his own lines and snorted them.

"Would you like to go with me this afternoon to pay your respects to our daughter, Charlotte? She would like that. She loved you so much, Charlie. Like myself, our daughter was a daddy's girl." Nicole offered.

"Let's go!" Charlie smiled.

Nicole grabbed her black leather Argots jacket hanging from the back of a kitchen chair. On second thought, the "Property of Bulldog" patch seemed out of place. She hung the black leather jacket in the hall closet, stashing the gym bag of cocaine on the floor in the closet. Then she chose to wear a multicolored winter jacket. On their way to the grave site, they stopped at a flower shop and Nicole picked out a beautiful wreath. Charlie insisted that he pay for it.

"Flowers aren't going to last very long in this cold weather," he added.

"I don't care." Peaches replied, flatly. "It seems like the right thing to do."

"Understandably so." Charlie agreed, a thoughtful look on his face. He knew that he would not mention it, but he hated anything to do with the dark side of life. Incurable diseases, dead carcasses, funerals, and especially graveyards. They gave him the heebie-jeebies; a strong case of the creeps. At a very young age, his older brother had teased and taunted him by using dead animals discovered in the woods near their home.

His brother had laughed in a high pitched voice, while chanting, "The worms crawl in, the worms crawl out."

Even now as an adult Charlie found himself hating horror movies, or anything that made his skin crawl. In all truthfulness Charlie would not harm a fly. The time he grabbed Nicole by the hair and threw her out of his apartment had been out of character for him, and he was glad that Nicole had not held it against him. Arriving at the graveyard Nicole led the way to Charlotte's headstone.

"It's beautiful!" Nicole said, stopping to admire the concrete bench next to Charlotte's headstone. There was an engraved harp in the center with angels and flowers. She threw her arms around his neck and hugged him.

Charlie smiled, gently returning her hug. "The salesman said that it will never rust or rot. It came with a Lifetime guarantee."

Nicole fell to her knees and pulled weeds from around the headstone. She neatly arranged the bouquet of flowers, while Charlie sat quietly on the bench watching her. When she finished, she took a seat next to him.

"It's cold." Nicole said, shivering.

"Concrete retains warmth in the summer and cold in the winter," Charlie grinned in amusement.

Nicole suggested they say a prayer. They bowed their heads and Nicole thanked God for having giving them such a wonderful daughter to love. They sat in silence for another ten minutes before leaving. Charlie dropped Nicole off at the front door of her apartment building, then drove to his rented house in White Marsh.

Once inside her apartment, Nicole warmed herself, then called Manny. "I've got a problem and I'm hoping you will understand," she said.

"What's the problem, Nicole?" It made her feel warm to hear the touch of concern in his voice.

"It's my time of the month, so I won't be there today. I'm not going to be there next week either. I need to go home to Georgia and see my family."

"No problem." Manny replied, then thoughtfully asked. "Do you need some money for the trip?"

"No, but thank you for asking. I feel horrible for my not being there. Marsha may need the money."

"Don't worry about that. I'll call Marsha and tell her that I'm going on a hunting trip and that I'm giving you girls a two week paid vacation."

"Are you really?" Nicole asked, pleased to hear it.

"No, but that's what I'm going to tell Marsha. I don't want her bringing some other girl," Manny chuckled.

"She knows better than to share you with anyone else. You're mine and I love you, Manny."

"I love you too, Princess. Enjoy your trip."

All night, while Peaches was at work, she had the jitters. She could hardly wait for her shift to end, so she could see Bulldog. She needed to feel herself in his arms. Richard Allen Doyle was her man. She was sure of that. In his own way, he loved her. Being his property made her feel special. Thoughts of her looking up at him from the picnic table after he ate her pussy, and seeing his frosted beard made her laugh. For her, wearing his property patch was a badge of honor. She was thankful that no one had taken a photo of her naked.

Arriving home from work, she found Bulldog sitting on a couch in the front lobby. It was almost 3 a. m. Nicole stopped at the front door, beeped her horn, and motioned for him to come outside. Opening the passenger door, she said. "Get in!"

It was an amusing sight. Kind of like watching someone try to cram a five pound fish into a sardine can. She moved the seat back as far as it would go, but his knees were pressed against the dashboard and his head touched the roof of the little yellow Bug.

"I hope we're not going too far," he growled.

"I'm hungry. Thought we might grab a bite to eat at the White Coffee Pot."

"You're a woman after my own heart. I'm starved!"

Nicole parked near the front door of the restaurant, As they entered, Bulldog picked a booth in the rear preferring to sit with his back to the wall. It was a habit. As Sergeant of Arms for the Argot motorcycle club, over the years he had made more than his share of enemies. They ordered coffee and roast beef sandwiches with gravy covering the French fries. Their similarities in taste were blatantly obvious.

"So, what's so important?" Bulldog asked.

"I want to go home."

"We just fucking ordered!" He spat, in anger.

"No, I mean that I want to go home to Georgia to see my family. And, I want you to go with me."

Bulldog was already shaking his head. "I can't just take off. I would have to clear it with Ramrod. Where exactly does your family live?"

"My mother and sister live in a trailer in Adel, Georgia. It's on five acres. There's a pond, an acre of blueberries and lots of wildlife. I was really young when I got pregnant with Charlotte and left home. Charlie filled my head with a lot of stupid dreams. I had never been outside of the state of Georgia. Charlie promised to take me back someday, but he never did. It's been eight years since I've seen my mother, or little sister. I have plenty of money, so I'll pay for the trip."

"It's up to you to get the okay from Ramrod."

"Piece of cake. I'll give him a blow job."

Bulldog glared at her.

"Just kidding." She giggled.

* * *

Nicole was awake and on the phone to Ramrod before Bulldog crawled out of bed. When she explained the circumstances, he did not hesitate to give his approval.

As Bulldog stepped out of the shower there was a knock at the door. Nicole had just placed four slices of bread in the toaster, and was pouring a glass of orange juice for Bulldog. Nicole looked through the peephole of the apartment door. It was Harold Glazer. He was carrying a briefcase, and smiling broadly.

"I didn't know you worked at the Two O'clock Club. That was quite the performance." Harold continued to smile.

At that moment Bulldog stepped out of the bathroom with a towel wrapped around his middle. "What's up, Harold?"

"Good afternoon. I'm just here to take care of a little business for the club."

Bulldog grinned as he walked into the bedroom leaving them alone.

Nicole smiled, understanding why he would become so nervous at the towering figure of Bulldog. Harold began stacking money from the briefcase on top of the dining room table. Nicole opened the hall closet to retrieve the gym bag of cocaine.

"Did you ask your associate if he would prefer a Cashier check, or a bank to bank transfer?"

"I did. He prefers cash. Nothing traceable."

"I'm setting up a Trust Fund for your ex-husband, Charlie. He wants to buy a house in Millerville, and have it owned by the Trust Fund. I'm not sure if I'm supposed to tell you, but I'm also doing his Last Will and Testament. In the event of Charlie's death, he's making you his sole beneficiary."

Nicole hoped Bulldog had not overheard their conversation. She handed Harold the blue gym bag, and quickly ushered him out the door. "Have a nice day. I'll see you next week."

Bulldog walked out of the bedroom and sat down at the kitchen table, waiting for breakfast to be served. Nicole gingerly opened the refrigerator, grabbed a butter dish, a jar of marmalade jelly, and placed the items on the table in front of him. Next, she put four slices of hot golden brown toast on a plate and handed it to him along with a butter knife. She was proud of herself for not burning the toast.

Bulldog gave her a hard look. His eyes spoke volumes.

"Where's the rest?" He demanded.

"Two slices of toast is breakfast," she laughed. "Four slices is a meal fit for a King."

"Peaches, you are going to have to learn how to cook."

"'Well, you're going to love my mother's cooking," she promised.

"I've got to return to the cabin and pack some clothes while you're at work."

"Oh no, you don't. Whatever you need, I'll buy it new. Promise me that you won't go anywhere. Promise me that you will be right here waiting for me when I get off work."

"Okay."

"No, promise me."

"Okay, I promise."

"Get some rest. As soon as I get home, we're leaving, We're taking the Mercedes and you're driving, while I get some rest."

* * *

"I can't believe that you are leaving me like this! I've got one girl in jail and another out sick with the flu. It's not very good timing."

"My mother isn't in very good health, and I haven't seen her in eight years," Nicole replied, tears coming to her eyes.

Blaze sighed. "Go ahead. I guess I'll manage somehow."

"Oh, thank you so much." She gave Blaze a hug.

"Make sure you bring me back a peach."

They both laughed.

* * *

Nicole returned to her apartment to discover Bulldog sitting on a couch in the living room, watching television. His feet rested comfortably on top of the coffee table.

"You're still here." She smiled her happiness.

"I never break a promise," he grinned. Within minutes she packed a small suitcase.

"Whatever you need, I'll buy it new. The Green Frog motel is less than two miles from the trailer. We can rent a room there. On the premises, there's a restaurant and clothing store."

"Sounds good. But we're not going to be renting a room with the twenty-two dollars in my wallet." Bulldog grinned.

Nicole opened her purse, and handed him five crisp One Hundred dollar bills. "I don't want you walking around without money. I'm taking five thousand dollars, which should be more than enough."

"I seriously doubt if I spend that much money in a year." Bulldog chuckled.

They uncovered the Mercedes-Benz, stopped to fill the gas tank, and drove throughout the night. Bulldog drove for the first five hours, while Nicole curled up in the passenger seat for some much needed rest. They stopped only for rest-room breaks, fuel, and to switch places driving. The weather slowly gave way from a bitter cold to the warmth of a beautiful summer day. They were quick to shed their winter coats and let down the roof of the convertible Mercedes.

At 3 p.m. the following day they pulled into the parking lot of the Green Frog motel. Nicole rented a room, then she and Bulldog walked hand in hand to the wholesale clothing outlet. Bulldog purchased new Levi's, shirts, underwear, and socks. Nicole purchased an outfit, toothbrushes, deodorant, shampoo, and soap. They showered, dressed, then drove to the trailer. Charlotte Lynn, Nicole's younger sister, was the first to see the silver Mercedes pull into the driveway. Her mother Beverly was standing at the edge of the small pond, her back to the driveway, tossing bread crumbs to a flock of wild ducks.

Nicole brought the car to a stop, her eyes already beginning to fill with tears. Turning off the car, her and Bulldog exited the car together.

"Mama!" Nicole called.

Beverly Scott paused in the motion of throwing a handful of crumbs, unable to believe it was true. She spun around, her eyes going wide in shock. "Nicky!" She cried.

Suddenly the two women were running across the uneven ground towards one another, stumbling and crying all the way. They came together in a fierce hug, tears of happiness pouring from their eyes.

Her mother ran her fingers through her hair, moving long strings back to expose the beauty of her face. Beverly kissed her eyes, feeling the moisture from her tears wetting her lips. "Oh, thank you, Lord. Thank you for keeping my baby safe, and bringing her home to me." Beverly pulled her back into her arms, holding her tight, and gently rocking from side to side.

Charlotte Lynn who had been watching from a window in the trailer, came running from the trailer in excitement. "Nicky! Nicky!" she screamed.

Bulldog stood smiling with his arms crossed, while resting a hip against the car. Watching the reunion and Nicole's happiness, he thought the trip to be worthwhile.

"Look at you!" Nicole pulled away from her mother to hold her sister at arms length,. "You were in pigtails the last time I saw you."

Charlotte Lynn was now twenty-one, taller than Nicole by a few inches, and more filled out in the breast and hip areas. Her brown hair fell in waves to a narrow waist, accenting her olive skin and bedroom brown eyes. She was truly gorgeous.

"Boy! I bet Mama has a hard time keeping the boys away from

you," Nicole said with a whistle.

Charlotte laughed. "She tries." She glanced over at Bulldog, and added. "But I see you've brought me a present."

"Sorry baby girl," Nicole shook her head. "Mama, Charlotte Lynn. This is my boyfriend, Bulldog."

"Please to meet you, ladies," he said, still smiling.

"Hello, Bull...dog." Beverly offered a hesitant smile.

"Hi." Charlotte smiled, then added. "When Nicky was a baby she couldn't say Mommy. She always said, Mama. So it stuck. I wish it wouldn't have."

"I like it." Bulldog smiled down at Nicole.

"Come on inside. You two have got to be hungry, and we've got a lot of catching up to do."

"I sure hope you're a better cook than your daughter." Bulldog said, making them laugh. He then added, "I'm so hungry I could eat the ass end of a mule."

CHAPTER SIX
THE HAUNTED MANSION

"Charlotte, how old were you the last time I saw you? Twelve or thirteen."

They were seated around a small kitchen table. The double wide trailer provided a little nook of a kitchen, a tiny living room area which double as a second bedroom with a pull out sofa, and surprisingly a nice sized bathroom.

"Thirteen." Charlotte answered Nicole's question. "I still wore braces, remember? I didn't get those off until I was fourteen."

"There's no car in the driveway. How do you and Mama get around? Do you have a driver's license?"

"Nope. We don't have a car and I don't have a license. Someone from the church usually volunteers to take us shopping. We can't afford many luxuries living on Mama's Social Security checks."

"Do you have a boyfriend?"

"I do now!" Charlotte Lynn smiled in Bulldog's direction. Nicole laughed. "I see now that I' m going to have to keep a watchful eye on my little sister when she's around you."

"She doesn't look that little to me," Bulldog grinned. He could easily see where both daughters got their looks from.

For a woman in her mid forties, Beverly was still an attractive woman.

Beverly looked through the curtain of the kitchen window. "Whose car is that?" She asked.

"It's mine, Mama."

"Sure looks expensive. What's that say on the license plate."

"Maryland." Nicole laughed.

"It reads P-E-A-C-H-E-S," Bulldog spelled it out.

"Why Peaches?" Charlotte Lynn asked.

They all stared at Nicole anxiously waiting for a response.

"Peaches is my stage name. I'm a performer."

"What do you do?" Charlotte inquired.

Beverly interrupted by asking. "What happened to that no account boy you ran off with?"

"Charlie?"

"That's him. I never figured he would amount to much." Her mother looked at Bulldog with only a look a mother could give a man that was hanging around her daughter.

Bulldog gave her a bright smile. Beverly frowned in return. "We're divorced. He lives by himself in White Marsh, Maryland."

"Where's my granddaughter?"

There was a moment of silence as Nicole dropped her head for a brief second. When she raised her head there were tears in her eyes. She knew that the question was unavoidable, but it hurt so much to talk about her daughter, Bulldog reached over to hold her hand.

"What is it?" her mother asked.

"Mama, a little over a year ago Charlotte was killed by a hit and run driver. She was killed instantly." Tears poured slowly from her eyes.

"Oh, my God'" Charlotte covered her mouth, tears filling her own eyes. Nicole named her daughter after her little sister.

"I'm so sorry, Nicky." Beverly said, trying to hold back her own tears, while getting up to go comfort her daughter.

"She was only six years old, Mama." Tears now streamed from Nicole's eyes.

Bulldog sat quietly at the kitchen table. He had never felt so helpless in his life, It was at that moment, he realized, he was in love with Nicole. Someday, he thought, she would carry his last name and bear his children.

It was some time before they were composed enough to start preparing dinner. Charlotte Lynn busied herself peeling potatoes, placing the peeled potatoes in a pot of boiling water on the small stove top. Beverly quickly mixed eggs and milk in a bowl, dipped chicken in it, then rolled the chicken in flour, carefully placing the pieces in a skillet of hot grease. While the chicken fried, Nicole stood beside her mother helping snap green beans. After peeling the potatoes, Charlotte began kneading dough to make homemade dinner rolls.

Bulldog sat at the kitchen table sipping on a beer. "Smells mighty good," he grinned.

"I bet you've never had fresh baked dinner rolls." Nicole smiled at her man.

"Can't say that I have."

"Well, you're in for a real treat."

It was getting hot in the small kitchen. Nicole took her black leather jacket off, hanging it on the back of a wooden chair. Charlotte studied the patches on the jacket.

"What does Property of Bulldog mean?" she asked.

Nicole laughed, then moved over to whisper in Charlotte's ear. "He thinks he's my boss."

"It's to let everyone know that if they mess with her, they will have to answer to me." Bulldog grinned, then added. "And, I am the boss."

"I bet!" Charlotte said, recalling how crazy her sister could get. She seriously doubted if his words were true.

"What's an Argot?" Beverly asked.

"It's a biker gang." Charlotte Lynn answered for her sister.

"No, it's not!" Nicole snapped.

"The club was formed three years ago by Vietnam veterans, who after preserving the freedom of this country were shunned when they returned stateside. So, they dubbed themselves one percenters, the one percent representing those that didn't fit in with the norms of society." Bulldog paused before continuing his explanation. "The club represents a brotherhood, It's much like in the military where your life may depend on the guy in the foxhole next to you to have your back. I'm proud to wear the Argot patch."

"So am I." Nicole smiled. She jumped onto his lap to kiss him with a loud smack.

"Well, I suppose there's a lot of things in this world I know very little about. But I can see my baby is happy and my motherly instinct tells me that you will keep her safe. That's all that matters to me," her mother said smiling.

"What kind of motorcycle do you have?" Charlotte wanted to know.

"There's only one real motorcycle, a Harley. I ride a pearl white 1949 Panhead. The engine is bored forty-over, and it has a roller cam. It's tricked out!" Realizing that Charlotte had no clue as to what 'tricked out' meant, he simplified it. "By that I mean it has a lot of chrome."

"I have never been on the back of a motorcycle," Charlotte frowned.

"Nicky, why don't you and Bulldog go out back and pick me two pints of blueberries. For dessert, I'll make a homemade blueberry pie."

Nicole grabbed two red plastic one pint containers from a shelf on the front porch, took Bulldog by the hand, and led him to the blueberry patch.

"Look!" Nicole pointed. There was a doe and her fawn standing at the edge of the pond drinking water. "Aren't they beautiful?"

"It's moments like this." Bulldog grinned. "That makes me wish I had a gun."

"Mama would kill you if you harmed so much as one hair of any of the wildlife around here. This is their sanctuary. It always has been and it always will be."

"I was only teasing."

Walking along a well traveled trail they approached a large wooded area, entering into a deeply shaded area.

"Watch out for snakes." Nicole cautioned, handing Bulldog an empty pint container. "I'll bet that I'm finished picking a pint before you," she wagered.

"What's the bet?"

"If you beat me I'll give you a blow job tonight."

"And, if you beat me?"

"Whatever I want," Nicole giggled.

"Bet."

Bulldog never saw or looked for a snake. They found the desired bushes and the race was on. He figured she made the comment about the snakes to slow him down. Bulldog finished picking berries a good two minutes before her, and he was damn proud of himself. Nicole looked at his fingers, and laughed heartily.

"It's obvious you're a city boy. You've never picked blueberries, huh?"

While her little hands were almost snow white, the palms of his hands and fingers were a purplish color.

"I hate to have to be the one to tell you this," Nicole chuckled. "But that's not going to wash off. It's like ink."

Bulldog looked at his hands. "This is a good time to tell me," he growled.

Nicole laughingly led the way back to the trailer. She handed her pint of blueberries to her mother. Bulldog walked in and sheepishly handed his over. Nicole's berries were picked clean and were easy to rinse. Bulldog rushed to win the race. Most of his berries were mushy. Seeing his hands Beverly looked at Nicole and laughed. "You should be ashamed of yourself."

Nicole giggled, remembering the time at the cabin and thinking it evened the score.

"Wash your hands in vinegar, then scrub them with Comet cleanser. That will take most of it off." Charlotte Lynn volunteered.

"Thanks, baby girl."

After being supplied with the necessary cleaning supplies, Bulldog excused himself to go wash his hands. Beverly started making blueberry pies. When the hot dinner rolls came out of the oven, the pies would go in.

"Would you set the table." Beverly asked Charlotte Lynn.

Half an hour later they sat down to eat. Bulldog and Nicole were seated across from one another, while Charlotte and Beverly sat opposite each other.

"I owe you one!" Bulldog said looking into Nicole's eyes.

"Don't be shy." Beverly told Bulldog. "Help yourself."

Without hesitation, he helped himself to a breast of golden fried chicken, mashed potatoes topped with thick brown gravy, and a large serving of fresh green beans. He generously buttered two hot dinner rolls. The rolls were soft and sweet. Bulldog ate the first plate of food in record time, then helped himself again and again.

"I told you Mama was a very good cook." Nicole boasted.

"I wish you had kept your butt home a little longer. Your daughter has trouble making toast," Bulldog complained.

"Nicky never liked to cook. Instead, she washed clothes." Charlotte offered.

"I'm full as a tick. I couldn't eat another bite if I tried. But it was delicious." Bulldog declared.

Beverly pulled the hot blueberry pie from the oven and placed it on the table. The aroma was overwhelming. "Well, maybe just a small piece." Bulldog grinned.

The women laughed. A little later, while Nicole and Charlotte washed dishes, Bulldog and Beverly stepped outside. They sat on the front porch in twin rocking chairs watching the sunset turn to twilight, a slight chill replacing the summer heat. The only sound in the darkening night was the sound of crickets chirping down near the pond.

"It's very peaceful here." Bulldog said.

"Yes, it is. Where does your family live?"

The question caught Bulldog completely off guard. He hung his head in sadness. "My mother, father, and younger sister were killed in a car accident."

"I'm sorry!" Beverly replied sincerely.

"I've a brother three years older than me. I haven't seen him since the funeral. The last I knew, John was selling insurance somewhere out in the Midwest. Arizona, I think."

"It's getting a little chilly. I think the girls are finished. Whattaya say we go inside and join them?"

Nicole and Charlotte had retired to the den, an addition added to the trailer years ago. Cheap pine paneling covered the walls and the floor was covered in dark brown carpet. In the far corner was an old pot belly stove. Nicole had just lit the fire and she was stoking it.

"I bet we haven't used that in a very long time." Charlotte Lynn reported. She sat down in an armchair, folding her legs beneath her. Then, she picked up a fashion magazine, thumbing through it until she came upon the horoscopes.

"Let's do our Horoscopes." Charlotte Lynn suggested. "I was born February twenty-seventh, nineteen fifty. That makes me a Pisces." My Horoscope reads 'Sometimes you like to swim against the tide and with Mars being an adventure on Friday you will enjoy bucking trends and breaking rules.' Travel is also an appealing option this week. That's pretty good, huh? Now, let's take a look at Nicky's. Ester Nicole Scott was born December third, nineteen forty-three, That makes her a Sagittarius."

"Ester?" Bulldog chuckled.

"I'm going to kill you, Charlotte Lynn!" Nicole shouted.

"No, you're not." Her mother smiled.

"Ester?" Bulldog repeated, laughing heartily.

Charlotte continued, "Your horoscope reads: Someone who envies your popularity is telling tales and you need to shut them down. You may be nice by nature, but sometimes you have to be nasty, even if it's only an act. Do what you must do to stop them now, or they will cause more trouble for you later."

"You're dead." Nicole said through sudden laughter,

Charlotte stuck her tongue out at her sister, then asked Bulldog when he was born.

"Baby girl, I was born in the State of Idaho on July fourth, nineteen thirty-nine."

"Your sign is Cancer. It reads: You' re sick of promises and tired of playing second fiddle to lesser talents. It's time to show the world what you can do. But be warned that's fighting talk, and someone is sure to take you up on your challenge. They won't stand a chance, you're a winner."

"Bulldog's name is Richard Allen Doyle." Nicole announced, sticking out her tongue at him.

"That's true, Ester." He laughed.

"Well, I guess we better start thinking about making some sleeping arrangements." Beverly said thoughtfully.

"We've got a room at the Green Frog motel."

"How long are you staying?"

"We don't know for sure." Nicole explained.

"Well, there's plenty of room here." Her mother offered again.

On their way back to the motel, Bulldog said. "You've got a beautiful mother and sister." As an after thought, he added. "Ester."

Nicole slapped his hand hard. "Stop it! I hate that name." Bulldog grinned. He knew how to get her dander up now, anytime he wanted to.

By the time they entered the motel room they were both exhausted. They undressed, pulled back the covers on the large Queen sized bed and cuddled into each others arms. Within minutes they were both fast asleep.

The next morning Nicole was glad to discover she was no longer bleeding. She discarded the tampon, showered, and returned to a still sleeping Bulldog giving him a blow job to wake him up. Aroused he came awake with a groan of pleasure. No sooner than his manhood hardened, she mounted him and rode him until they both exploded in satisfaction.

They showered together, dressed quickly, then walked to the name brand wholesale clothing outlet to purchase more new clothes. "I could get use to this." Bulldog grinned, watching Nicole pay for the clothes.

Exiting the store the smell of freshly cooked bacon waffled through the crisp morning air.

"Let's stop at the restaurant and grab a bite to eat." He suggested.

"Mama would kill us both. I guarantee she's planning on feeding us."

Returning to the motel room, Nicole turned on the television hoping to catch the early morning weather report. The forecast was clear skies, sunny in the mid 70's by noon. After putting on their new clothes, they left to visit Nicole's mother.

Standing over the sink washing dishes, her mother looked out of the kitchen window and saw the silver Mercedes pulling into the driveway. She rushed to turn the oven on to start cooking homemade biscuits. The table was set for four and topped with butter, marmalade jelly, blueberry jam, and honey. Breakfast would be bacon, ham, sausage, and fried eggs. As they entered the kitchen, Nicole's mother, Beverly, was standing over the stove making sausage gravy in a skillet. The smell of fresh bacon frying made Bulldog all that much hungrier.

"I'm starving!" Bulldog announced.

"Son, what would you like with your breakfast? Coffee, juice, or milk?" Beverly asked, smiling.

"One of everything. I just might trade the daughter in for the mom." Bulldog grinned.

Beverly blushed. "Nicky is a work in progress."

Bulldog made a plate with fresh biscuits and gravy, and a second one with fried eggs, bacon, ham, and sausage. After eating all of that, he buttered two biscuits and covered them with honey.

"You guys should go to Disneyworld." Charlotte suggested. "I've never been there myself, but it's just outside of Orlando. I've heard that's only a three hour drive from here."

Nicole and Bulldog looked at one another, more to see if the other was interested.

"Do you want to go to Disneyworld?" Bulldog asked Nicole.

"I wouldn't mind going." She admitted.

"You should go, Nicky," her mother said, offering her opinion.

"Sounds like a plan," Bulldog grinned. "Just as long as we stop here on our way back to Maryland."

"You better!" Beverly insisted.

They sat at the kitchen table for what seemed like hours talking. Mostly about girlish things that were of little interest to Bulldog, and they paid no attention to him when he buttered another biscuit or helped himself to another slice of bacon or ham.

At 11:00 a.m., they hugged and said their goodbyes. Bulldog unlatched the convertible top letting it down and snapped the protective cover in place. As they drove away, Charlotte Lynn and Beverly returned their waves of goodbye. Nicole felt sad leaving her mother and Charlotte behind.

Returning to the Green Frog motel, they gathered their things and checked out. Stopping for gas, the attendant confirmed Disneyworld was about a three hour drive. The directions were simple. "Take Interstate 75 until you see exit for Disneyworld, and be sure to visit the Haunted Mansion. The line will be long, but it's well worth the wait."

It was nearly 4 p.m. when they parked the Mercedes in the parking lot of the United Kingdom. The sign read Section Pluto, row five. They hopped onto a train of covered wagons seating themselves. When the train came to a stop, they walked to the entrance and purchased tickets at the booth.

"Do you want to take the ferry or ride the tram to the Magic Kingdom?" Bulldog asked Peaches.

"The fastest way is the tram, so let's take that." She replied, pleased at her choice.

Soon they were walking down Main street. At the end of it was Cinderella's castle. It was like a fairytale come true, Charming, beautiful, and enchanting.

Nicole stopped at a gift shop, purchasing a camera, film, and a pair of Mickey Mouse ears. She loaded the camera, placed the Mickey Mouse ears on Bulldog's head, and quickly snapped a photo capturing the sad look on his face. He looked hilariously funny. Then she bought matching tee-shirts, one for herself, the other for Bulldog. It took only a few threats before she managed to get him to wear it. Before leaving the store, she asked for directions to the Haunted Mansion.

They stood in a long line waiting their turn to go inside the Haunted Mansion. Just when they neared the entrance, the line turned and went back in the other direction. "You've got to be fucking kidding me," Bulldog growled. "You've got to stand in line to get in line!"

Finally, they hopped into a moving amusement park car, a bar fell down locking them inside, and the car slowly moved into the darkness. They heard a howling of ghosts, followed by the sound of creepy music. On Nicole's right, ghosts appeared flying through the air. Others danced in a ballroom below while another ghost sat on a stool playing a piano. It looked all too real. She held tight to Bulldog's arm, squeezing harder when she was frightened. They rode past three singing heads without bodies, the entire experience becoming terrifyingly eerie causing goose-bumps to rise on her arms. She closed her eyes. She opened her eyes to see a mirror on the wall reflecting her and Bulldog in the car.

A ghost appeared sitting in her lap and she screamed making Bulldog laugh. That was enough for her. She was ready to get the fuck out of there.

Next they visited the 'Hall of Presidents'. They were wax figures that stood, looked around, and spoke. Abe Lincoln gave a speech which started a debate amongst the other Presidents. Nicole laughed in delight. It was amazing. They looked so real. From there it was on to the Mickey Mouse Revue and a boat ride through 'It's a Small World' which was Nicole's favorite. They walked past the submarine ride 'Twenty Thousand Leagues Under The Sea' stopping at the 'Tiki Hut' for a cold beverage.

At the closing of the park, Nicole told Bulldog. "We've got to come back tomorrow."

There was no argument from him. They opted to ride the ferry back to the mainland. It was powered by steam and a huge paddle wheel at the rear of the boat. Nicole leaned against the railing. Bulldog wrapped his arms around her from behind.

Fireworks lit up the sky as he whispered in her ear, "I love you."

It was a beautiful moment. The perfect ending to a perfect day.

CHAPTER SEVEN
DAYTONA BEACH

"Where did we park?" Nicole asked.

"You're asking me?" Bulldog laughed as they made there way away from the Magic Kingdom.

"Fuck!" Nicole shouted racking her brain. "I think the section was called Pluto. I remember it was a single number. I should have wrote it down."

The train came to a final stop, and they hopped into a covered wagon. Nearing the section Pluto, the Mercedes became clearly visible. Within minutes they were driving out of the parking lot with Bulldog behind the wheel. Nicole turned on the radio, twisting the dial to tune into a local radio station, they heard. "Thank you for visiting the magical world of Disney. We hope that your journey was a pleasant one, and that you will be back to visit us again real soon…"

"Tomorrow!" Nicole laughed.

They stopped at one motel after another, discovering each of them to be booked full for ten miles. Just outside of Orlando on highway 17-92 in Kissimee, they found a motel with individual teepees, white wigwams made of concrete with solid doors. Nicole thought them to be cute, but Bulldog found them to be utterly ridiculous. There was not much of a choice, nothing else was available. Once inside there was a bed, television, and a bathroom with a shower.

Down the street there was a local dive with several Harleys parked at the curb. Bulldog suggested they stop in, have a drink, and inquire where they should go for dinner.

* * *

The sign hanging from the pole at the street's edge read 'JOLLY ROGER'S'. The bar was not more than a hole in the wall with a crushed stone parking lot. The Mercedes-Benz pulled in and parked, leaving a trail of dust.

Bulldog walked through the front door with Peaches in tow, taking note of his surroundings. Five bikers, wearing black patched leathers were bellied up to the bar and a biker chick was standing at a jukebox with a handful of quarters. The bikers' upper rocker read 'HEATHENS' and the lower rocker claimed their territory to be FLORIDA. One by one they turned to watch as Bulldog and Peaches entered wearing their black leathers. The upper rocker on their jackets clearly reading 'ARGOTS'. The bottom rocker on their jackets claiming their territory as PENNSYLVANIA. The furniture of the bar consisted of a few scared wood tables and a large wooden bar top with matching stools. The wood floor was covered in a layer of dust, very much in need of a good sweeping.

The leader of the motley crew introduced himself as, Big Moose. He stood six-three, weighing two hundred and forty pounds of solid muscle, with red hair and a full beard. The bikers looked as if they had not showered in weeks and their Harleys were covered in dust and grime.

Bulldog let out a shrill whistle, attempting to get the barmaid's attention. With hard eyes she turned to acknowledge his presence, "Just a minute," she shouted.

"You're a little out of your territory, aren't you brother?" Big Moose asked, grinning.

"Just here on vacation." Bulldog replied, giving a smile of his own.

"Well, in that case, let me buy you and your tramp a drink. Maggie, give our guests whatever they want to drink and put it on my tab."

"That's mighty generous. I'm Bulldog, and this is my woman, Peaches."

"And, I'm not a tramp." Peaches snapped.

"Well, excuse the Hell out of me." Big Moose chuckled, then introduced his crew. "This is," he pointed out each member in turn, "Crank, Bones, Shyster, Craven, and of course my scooter tramp

Nasty, over there spinning records."

Nasty lived up to her name. She was short, thin with brown hair falling to her waist and light brown eyes. She had a nice round ass and a pretty round face that was devoid of makeup. Her vocabulary seemed to be limited to mutha fucker, son of a bitch, cocksucker, bitch, bastard, shit, and stupid bastard.

"We just came from Disneyworld," Peaches said.

Big Moose laughed. "I thought you were here for bike week."

"What's that?" she asked.

"Once a year all of the clubs meet in Daytona beach. It's a huge party. Starts tomorrow."

"Where's a good place to get something to eat." Bulldog asked.

"Depends on what you're looking for?" Big Moose smiled.

"Grub. Good food, and lots of it."

"There's an all you can eat buffet five miles down the road. When you leave the parking lot, turn right. Turn left at the third light. That's Orange Blossom Trail. It's two miles on your left. You can't miss it! There's a sign out front that reads 'Big Mamma's Country Kitchen'."

Nasty was standing at the jukebox dirty dancing to some funky rock music.

"It's show time tramp," Big Moose shouted across the bar.

Nasty walked over to the bar and Big Moose lifted her on top of the bar with a booming laugh. Nasty began to strut her stuff, stopping only long enough to rub her jean covered pussy in Bones' face.

Bulldog grinned, reached in his pocket, pulling out a plastic baggy of crystal meth, asking Moose if he would like a treat.

"Don't mind if I do," he grinned.

Bulldog laid out enough lines for everyone, including Peaches and Nasty.

After he snorted two lines, Big Moose asked. "What is it?"

To him it looked like cocaine. He had assumed it was, but it was a different high sending a slight burning sensation through his nose, and his head becoming tighter than Dick's hat-band.

"Whatever it is, it's fuckin' good stuff." Big Moose declared.

"It's crystal meth. My club makes it. We call it 'crank', but it's also referred to as 'speed'. If your club is interested, we might be able to do some business."

Nasty finished dancing on top of the bar. Bulldog signaled to Peaches. "Strut your stuff." He handed her a quarter for the jukebox, then gave her a gentle pat on the ass.

Peaches selected an upbeat song, hopped on top of the bar and worked it from one end to the other. She was in her element, doing what she loved to do, and did best, taunting the desires of hungry men. She loved being the center of attention, all eyes watching the movements of her hips and hard nippled breast, which could be clearly seen through the tight T-shirt she wore. Peaches captured the heart of every man who dared to look her way.

"Most times you can reach me at this number," Bulldog said drawing Moose's attention back to him and away from Peaches.

He handed over a business card. "That's where I lay my head at night. We have a hundred acres and a cabin where we throw huge parties every year. If we do business, your club will be invited."

"What' s the price of the crystal meth?" Bulldog paused to help Peaches down off the bar before replying.

"Depends on the quantity and who's transporting it. In quantity, it can be as little as three hundred an ounce.

It sells on the street for eighty to a hundred dollars a gram."

"I've never seen or heard of it before today." Big Moose grinned, seeing dollar bill signs.

"It's popular out West, mostly in California,"

"It will make your dick hard for hours." Peaches giggled, grabbing Bulldog's crotch.

Everyone laughed.

"She's more than a handful." Bulldog smiled down at Peaches, pulling her close to his side.

"So are you, baby." Peaches looked up at him with a big happy smile.

Once more, Bulldog covered the counter of the bar with crystal meth. When Peaches reached for the rolled up dollar bill, Bulldog grabbed her wrist. "I think you've had enough."

She pushed her bottom lip out in a pout, then stuck her tongue out at him before stepping away from the bar.

"Would you be interested in doing some trading?" Big Moose asked.

"Depends on what you have to trade," Bulldog replied cautiously.

"Our club has the best cocaine in Florida. Would you care to do a line?" Big Moose offered with a broad smile.

"Sure," Bulldog agreed.

Big Moose laid out eight generous lines from a large plastic bag of white powder. Rolling up a dollar bill he handed it to Bulldog. Bulldog passed it to Peaches, letting her do the honors of going first. Nasty frowned, visibly upset that Peaches got to go first. But when Peaches offered her the bill next, all was forgiven. Bulldog snorted a line into each nostril, tilted his head back and gave a hard sniff.

Big Moose offered the cocaine to them for $28,000 per kilo. Bulldog and Peaches shared a brief look. They both knew that the cocaine they had just snorted was the same as theirs, which meant it was from the same supplier. Bulldog admitted to Moose that the cocaine was excellent, stopping short of commenting further. The Argots were not going to be happy hearing his report.

After a few more beers, idle chit chat, and snorting a few more lines of cocaine and crystal meth, Bulldog and Peaches bid the Heathens a good night and headed out the door.

The top of the silver Mercedes-Benz was down and the silver leather seats were hot to the touch.

Pulling out of the parking lot, Bulldog announced. "The Heathens are getting their cocaine from your supplier."

"You noticed that too," Peaches shook her head.

"It was friggin obvious! The club may sell them crystal meth, but there's not going to be any trades."

"Where are we headed now?"

"Big Momma's Country Kitchen. I'm friggin starved! When we get back to Maryland you are going to have to learn how to cook." Bulldog growled.

"I'm fuckin' horny." Nicole giggled, reaching across the seat and unzipping his pants. In one quick motion she pulled out his dick. His thoughts of ordering golden fried chicken, mashed potatoes with rich thick brown gravy was lost with Nicole's head bobbing up and down in his lap.

"You're a bitch, you know that?" He told her, driving away from the restaurant.

Peaches gently bit down on his dick.

"Hey!" He shouted.

"I'm giving you a blow job and you call me a bitch. That's not very smart of you." Peaches laughed.

"I guess I can forget about something to eat," he chuckled.

"Eat me!" Peaches suggested laughing.

Within minutes, they were inside the teepee motel ripping the clothes off of each other. Peaches was on her knees on the bed. Bulldog grabbed her waist. Standing behind her he placed his hand on his dick and guided it into her moist needy pussy. He pumped her hard for several minutes before pulling out. He took a seat in the room's only chair, allowing her to mount him. Face to face they were going at it like two dogs in heat, kissing and caressing each other wildly. Picking her up in his arms, he carried her across to the bed to mount her from the top. Holding her legs in the air, he pounded her until they both came with a collective groan. They next moved on to the shower, turning the day into a long fuck fest.

* * *

Saturday morning at 8 a.m. when Bulldog ducked his head to step out of the motel room, Nicole snapped his photo.

"I hope you're having fun with this." He growled at her.

"I am." She laughed.

"Within minutes, they had the car loaded, stopped at the little office to check out of the room, and were on their way back to spend the day at Disneyworld.

"Oh shit!" Peaches yelled.

"What's the matter?" Bulldog asked.

"I thought I had forgot my watch. It was on the nightstand, but I'm wearing it," she smiled. Her words to Bulldog had been a blatant lie. There was no way she could tell him what the real problem was.

Stopping for gas she went to the ladies room and looked through her purse for Marvin Mandell' s phone number. She cursed when she could not find it. It was definitely in her personal directory at her apartment. How could she forget that her and Marsha had an appointment with Marvin for five p.m. Tuesday at the Hilton? She had to think of something quick.

They arrived at Disneyworld early and found a parking space within walking distance of the front entrance. Once inside, the lines were much shorter than the day before. Nicole immediately loved the Tiki Hut with the animated birds that sang and talked, but their favorite attraction was a giant roller coaster. They stepped into a moving car, a bar fell over their laps securing them inside, and the ride slowly climbed a huge hill, then fell. The entire ride was exhilarating. High speeds, sharp turns and dips that nearly made Nicole puke. She screamed throughout the ride and swore she would never do it again. Bulldog loved it, thinking the entire experience was great.

Bulldog took two photos of Nicole. He snapped a Polaroid of her standing in front of Cinderella's castle and another with her arms wrapped around Mickey Mouse, She snapped a photo of him pretending to fight Donald Duck, They faced each other with their fists up. She pleaded with him to lay on the ground and pretend that Donald Duck won the fight. He flatly refused.

"I'll give you a blow job tonight." She giggled the bribe.

Bulldog laid down on the asphalt paved road and Donald Duck placed his webbed foot on top of his chest raising his arms in the air claiming himself to be victorious.

Nicole and Bulldog walked through the park, hand in hand. It was a place where everyone acted friendly, appearing not to have a care in the world. Everywhere you turned there was laughter, children living in the excitement of the moment. It was like living in another world; a world of fantasy.

Before leaving, they stopped at a small gift shop. Nicole bought two pairs of Mickey Mouse ears. One as a gift to Ramrod as a joke, and another pair for herself. It would become part of a costume when she performed at the Two O'clock Club. She would give new meaning to the Mickey Mouse Revue.

They departed Disneyworld with the top down. Peaches and Bulldog were in perfect rhythm. She sang 'Mickey Mouse' while he chimed in 'Donald Duck'. They looked at each other, and laughed. It was fun to feel like a kid again.

* * *

Bulldog drove up Interstate 4. A sign at the side of the road read 'Daytona Beach 90 miles'. It was seventy-five degrees in Orlando, the sun shining brightly down on the racing car.

Nicole opened the center console, grabbing her sunglasses to put them on.

"Do you want to go to Daytona to check out bike week?"

"Sounds like a plan to me," Bulldog grinned.

Nicole placed her bare feet on the dashboard, making herself comfortable. Stopping for gas, Bulldog purchased a pair of dark sunglasses and a six pack of Budweiser beer.

Arriving in Daytona, they drove down Main Street. Traffic was bumper to bumper, moving along at a snails pace. The smell of the ocean was thick and salty, and thousands of bikers filled the sidewalks, drinking, laughing, shopping at the many novelty stores, and having an all around good time. The streets were lined with motorcycles backed up to the curb… full dressers, low riders, choppers, and three wheelers. Some bikers wore colors while others did not belong to any club. The bars were open for twenty-three hours, the law requiring them to close for one hour each day for cleaning. The last thing the bikers wanted to hear about were the Health regulations. In the minds of bikers there were only two requirements to be served alcohol. You had to have money and be able to reach the top of the bar.

Cocaine and marijuana were used openly. Cocaine was being used off counter tops, tables, and occasionally from a chuck's stomach, ass, or breast. The smell of marijuana filled the air. The police turned a blind eye to the drugs and outlaw bikers, only concerning themselves with keeping the peace. During Bike week the bars were permitted to remain open seven days a week.

Bulldog found a vacancy at the Sandpiper motel. It was a last minute cancellation. The room was located on the sixth floor, featuring a balcony overlooking the beach with a fantastic view.

After checking in, they walked to a nearby clothing store. Peaches purchased a white bikini, two beach towels, a pair of jeans, and matching shirts for her and Bulldog. He purchased a pair of jeans and settled on a pair of plain brown swimming trunks for swim wear.

"Good choice, they match your beard." Peaches laughed. There was never anything fancy in his wardrobe.

As a last thought, she purchased a bottle of Coppertone suntan lotion.

After going back to their motel room to change, Bulldog went out on the balcony and watched as a crowd gathered. A group of drunken bikers were tossing a naked girl in the air on a blanket. Up and down she flew. The crowd grew larger, making a cop come over to defuse the situation and rescue the girl. The bikers snatched him, stripped him of his clothes, and naked he flew up and down on the blanket while the naked girl ran away to safety. The cop's three-wheeler was driven into the ocean by a second group of bikers. Squad cars from three districts and two paddy wagons rushed to the scene, saving the cop and arresting bikers, when the paddy wagons left the crowd regrouped continuing the madness for the next two hours. Bulldog and Peaches watched it all from their balcony cheering the bikers on.

Bulldog left the room in search of a soft drink machine, promising to return with cold drinks. As soon as the door closed behind him, Peaches called Marsha to tell her that she was going to have to meet Marvin by herself.

"Tell Marvin I apologize, that I had a family emergency. I will call him as soon as I get home. Write this down. Hilton Hotel downtown. Tuesday night, room seven-fifteen, at five p.m."

"I'm not comfortable with this," Marsha admitted.

"You'll be fine. Have a good time." Peaches assured her, then quickly hung up the phone.

She was just in time. The key tuned in the lock of the door, and Bulldog entered the room.

CHAPTER EIGHT
FIELD OF DREAMS

Once again, Detective Marks parked the white Cadillac in the employee parking lot of the Baltimore City Police Department. While listening to the morning local news, he enjoyed his customary cigar. He took a sip of hot coffee from a paper cup, wishing in hindsight that he had thought to buy a donut when he stopped for gas on his way to work. After listening to the news he stepped from the car wearing his beige overcoat and matching hat, flipped the brim down, and flipped the collar of his coat up. Smoke filled the crisp morning air. The more he puffed, the more clouds of smoke drifted to his right. He looked up at his office on the third floor of the red brick building and methodically began his walk. The receptionist at the front desk bid him good morning. He nodded, grabbed a handrail and proceeded up the marbled steps. He could have taken the elevator but figured that the exercise would be good for him.

"It's your day to shine, Twinkle Toes." He said with a grin as he walked past Betty Crawford's desk.

After five years she was never surprised by anything coming out of his mouth. She had heard him rant, rage, scream, shout, and curse. But her favorite memory was of him holding his newborn son. He was a gentle giant with a tender touch. It was the first time she had seen that side of him, and knew she was unlikely to see it again anytime soon. At work he was all business. She watched as he went over to the coffee dispenser, making himself a fresh cup of coffee, while wondering what he meant by it being her time to shine. He did not leave her in suspense for long.

"Grab your coat and purse." He ordered, chuckling to himself. He could not believe he had just told her to grab her purse. In the good old days he pictured himself saying "Grab your guns." As fond as he was of Betty, he thought women had no place in this line of work. However, it did not matter what he thought, the Department's

Policy dictated otherwise. To her credit, she had long since earned his respect. She was both smart and tough.

"Good cop, bad cop." He asked.

"Sir?" she replied, not understanding what he meant.

"Do you want to be the good cop, or the bad cop." He asked slowly, then explained. "We are going to interview Charlie Redman this morning."

"Yes, sir." She stood up grabbing her coat off the back of her chair.

"Yes, what?" He stopped walking, waiting for clarification.

"Bad cop, sir. I'll be the bad cop." She replied, having gathered her thoughts.

They stepped lively out of the door and across the parking lot. Stopping at his car, he unlocked the driver's door, then pressed a button unlocking the passenger's door. Betty seated herself, immediately being hit with the foul stench of stale cigar smoke, Nothing was worse than having to ride in his car, she thought, the overpowering smell was almost too much for her to stand.

Charlie was laying in bed, with one armed draped over a pillow and a smile pursing his lips, dreaming that he was living in a huge castle, laying in the midst of a harem of gorgeous women. Three of the scantily dressed girls were taking turns feeding him green grapes from a vine, while belly dancers performed for his pleasure. In the distance, he heard a trumpet blow three times. The sound annoyed him, making him toss beneath the covers.

Moments later, a loud pounding had him sitting up in the bed. The noise was coming from the front of the house. Stumbling to his feet, he ran his fingers through his hair, wrapped himself in a soft blue cotton robe, and went to investigate. More pounding sent him to answer the front door.

"Charlie Redman." Detective Marks asked.

"Yes."

"I'm Detective Marks from the Baltimore City Homicide Division, and this is Detective Betty Crawford, We are investigating the murder of Roger Pickett. Did you know him?"

"Yes." Charlie answered flatly.

"We would like to ask you a few questions. Do you mind if we step inside?" Detective Marks asked.

"Yes, I do." Charlie retorted. "If you have any questions for me, call my attorney, Harold Glazer."

"Charlie, we are aware of the fact that Roger Pickett set you up."

"That's motive." Betty Crawford added sharply.

"We would simply like to get your side of the story," Detective Marks smiled.

"Talk to my attorney." Charlie repeated.

"I'm sure there were latent fingerprints found at the crime scene. If any are yours, you will be charged with murder. In this state murder carries the death penalty. Did you kill Roger for snitching on you? Where were you on the night of January first?" Betty Crawford pressed.

"Talk to my attorney." Charlie said flatly.

"If you cooperate now, you'll probably be spared the death penalty." Detective Marks offered.

"There's probably enough evidence to present the case to the grand jury right now," Betty Crawford added.

Charlie slammed the door in their faces.

"Well, that went well." Detective Marks chuckled. He stuck a business card in the door, looked sideways at Twinkle Toes, grinned and repeated her words. "We've probably got enough evidence to present the case to the grand jury?"

She shrugged her shoulders, smiled and replied. "It's all I could think of saying."

* * *

After a hard night of partying at The Landing with Big Moose and his crew, a very drunken Bulldog and Peaches returned to the motel and raced for the shower. They showered together, then collapsed on top of the bed butt naked, falling into a deep sleep. The balcony doors were wide open, allowing a gentle breeze to blow through the room. By 9 a.m. it was hot and humid.

Peaches screamed, kicking her feet wildly, causing Bulldog to come awake from a deep sleep to grab hold of her. Her eyes popped open and she sobbed.

"Are you alright?" he asked, holding her tightly in his arms.

"I had a terrible nightmare! It was about how my daughter was killed. Instead of the car disappearing around the corner, in my nightmare the car stopped, backed up, and ran over her again and again."

"You're okay now, baby." Bulldog reassured her, he patted her back and gently rubbed her shoulders to comfort her. But nothing could take her pain away.

Crying softly, Peaches jumped up and ran into the bathroom. Locking the door, she stepped into the bathtub to stand up under the hot shower, the weight of her loss bowing her down. She stayed in the shower until her tears had run their course. Going to the sink in the small bathroom, she brushed her teeth and combed her hair. When she exited the bathroom, Bulldog was dressed and waiting for her. He took her in his arms, holding her close. "I'm alright, baby," she assured him.

After dressing, she went out to stand on the balcony, tossing bread crumbs from a half uneaten sandwich to a flock of crying seagulls. When Bulldog stepped outside a few minutes later, she announced. "I want to go home."

"Home to Maryland," he asked.

"No. Home to Mama's."

He wrapped his arms around her from behind, kissed her neck, and replied. "Baby, whatever you want is fine with me."

Within minutes, the car was packed, the top was down, and the silver Mercedes-Benz was cruising up the coastal highway, going north on A-1-A.

Nicole's knees were resting comfortably against the dashboard, her hair blowing wildly in the wind. Despite wearing dark sunglasses to shield her eyes, she was still forced to squint into the glaring sun.

"What's that smell?" Peaches asked, sniffing the air. The fragrance was sweet and pleasant to her senses. "Look!" She exclaimed excitedly.

A sign on the left side of the road read WILLOW'S GARDENS AND RESTAURANT.

"Pull in there!" She pointed.

Bulldog slowed, signaling a left turn. They drove down a long single lane asphalt driveway. Sidewalks and paths on both sides of the driveway led from one flower garden to another.

"This is beautiful." Peaches marveled, trying not to miss anything. There were beds of yellow, pink, white, and red roses. There were Cherry Blossoms, shrubs, walkways, and a pond with a small bridge overlooking a wishing well.

"Would you like for me to find a parking space," Bulldog asked.

"No. But I want to rent a car and bring Mama and Charlotte here. I wonder if we need to make reservations for dinner?"

"Let's stop at the restaurant and ask." Bulldog suggested, happy to see her smile.

The restaurant had a rustic log exterior with huge Bay windows. A wooden sign hung from brass chains above the entrance. The sign read 'THE WILLOW'S', the name burned into the wood under a thick coat of glossy varnish. There were a dozen rocking chairs spread about the wooden railed and planked porch. Double doors led into the interior of the restaurant, one being used for the entrance, the other for the exit. The interior was decorated with knotty pine tables and chairs, while the tables were covered with red and white checkered table clothes. Huge ceiling fans with lights hung from the rafters, while to the left of the entrance an enormous stone fireplace ran half the length of one wall. Entering alone Bulldog stopped at the front desk.

"To eat here this evening, do I need to make reservations?"

"It's not a requirement, but it would certainly give you preferred seating," the female cashier replied.

Bulldog looked at his watch. It was 10 a.m. He wondered what would be a good time to make reservations?

"I would like to reserve a table for four. Could you make it for seven o'clock this evening?"

"Sir, what name do you wish to make the reservation under?" The spectacled hostess asked.

"Richard Doyle," he replied, acting as though he had made hundreds, maybe thousands of reservations.

"Seven o'clock it is, Mr. Doyle." The hostess smiled, patiently logging in the reservation.

Bulldog grinned, proud of his accomplishment.

Peaches noticed two pay phones on the covered porch and stepped out of the car to make a call to her sister. She told Charlotte to get herself and their mother dressed for dinner because she and Bulldog were on their way to pick them up. Bulldog stepped outside to find Peaches hanging up the phone. She dropped her sunglasses from her head to her nose and reported what she had done.

"I just called Charlotte Lynn and told her to get herself and Mama ready for dinner."

Charlotte Lynn was excited. It did not happen often where she was allowed to escape her boring every day life. Other than a trip to the grocery store or to church on Sunday, she was stuck in the house with her mother. Going out to dinner was going to be great.

The trailer was less than an hour's drive from Willow Gardens. Peaches pushed the sunglasses back on top of her head, grabbed the telephone directory and flipped through the Yellow pages in search of a rental car service. The closest one was at the airport, which was a two hour drive in the opposite direction.

"Shit! What now?" Peaches sighed,

"Look for a Limo service, or a cab." Bulldog suggested.

Peaches smiled, wondering why she hadn't thought of that. The only limousine service was in Gainesville, Georgia which was too far away to be considered. and there were no taxi cabs.

"Don't panic!" Bulldog growled. "Let's check into the Green Frog motel, buy some new clothes, and talk with the locals. They are more familiar with the area than we are. I promise, I will figure something out."

After purchasing new clothes, they rented a room, and while Peaches was busy getting herself together, Bulldog stepped outside to smoke a joint. On the far side of the restaurant, he noticed there was a U-Haul rental dealership. Parked alongside the yellow building, he saw a bright orange, black stripped, windowed extended van. U-Haul was painted across the sides and back doors in bold black letters. Upon closer inspection, the van had two front seats, a sliding door, and two bench seats.

Several minutes later, Peaches heard a strange horn honking outside the motel room. It was very annoying horn. It sounded like someone playing an instrument that was badly out of tune. She opened the door to the motel room, peered out, and laughed. Before her was the ugliest Dodge van she had ever seen, and Bulldog was sitting in the driver's seat with a joint dangling from his mouth. It was a hilarious sight. Laughing, she ran back inside to get her camera, capturing the moment before he could move a muscle. This photo was right up there with his wearing those ridiculous Mickey Mouse ears.

"I love you," she told him with a smile, opening the door to hop inside the passenger seat.

"Your chariot has arrived," he laughed.

The van was surprisingly spotlessly clean, but with no amenities. No air conditioning, power windows, seats, or locks. Luckily, it boasted an AM-FM radio.

"It's going to get us there and back," he promised her.

"It's fine." Peaches smiled, excepting the joint he passed.

"Then let's go get the troops," he grinned.

Beverly looked out of the kitchen window, saw the van turn into the driveway, and burst out laughing. "Here comes Nicky."

Fifteen minutes later they were in route to Willow's Gardens. Bulldog looked at his watch, it was 1:30 p.m.

As they parked, Beverly asked. "What is this place?"

"It's a pleasure garden. Acres and acres of flowers with paths and walkways. We are going to take in the sights, then have dinner. Bulldog made reservations for seven o'clock."

They walked over a wooden bridge. In the pond below were huge pink, gold, and albino fishes.

"Look at the purple violets." Charlotte gushed, pointing out the delicate flowers.

"They're gorgeous! How did you find this place." Beverly wanted to know.

"We were driving back from Daytona Beach when I smelled the roses." Nicole explained.

They wandered upon a field with a sign that read 'FIELD OF DREAMS'. The grass was green and plush like expensive carpet, the grass feeling velvety soft to the touch. The field was filled with dandelions and butterflies. Nicole and Charlotte Lynn took off their shoes, the grass cushioning their bare feet as they ran into the field, spinning around in circles with their arms outstretched.

"What are they doing?" Bulldog asked Beverly.

"Dancing with the butterflies." She replied, smiling proudly. The girls would forever be her babies.

It was a sight to behold. The sisters were graceful as two ballerinas and the butterflies fluttered around them playfully.

"Well, I'll be damned. Just when I thought I'd seen everything." Bulldog grinned, watching in awe.

CHAPTER NINE
HAPPY TRAILS

The Willow's restaurant was a warm, friendly, and relaxing atmosphere. The hostess had reserved them a table near the fireplace overlooking a scenic view of the meadow where the girls had danced with butterflies. It would be a moment that would be trapped in his mind forever. Words alone could not do the sight justice.

The waitress brought them menus, water, and hot dinner rolls. They all ordered prime rib, a baked potato, fresh vegetables, and a salad. Talking quietly to themselves about nothing in particular, they did find reason to comment on how delicious the meal was; the prime rib tender and juicy.

After dinner Nicole turned to Charlotte. Smiling, she announced. "I've got some photos from Disneyworld. Would you like to see them?"

Before Bulldog could get a word in edgewise, Nicole grabbed a stack of Polaroid photos from her purse. As she flipped through them, Charlotte and her mother watched. With Charlotte practically leaning over her shoulder, she passed each photo over after reviewing it herself first.

Bulldog cleared his throat twice.

Nicole ignored him, her face turning beet red as her slender hands quickly moved a photo to the bottom of the stack. Her eyes darted over to Bulldog.

"I was trying to warn you," he grinned sheepishly.

The photo was a picture of her laying butt naked across the bed in the hotel room in Daytona beach.

Having caught a glimpse of the photo, Charlotte Lynn burst into laughter.

"What's so funny?" Beverly asked, completely clueless.

"Nothing." Nicole gave her sister a sharp poke of her elbow.

"Well, what are you two laughing about?"

"Nothing, Mama." Nicole repeated, smiling.

* * *

"Harold Glazer's office." The receptionist answered.

"Is Mr. Glazer in?"

"May I ask who's calling and what it's regarding?"

"Charlie Redman. I had some detectives from the Baltimore City Homicide Division at my house this morning. They wanted to question me about a murder." The tone of his voice was that of a desperate man.

"Just a moment, please."

The receptionist buzzed Harold's office. When he picked up the phone, she said, "Charlie Redman is on line one. This morning he had visitors from the Baltimore City Homicide Division wanting to Question him about a murder."

"Thank you." Harold said, dismissing the receptionist.

After a count of ten, Harold answered. "Good morning, Charlie. What can I do for you?"

"Two detectives were at my door this morning, threatening to charge me with a murder."

"This doesn't sound like something that we should be discussing over the phone. When can you come to my office?"

"I can be there in forty-five minutes."

"I'll see you then." Harold said, hanging up the phone.

As Charlie was leaving the house, he found a card of Detective Mark's stuck in the door. He grabbed the card and stuck it in the top pocket of his shirt.

Harold Glazer's office was downtown, located on the ninth floor of the Keiser building. The outside was made of gray granite stone. Inside, there were marble floors in the foyer, and a waterfall was centered on the back wall. There were four elevators, two directly across the lobby from one another. Plush, dark red carpet ran the length of the Hallways.

Harold greeted Charlie at the receptionist's desk when he opened the outside door and stepped into the waiting area.

"Come on back to my office." Harold smiled, motioning for the door behind them.

Charlie reached into his shirt pocket to pull out the detective's card. He passed it to Harold as he moved around behind a large oak desk. "This detective, along with a female detective paid me a visit this morning. They reminded me of Jackie Gleason and Audrey Meadow of the hit 50's TV show, 'The Honeymooners.'"

Without looking at the card Harold chuckled. "That would be Detectives Marks and Betty Crawford."

"It appears that I am the prime suspect in their murder case and she told me I can expect to be indicted because I had a motive."

"Did you do it?"

"Of course not!" Charlie snapped. "I had nothing to do with that."

"Do you know who did?"

"No." Charlie sighed.

"Where were you when it happened?"

"I don't know. Probably home in bed."

"Don't lie to me, Charlie. This is serious business."

"I swear, I don't know anything."

"We need to clear you of this as soon as possible. Do you have any objections of my volunteering you to take a polygraph? It would be no cost to you."

"A polygraph?" Charlie frowned.

"If you intend to purchase the house in Millerville, you can't afford to be the focus of a murder investigation." Harold explained.

"Whatever you say." Charlie agreed after a moment's hesitation.

Harold picked the card up from his desk and dialed the number on its face.

"Detective Marks." The voice on the other end answered. "Harold Glazer. I understand that you have been harassing one of my clients."

"Any one in particular?" Detective Marks chuckled.

"Charlie Redman. I believe you and Betty Crawford paid him a visit this morning."

"We did. Your client didn't invite us inside, or offer us coffee and donuts. He slammed the door in our faces. Imagine our disappointment."

"Well, my friend. You are a donut short of a heart attack. I wouldn't care to defend Charlie for his having contributed to your demise."

"What can I do for you, Harold?" Detective Marks demanded.

The two men had known each other for too many years to count. They played golf, bowled, and matched wits on the opposite side of the law.

"My client would like to cooperate."

"Twinkle Toes!" Detective Marks shouted across the squad room. "Sharpen your pencil, Charlie Redman wants to make a confession."

"I didn't say that." Harold corrected him. "Charlie would like to clear his good name. He will freely give you fingerprints, palm prints, even toe prints if you want them. He will give a statement and he's agreed to take a polygraph."

"If he didn't do it then he knows who did," Marks growled.

"No, he doesn't. Ask him on the polygraph. You are barking up the wrong tree. Rather than have you waste your time, Charlie would rather have this matter cleared up."

"So would I." Marks suddenly began to consider the possibility that Redman had nothing to do with the death of Pickett. If Charlie did not kill Roger Pickett and had no involvement, then the investigation would return to square one. "Would Charlie be willing to come in this afternoon?"

"Absolutely."

"Then I'll see you at three-thirty."

Later that afternoon, Charlie walked into the Police Department escorted by his attorney, Harold Glazer. He gave a very brief statement claiming to have no knowledge concerning the demise of Roger

Pickett. Shortly thereafter he passed a polygraph test with flying colors. A frustrated Detective Marks watched him exit the room where the polygraph had been held. As Harold and Charlie left the police station, Charlie glanced over his shoulder.

"Happy trails to you... until we meet again." He sang. Harold chuckled.

"Can I buy my house now?" Charlie asked.

"How much money would you like to put into the Trust Fund account?"

"Can I receive a monthly check from the Trust Fund?"

"Of course."

"That's great. I intend to start by putting in seven hundred and fifty thousand dollars."

"What's the price on the house in Millersville?" Harold asked.

"Two hundred and fifty thousand. Would it be possible for the Trust Fund to send me a monthly check of twenty-five hundred dollars?"

"No problem." Harold grinned.

"It's kind of ironic."

"What is?"

"More than likely I'll be putting two hundred and fifty thousand into the Trust Fund each month," Charlie laughed. He immediately had another thought. "Am I going to be required to claim the money I receive and pay taxes at the end of the year?"

"Of course!" Harold laughed. "But I can arrange for the accountant that handles the Trust Fund to take care of that for you. All you will need to do is sign your name, and that will keep the I.R.S. from knocking on your door."

"How soon can the Trust purchase the house?"

"As soon as you give me the money to open the account." Harold said, a smile lighting his face.

"I will bring the money to you in the morning."

"Meet me at my office around seven in the morning. Don't be late because I have a court hearing at eight. Call the Realtor and have him call my office. I'll take care of everything," Harold promised.

Charlie grinned. He was happy with Harold's performance and even more pleased with himself. He had handled things just as Peaches suggested. If he was any prouder of his accomplishments, he would have to pat himself on the back.

Charlie and Harold shook hands, separating to go in different directions. Charlie stepped lively to reach the underground parking lot where his car was parked. He dreaded having to park his prized Corvette downtown, having heard somewhere that in New York a Corvette was stolen every seven minutes. He reasoned that in Baltimore there was not nearly as much day time theft. He was still happy to find his Corvette parked where he had left it.

* * *

After dinner, Nicole excused herself to go to the powder room. A few minutes later Charlotte Lynn excused herself to follow her sister. Stepping into the ladies room she saw Nicole standing over two lines of white powder laid out on top of a compact mirror. Nicole was in the process of rolling up a dollar bill.

"What is that, Nicky?"

"It's crystal meth. It gives you an indescribable feeling."

"Can I have some?"

"No! Mama would kill me!"

"If you don't give me some, I'll tell Mama."

"You're a conniving little bitch." Nicole giggled.

Charlotte Lynn took the rolled up dollar and snorted a line. She immediately felt a burning sensation and sneezed hard. Nicole laughed. Recovering from the unfamiliar burning sensation, Charlotte smiled.

"What do you do for fun?" Nicole asked, concerned for her little sister not having any fun.

"The highlight of my week is when someone picks me and mama

up for church on Sundays," Charlotte sighed.

At that point Nicole knew that her little sister's entire life consisted of her being there with their mother, never grumbling, complaining or feeling sorry for herself.

"I love you, Nicky." Charlotte Lynn whispered softly.

"I love you too." Nicole replied, her eyes filling with tears.

"When will you be leaving?"

"Probably tomorrow night."

"How long is it gonna be before I see you again?"

"I don't know." Nicole replied honestly. "Maybe you could come spend a week with me sometime. I'll pay for everything."

"That would be fantastic. But who would keep Mama company? I wouldn't feel comfortable leaving her by herself."

"Maybe someone from the church. I would also pay someone to stay with her." Nicole offered.

Charlotte was overwhelmed at the mere thought of her going to visit Nicole in Maryland, She had read stories and watched movies about big cities. But before now she had only dreamed of visiting such a place.

High on crystal meth, they returned to the table wearing big smiles. Nicole and Charlotte turned their conversation to their younger years of boys and a creek they all swam in. Beverly and Bulldog could not get a word in edgewise.

"What's wrong with these two?" Beverly asked laughing.

Bulldog had a pretty good inclination. He excused himself, went to the men's rest-room, laid out two lines, deciding to join the party.

Bulldog sat back down at the table drawing looks and laughter from Nicole and Charlotte. They knew what he had done.

It was 9 a.m. when they pulled into the driveway at the trailer. The headlights fell on a small critter in the middle of the driveway. It was brown and furry with fiery red eyes.

"It's a raccoon!" Nicole shouted, excited to see it after spending so much time living the life of a city girl.

Bulldog and Nicole were anxious to return to the comforts of their motel room. After escorting Beverly and Charlotte inside the trailer, they sat down for a few minutes to talk. Finally, it was time for them to go, promising they would return in the morning.

Within minutes they pulled up in front of their motel room. The second they entered the room Nicole began taking off her clothes. "I want some." She demanded, shoving him backwards onto the bed.

"You'll get no argument from me," he laughed.

Nicole smiled, already unzipping his pants, and tracing his happy trail with her tongue to his already throbbing dick. She wrapped her little hands around it, placed it in her mouth and began sucking hard.

Jerking away from her Bulldog took over. He unzipped her jeans, shoved them down over her knees, then pushed them off using his right foot. He grabbed a bare tit and squeezed a hard nipple.

Nicole moaned. He threw her on the bed and mounted her, holding her legs in the air, and fucking into her hard. Within minutes she cried out in sheer ecstasy, causing him to explode deep inside her tight, warm pussy.

She lay with her head on his shoulder, her right hand busy caressing his pounding chest.

"I love you," she whispered.

"I love you, too." he replied.

"What did you say?" Nicole smiled.

"If you didn't hear it the first time, you're out of fuckin' luck." he grinned.

"I heard you!" Nicole declared happily.

CHAPTER TEN
JUSTIFIED

Beep... beep... beep. The alarm next to Harold's enormous king sized bed went off at 6 a.m. He quickly shut the alarm off, not wanting to disturb his wife. Emily was a bitch from the time her head came off the pillow. Lord knows she needed her beauty sleep, he thought to himself as he slowly crawled from the bed.

Harold stumbled to the bathroom to shower and shave. He looked at himself in the mirror, taking careful note of his plump, rosy red checks. He knew that a twenty pound weight loss would make him happy and do much to improve his appearance. Exiting the bathroom he walked to the walk-in closet and picked out a blue pin-stripe suit, a light blue dress shirt with matching tie and a pair of black alligator loafers with tassels.

He wore gold cuff links engraved with his initials, a diamond tie clasp, and a gold Rolex watch. Harold never left the house without first considering how he might look in the public eye. His motto was to always dress for success.

Harold looked over at Emily, who was still sound asleep. Her hair was a complete mess, the pink plaid pajamas she slept in doing her no favors in making herself more appealing. She had become the kind of woman that could only be helped with tons of make-up and body supports. Shaking his head at such a waste of a California King sized bed, he exited the bedroom to go downstairs to the most modern kitchen that money could buy. After drinking a tall glass of Minute Maid orange juice, he left the house through the front door.

Daylight was just breaking over the horizon, the morning air crisp and chilly. Harold unlocked the door to his brand new Cadillac Coupe Deville, climbed in, and keyed the ignition.

He drove straight to his office, parking in his designated space in the underground parking lot of the Keiser building. His space was reserved by a metal plaque fastened to the wall with his name engraved on it.

Charlie was awake most of the night counting money, going through the process twice to make sure there were no mistakes. Finally satisfied with the results, he showered, combed his hair and dressed in beige pants, a white sweater, and soft imported brown Italian loafers. For breakfast he made himself two slices of buttered toast smothered in strawberry jam and a black cup of coffee. Wearing a soft brown leather bomber jacket, he walked out to his car, dreading the thought of having to park his prized Corvette in the downtown underground parking garage. He was relieved when he arrived at his destination to discover a parking space near the attendant's booth.

Carrying an oversized gym bag in each hand, he rode the elevator to the ninth floor. Harold was there to meet him as he stepped off the elevator, holding the door to his office open for his entrance. Charlie led the way inside. As the door closed, Charlie chuckled to himself placing the two bags on top of the receptionist desk.

"They match your suit," he said already unzipping a bag.

"Would you like to count it?"

"I'm not counting that," Harold grinned. "The bank can count it!"

"I talked to the Realtor last night. He will be calling the office for you around ten."

"I won't be here." Harold quickly replied. "I will leave instructions with my secretary to take care of that. One of my junior associates will be spending his day setting up the Trust Fund. Before I forget, I need the name of someone in your family who died and could have left you a sizable inheritance?"

"I had a wealthy uncle in Florida who passed away last year. During the depression he had no job or money. He went out and bought a brand new Cadillac and a set of golf clubs. On the golf course he met Harry Reese. Harry was a Taxidermist with displays all along the gulf coast. Harry was a millionaire and he backed my uncle Walt so he could start a welding company in Fort Lauderdale. From there…"

"I don't need his life history, Charlie." Harold interrupted him. "I just need a name."

"Walter Ryan Redman," Charlie chuckled.

"Thank you."

"How soon can I move into the house?"

"How fast can the Realtor close? I will suggest he allow you to move in, pay rent, and apply the rent towards the cost of the house. If he agrees to that, you could have the keys this afternoon, I intend to make it known there's no financing involved. The money to pay for the house will be placed in Escrow. At the closing, I will present a Cashier's check for the full purchase price."

"I will give you a call this afternoon." Charlie promised with a smile before leaving the attorney's office.

Charlie found his thoughts drifting to Nicole. He wondered where she was, what she was doing, and when she would be back. In a strange way, he missed her.

* * *

Nicole was sleeping peacefully with one hand on Bulldog's chest and her left leg covering his. She awoke, startled by the annoying short snorts coming from Bulldog. She rolled over being careful not to awake him as she crawled out of bed. Bulldog's watch on the bedside table told her that it was 9 a.m., and she already knew it to be Wednesday. Her first thought as she came fully awake, was to wonder how things had gone with Marsha and the governor. It had probably been awkward for Marsha, especially with her not having been able to call before her arrival. Hopefully, Marvin had not been upset. Manny had kindly covered her with his claim of a hunting trip. The only thing making her feel guilty was leaving Blaze in need of help. It would be a small consolation, but she had not forgot Blaze's request for peaches.

Nicole showered and dressed. She put the room key in her pocket, grabbed her sunglasses from the nightstand and quietly closing the door to the motel room, she stepped outside into the early morning warmth. If the present warmth was any indication, the day promised to be bright and sunny. She wore a pair of cut-off jeans, a white windbreaker, and a pair of tan leather moccasins. She loved the moccasins because they were not only unique but unbelievably comfortable. Nicole decided that she should buy four more pair. One for Marsha, a pair for Blaze, and at least two more for herself.

On the other side of the clothing store stood a large fruit stand. Peaches ordered six baskets of oranges, grapefruit, and tangerines to be shipped to Blaze, Charlie, Marsha, Ramrod, Manny, and governor Marvin Mandell. To Blaze's shipment she added a large shipment of the promised peaches. Then she stopped at the restaurant and ordered two large cups of black coffee, to go. When she returned to the room Bulldog was awake and in the shower. She peeked inside the bathroom, saw the silhouette of his body in the frosted glass and stood there for a minute before announcing. "I got you a cup of coffee."

"Thanks, baby. I'll be right out."

She took a second look at his naked body, giggled, and left the door partially open. Just for her to lay on the bed and sneak a peek when he stepped out of the shower. Damn, he was good looking, she thought to herself with a shake of her head. She picked up the phone and called the trailer to let her mother and Charlotte know they would be there in less than thirty minutes.

After Bulldog dressed, they checked out of the Green Frog motel. Arriving at the trailer, they discovered a large breakfast waiting for them.

"Seat yourself, son." Mama told Bulldog, having warmed to him over the previous night's dinner. "Nicky, would you please get the milk, orange juice, butter and jelly from the refrigerator and set it on the table."

"Yes, Mama." Nicole smiled, pausing to give her mother a quick peck on the cheek.

When Charlotte Lynn walked into the kitchen, Bulldog's eyes

almost popped out of his head. She was wearing cut-off shorts, exposing the cheeks of her ass, even more so than Nicole's. Charlotte had taken the time to tie a blue halter top above her waist, exposing her bare midriff, her auburn hair was brushed to hang down her back, She was wearing pink lipstick with blue mascara under her eyes, and her cheeks were powdered a rosy red.

"Where do you think you're going?" Nicole laughed.

"Back to the bathroom so she can wash her face and dress in something more appropriate." Beverly spoke sternly.

"What's wrong with the way I'm dressed? You never say anything to Nicky about how she dresses!"

"You look pretty good to me," Bulldog grinned.

"Thank you, Bulldog." Charlotte gave him a pleased smile.

Nicole smacked the back of his head with the palm of her hand. "Get your eyes back in your head. That's my little sister!"

"She don't look so little to me," he teased.

"Bulldog, you stop encouraging her." Beverly told him with a tolerant smile.

"Yes, Ma'am," he smiled.

"And you, young lady." Beverly continued, pointing an accusing fork at Charlotte. "Get your butt back in there this instant."

"It's not fair. I'm twenty-one years old now, Mama." She yelled and stomped off.

"Life's a bitch!" Nicole shouted after her.

"Nicky!" Beverly snapped sharply. There was no need for her to antagonize her little sister.

After a hearty breakfast Bulldog walked outside to enjoy the fresh air. The women chatted while washing and putting away the dishes. Bulldog found a seat in a folding lawn chair and looked out over the pond. The water was like a sheet of glass. It rippled when an occasional small fish broke the surface, the tall pine trees and golden reeds mirrored in their reflections. A mother and her baby duckling waddled into the pond for a swim.

Bulldog walked back into the trailer and asked for some bread to feed the ducks. Smiling, Beverly gave him several slices of stale bread. Going back outside he stood at the edge of the pond, breaking the bread into smaller pieces and tossing them to the ducks. The bread caused a brief feeding frenzy with the fish, scaring the ducks away.

Watching from the kitchen window the three women broke into hysterical laughter.

"If you want to feed the ducks, sprinkle the bread on the ground." Beverly yelled out of the window.

Bulldog hoped the ducks would get out of the water quickly before the birds ate the bread.

"When are you leaving?" Beverly asked.

"Sometime before noon."

"It's been so good having you here." Beverly said, her eyes suddenly tearing.

"It's been wonderful, Mama. I promise I'll return again real soon."

"You better keep your promise." Charlotte Lynn warned.

"What promise?" Their mother asked.

"It's between sisters, Mama."

Nicole smiled. She looked at her sister and assured her. "I won't forget."

They all hugged saying their goodbyes. They stopped to fill the gas tank before getting on highway 301 North. By 3 p.m. the State of Georgia was in their rearview mirror.

"I had a good time." Nicole smiled, reclining back in the passenger seat.

"So did I." Bulldog grinned.

They were both looking forward to returning to their normal lives. Bulldog was driving with the convertible top down, and Nicole's hair blowing wildly in the wind. She was lost in her own thoughts, thinking about how she never regretted leaving home. When they stopped to refuel and stretch their legs, Bulldog called Ramrod to let him know they were on their way back.

Back in Pennsylvania the cabin was filled with brothers coming inside to get out of the cold. The weather between Florida and Pennsylvania was like comparing night and day. It was bone chilling cold in the hills of Pennsylvania. Dollar had just rode in on his Harley from Harrisburg and he was warming his hands by the fire.

* * *

Bulldog and Nicole took turns at the wheel and drove throughout the night. It was 2 p.m., when they arrived at the cabin. Ramrod stepped outside to greet them.

"I sent you a basket of fruit." Peaches announced with a smile.

Ramrod grinned. "I can't remember the last time anyone gave me anything. The last time was a girl in Kentucky and I had to go to a Doctor to get rid of it," he laughed. "What's the catch? What do you want, Peaches?"

"A gun. I want a gun for protection."

"You don't need a gun." Ramrod chuckled, recalling the time she caught Bulldog in bed with two other women.

"A gun?" Bulldog repeated. "Have I done something that I'm not aware of? This is news to me too!"

"I don't want to shoot you, it's for protection. I've been kidnapped before."

"I've got just the thing for you."

Ramrod led them back into the warmth of the cabin. He left them to go into his bedroom, returning a few minutes later with a .25 semiautomatic pistol.

"I don't want that!" Peaches snapped, drawing laughter from the other club members. "I want something that's going to get someone's fuckin' attention."

Peaches took it upon herself to go into Ramrod's bedroom. On the night-stand next to his bed was a phone and a pearl handled Colt .45 automatic. Peaches snatched up the gun and returned to the front room. "This is what I want!"

"I'm not so sure she can handle a gun that big," Bulldog laughed. The mere thought of her holding the gun in her tiny hands amused him.

"She's justified in wanting to protect herself." Ramrod admitted.

"Would you care to find out if I can handle it?" She challenged. "Have the Prospect set-up five empty beer bottles on top of a picnic table and count off twenty-five yards. If I can hit three out of five, give me the gun."

"Sounds fair to me." Ramrod agreed.

There were loud shouts of approval, then a mad scramble for coats and hats. Once outside, the Prospect lined the bottles up on top of the picnic table, then counted off twenty-five yards by taking giant steps.

"I've got ten bucks on Peaches!" The Prospect shouted, hustling to get out of the line of fire.

"I'll take that bet!" Ramrod called out.

Wagers were soon being made amongst the club members, half of them for Peaches and half against. Most were shocked to watch Peaches expertly checking the gun, making sure that it was loaded and in good working condition. She walked to the picnic table, paced off her own thirty yards and turned in one swift motion. Flipping off the safety, she looked down the sight and began firing, hitting one bottle after another. There was a moment of complete silence, then the brothers erupted in shouts of stunned approval.

"Where in the fuck did you learn to shoot like that?" asked a stunned Bulldog.

"You saw where I grew up. There wasn't much to do for entertainment. I went hunting and fishing with my daddy since I was ten years old."

"I wish you had learned to cook," Bulldog cracked.

Ramrod gave Peaches a box of ammunition to go along with his prized Colt .45. Then, he begrudgingly handed a ten dollar bill to the Prospect.

CHAPTER ELEVEN
SCRUFFY

Peaches stayed the night at the cabin. The next day she drove home to her apartment, and immediately placed a call to Marsha. On the third ring Marsha answered. "Hello?"

"Hi girl. How was your week?" Peaches giggled, anxious to hear about her date with the governor.

"It was interesting. Thanks for the basket of fruit! It arrived this morning."

"Did you fuck the governor?" Nicole asked bluntly.

"I did," Marsha laughed. "But not before I gave him a blow job. I was in his room for four hours."

"Well, he certainly got his moneys worth." Nicole laughed.

"Did he appear upset because I wasn't there?"

"Not at all. He was happy you sent me."

"Great! I sent him a basket of fruit."

"Did you?" Marsha laughed. "I don't know why that should surprise me."

"I' m looking forward to our seeing Manny Wednesday." Nicole said, wondering if Marsha knew that he had not gone hunting.

"Me too!" Marsha replied.

"Well, I just wanted to give you a jingle to let you know that I was back."

"Bitch, you just wanted to know if I fucked Marvin." Marsha laughed.

"That too."

"Did you enjoy the trip?"

"It was fantastic. I took some photos. I'll bring them with me Wednesday."

"Sounds great. I'll see you then."

Nicole' s second call was to Manny. He thanked her for the basket of fruit, said that he missed her, and was looking forward to seeing both her and Marsha on Wednesday.

The third call was to Charlie. He excitedly told her about his new Trust Fund, explaining that he would be moving into the house in Millersville in the morning.

"Have you heard anything else about Roger Pickett." Nicole asked.

"Yeah. Harold Glazer called the two detectives that threatened to charge me with murder. I gave them a statement, took a polygraph, and they cleared me."

"That's great news, Charlie."

"What are you doing tonight? Will you help me pick out some new furniture? I really want to show you my new house. Besides, you need to know where I live."

Nicole agreed. "Okay, Charlie. I'll meet you at the White Coffee Pot in Glen Burnie at four o' clock, I'm not going to stay out all day. I need to get some rest tonight."

"That's fine. Thanks," he replied.

Nicole's final call was to Blaze at the Two O'clock Club. When Blaze heard her voice on the other end, it was as though a heavy weight had been lifted from her shoulders.

"Peaches? Are you back?"

"I'm at home."

"I just received a basket of fruit this morning. Thank you for the peaches."

"I didn't forget." Peaches giggled.

"Can you come in to work tonight? It's been crazy since you left. The court appointed Natasha two attorneys and she fired them both. Then she tried to commit suicide. She's got it in her head that shooting the no good bastard was justified. Also, you should know that I hired two new girls. Neither one of them has any talent. I really need you on the stage before all of my regulars go elsewhere."

"I'll be there by nine." Peaches promised, realizing that her plans to go to bed early weren't going to happen.

"I'm so glad you're back." Blaze said, giving a sigh of relief.

Nicole opened her purse, pulled out a baggy of cocaine, snorting two lines of cocaine. It felt good to be home.

* * *

Charlie's blue Corvette was parked in front of the White Coffee Pot when Nicole arrived. She parked her silver Mercedes beside his Corvette, stepped out, and immediately slipped on the frozen ice.

"Damnit." She cursed.

Watching from the comfort of a warm window booth, Charlie chuckled.

Entering the restaurant, Nicole caught the tail end of his smile. "That was funny, huh?" She asked seating herself across from him.

"Not really. But the look on your face and imagining you cursing was." He admitted.

"Fuck you, Charlie!" She smiled.

"That's the best offer I've had all day." Charlie grinned.

Peaches immediately changed the subject. "What kind of furniture are you looking to buy? Modern, contemporary, or antique?"

"Modern. I want a king sized bed, a complete living room set, a dining room table with a hutch, a soft leather group for the den, and maybe some patio furniture."

"Keep in mind that if you spend more than ten-thousand dollars in one store, they are required to report the transaction to the I.R.S."

"I'm sure glad you're with me because I would have fucked things up, for sure."

Charlie ordered a BLT sandwich, fries, and a Coca-Cola. Nicole ordered hot chocolate with marshmallows.

Nicole left the Mercedes at the restaurant and went with Charlie from one store to another, furniture shopping. Deliveries were guaranteed for the following day before five p.m.

Charlie's new home was impressive, especially the back yard.

There was an Olympic pool with a waterfall feature. The pool was covered and winterized, but she could see the rock formation the waterfall would cascade from in the summer. A detached plain white cinder block building hosted his and her restrooms, and on the patio there was a large built-in grill.

"I see what you mean about this being a great place for entertaining," Nicole smiled.

"I owe it all to you, baby." Charlie admitted, then thoughtfully added. "And thanks for the basket of fruit."

Returning Nicole to her car, they said their goodbyes, promising to hook up again real soon.

Nicole rarely drove the Mercedes to work. Instead, she drove the yellow Bug, and today there was no exception. The Bug was less likely to be stolen or vandalized. After parking, she walked into the Two O' Clock Club at precisely 8:45 p.m. When she went backstage, she was shocked to see her name "Peaches" stenciled on a private dressing room door. Nicole opened the door and stepped inside. Their outfits were neatly hung from a shiny metal rack. Against the wall directly in front of her, was a vanity with a huge mirror and a row of low density bulbs recessed above it. Two bouquets of flowers were thoughtfully placed on the counter of the vanity. She read the cards. One was from Manny, the other from Marvin Mandell. She felt like a movie star.

"Do you like it?" Blaze peeked her head in the door.

"Like it? I love it!"

Fifteen minutes later, Peaches went on stage wearing a three quarter length black fur coat with black mesh stockings. Beneath the coat, she wore a black wrap around skirt and a black g-string with black tassels covering her nipples. On top of her head, she wore a pair of black Mickey Mouse ears.

"Guess where I've been?" She announced to the crowded club.

Amidst sudden loud calls of welcoming her back, she dropped the fur coat to the floor of the stage. She strutted up and down like a lioness stalking its prey. She methodically unwrapped the skirt and let it fall away from her body. Starting slow to a steady buildup, she gave a performance that was worthy of an Oscar, capturing the audience in her spell like a spider weaving its web. None of the other dancers could bring a crowd to their feet like she could, not even the legendary Blaze Starr. Blaze's perfect set of double D's were certainly a crowd pleaser, and her flaming red hair caught the attention of every man in the room. What Peaches lacked in God given assets, she more than made up for in personality. When she took the stage she became every man's fantasy.

Nicole loved being the one to give so many people so much pleasure. She loved the limelight. There was no feeling in the world that compared to the high she reached when performing on stage.

* * *

At the weekly meeting of the Baltimore City Homicide Division, Detective Marks was asking. "Does anyone have any new information regarding the Pickett murder?"

There was no response.

He directed the next question to Betty Crawford. "Nothing, Twinkle Toes?"

"No, sir," she replied. "Charlie Redman passed the polygraph. He had nothing to do with the murder, and he doesn't know who did. So, we are back to square one. Hit the streets, somebody knows something." Detective Marks snarled at the other detectives.

"Sir, with all due respect." Detective Wyatt retorted. "Polygraphs aren't always a hundred percent accurate. We were taught that in training."

"In training, huh?" Detective Marks barked. "Well, in this case it's ninety-nine point nine percent accurate. Is that sufficient enough for you?"

"Yes, Sir."

* * *

Three weeks passed, placing Charlie firmly in his new house in Millerville, and everything had returned to its normal routine. On Tuesday, Charlie dropped a blue gym bag filled with ten kilos of cocaine off at Nicole's apartment. Like clockwork, Wednesday at two o'clock Harold Glazer knocked on the apartment door, picking up the gym bag, and leaving behind two hundred and fifty thousand dollars on the kitchen table. Nicole took out twenty thousand dollars for herself, then she put his money into a brown paper grocery bag and placed it on the floor of the hall closet. Leaving the apartment she drove straight over to Marsha's house and they went together over to Manny's penthouse suite. Before going to work on Thursday, Nicole stopped by Charlie's house, giving him the proceeds from the sale of the drugs.

* * *

Charlie was neatly stacking wood next to the fireplace when the phone rang.

"Hello." Charlie answered.

"Peanut?" The voice on the other end asked, the sound of humor clearly heard over the line.

"Juice!" Charlie exclaimed, happy to hear his friends voice. Charlie shared many fond memories with Brad 'Juice' Bernhagen. Their friendship beginning when they shared a cell at the Maryland House of Corrections. The locals called the prison 'Jessups Cut' due to the daily stabbings.

"Pack a bag! I need your help this weekend." Juice reported.

"I'll be there." Charlie said without any hesitation.

"I'll see you then, my friend." Juice said flatly, ending the conversation.

CHAPTER TWELVE
OPEN WATERS

Friday morning, Charlie caught the early bird flight from Baltimore International Airport to Tampa, Florida. Upon his arrival in Tampa, he took time out to make arrangements for a Monday afternoon return flight before renting a small, white, compact Ford from Avis rent-a-car.

Enjoying the warmth of the sunny day, Charlie drove to the condo on Marco Island to meet with Brad Bernhagen, better known as Juice. Juice stood an easy six-one, weighing a solid two hundred pounds with brown hair and blue eyes. With his rippled washboard stomach he looked like a Greek god. Charlie was shorter with brown hair, the only six pack he ever had was in his dreams. No one would ever mistake the two men for brothers. It had been a little over a year since the two men had seen each other, their last meeting ending in Juice introducing Charlie to John Leder. They had partied in Miami afterwards, and it was also the place where Juice purchased their matching gold chains and medallions made from Pike's Peak gold. Charlie had sworn to never part with the gift.

It was eleven a.m. when Charlie pulled into the parking lot of the staggered high-rise buildings. Just beyond them was the ocean and miles of sandy beach. Charlie parked the rental car, catching sight of Juice in the distance walking the shoreline, wearing light Bermuda shorts and a lightweight white windbreaker, unzipped, displaying his bronze physique. His blonde curly hair was blowing wildly in the wind.

Charlie honked the horn, waving as he stepped out of the rental car. Juice waved back, already heading his way.

"Why didn't you call?" Juice asked, greeting his friend with a firm handshake, a half hug, and a slap on the back. "I would have picked you up in a Limo."

"I caught the early bird special to Tampa on American Airlines.

I think we both know that you don't do mornings." Charlie grinned, grabbing his suitcase from the back seat.

"I'm glad you're here. We are meeting a shrimp boat tomorrow morning at four a.m. The timing is critical because it starts turning daylight around five-thirty. We've got to be back at the dock by then." Juice explained.

"No problem. But tonight we party." Charlie grinned.

"I'm with you on that." Juice laughed.

"My ex was in Florida last month. Orlando, I think, Nicole took her boyfriend to Disneyworld." Charlie explained as they headed for Juice's high rise condo.

"Are you still talking to that skinny bitch?" Juice said, recalling the stories Charlie had told him about her. She was the reason Charlie went to prison, and while he was there she divorced his ass.

"She's changed. She put on a few pounds, performs burlesque, and even gets high. Honestly, she probably the coolest chick I know."

"Uh-oh." Juice said, stopping to look at Charlie.

"Uh-oh what?" Charlie laughed. "Can't I be friends with my ex-wife? We're just friends. Her stage name is 'Peaches' and she helped me pick out the furniture for my new house."

Juice chuckled as they continued on their way, entering the building past a uniformed doorman, who nodded a greeting to Juice.

"Good afternoon, Mr. Bernhagen!" The middle aged man spoke respectfully.

"George." Juice returned the greeting turning his attention back to Charlie. "She helped you pick out the furniture? Has she helped you try out the new mattress?"

"No. The bitch charges me for sex. She says that when it was for free that I didn't want it."

"She makes you pay to have sex with her?" Juice laughed in disbelief.

"Well, she does have some good pussy." Charlie admitted laughing.

Juice shook his head in disbelief. They entered the private elevator leading up to the penthouse. He could not believe his own ears. Charlie Redman was paying to fuck his ex-wife. She never took time out to visit him during his stay in prison, then she divorced his ass. It made absolutely no sense to him.

Friday night, Charlie and Juice went to Apples Place, a local bar where drug dealers and girls looking for a good time gathered to party. Juice's entrance into the dimly lit bar drew the attention of a group of beautiful woman, who fought to hug and claim him as their own. The loud music made it difficult to hold a conversation so Charlie stood back smiling. It reminded him of bees swarming their nest to protect it. Smiling, Charlie went along with the flow, following the group in the direction of a large half circular booth at the rear of the bar. It was a common sight to see people snorting lines of cocaine from the tops of tables and compact mirrors.

Charlie zeroed in on a short brunette. She appeared to be shy and much quieter than the other women.

"Wanna dance?" He approached her.

"Sure." She smiled, taking in his expensive clothing of slacks and silk shirt opened at the neck.

"I'm Charlie. What's your name, gorgeous?"

"My friends call me Dee Dee. I'm just here on vacation for a few days. I'm visiting a friend."

"Me too." Charlie grinned. "Where are you from?"

"Harrisburg, Pennsylvania."

Charlie laughed. "We're practically neighbors. I live in Millersville, Maryland. I'm visiting a friend for the weekend."

Charlie and Dee Dee danced, laughed, and partied the night away. Juice finally settling on Dee Dee's girlfriend, Crystal. At closing, the two couples retired to Juice's condo. Charlie and Dee Dee took off their shoes, going for a walk along the beach, deep in conversation and holding hands. There was a full moon, waves breaking along the shoreline, leaving a white froth at the waters enge. The bright moon and stars lit up the darkness of the night. Dee Dee pointed a finger skyward.

"I think that's the big dipper."

Charlie looked in the direction she pointed. "I wrote a poem about the stars."

"Do you remember it?" She asked.

"Yes. The name of the poem is 'Futurity'.

As God created the Galaxy

with His heavenly touch of reality

a star spangled banner clustered gallantly.

And somewhere within the celestial sphere,

our father's home we know is near.

With tongues well oiled we fluently

named each shining star construently.

Pluto, Venus, Neptune, and Mars

and the Goddess of love among the stars.

The big dipper, the little one and Leo the lion

the falling star, our wishful sign.

The cosmic system and the Milky Way

and the Northern star that shines it's ray

radiates the night of our worldly dome

the abode of Saints our eternal home!"

"You didn't write that, did you?" Dee Dee questioned.

"I promise you, I did." Charlie smiled proudly.

"I think you should publish it," she declared.

"What is your full name, Dee Dee?"

"Promise not to laugh."

"Scouts honor."

"Dorothy Dawn Carusso."

"That's a very pretty name. Why would I laugh?"

"What's your name," she asked.

"Charlie Ryan Redman. Juice sometimes calls me, Peanut. It's a nickname that he gave me."

"When I was a little girl kids teased me. They said that I was

Dorothy from the Wizard of Oz. I was happy when my friends started calling me Dee Dee. Someone took the 'D' from Dorthy and the 'D' from my middle name Dawn, and Dee Dee became my nickname."

"I like it. But you're still little." He smiled, brushing the dark hair from her face with his hand. She stood on her tip-toes to kiss him passionately. The kiss lasted for a long time.

Juice and Crystal were standing on the balcony of the condo watching Charlie and Dee Dee. Out of the darkness Charlie and Dee heard cheers. They looked up and laughed. A few minutes later the balcony was empty and the light from Juice's bedroom went out.

"It looks like someone's getting lucky." Charlie chuckled.

Dee smiled, then quietly asked. "Would you like to get lucky?"

Charlie grinned from ear to ear. Ten minutes later they were in the spare bedroom, between the sheets, feeling the warmth of each others body. Once again they kissed passionately. Dee Dee broke the kiss to disappear under the covers. She wrapped her hand around Charlie's cock, took it in her mouth and sucked hungrily.

Charlie felt like he was going to explode in her mouth and wanted to fuck her. Grabbing her by the back of the head he pulled her up to ravish her mouth with his tongue, then took the plunge deep inside her moist warmth. He held her legs in the air as she bucked wildly beneath him. Fifteen minutes later she rested her head on his shoulder, content to lay in his arms.

It had been eight months since Charlie had been with a woman other than Nicole, his time having been occupied with handling his drug business. Nicole was the only woman he had ever loved, but he felt there was something special about Dee Dee. They had great chemistry, making him want to see more of her, for sure.

At 4 a.m. Dee Dee and Charlie exchanged addresses and phone numbers. Before the girls left the condo, Charlie kissed Dee Dee goodnight, promising to meet her at the bar around 8 p.m. that night.

* * *

The morning news reported tropical storms moving in from the southeast. Charlie guessed that the storm front would be coming across the Bermudas to Marco Island. It certainly was not the weather report Juice was hoping to hear. But under the circumstances they had no choice but to meet the shrimp boat. Come Hell or high water, at four o'clock in the morning they had to be there to pick-up the two hundred kilos of cocaine.

"The Donzi is fueled and ready to go. We're going to have to leave the bar no later than midnight, Charlie. In bad weather it could take us hours to travel twelve miles out to sea." Juice said decisively.

"Why do we always meet the boats twelve miles out to sea?"

"It's International waters, Charlie. There's no risk during unloading or loading of our boat. That's out of the jurisdiction of the United States. Our risk is taken when we bring the cocaine into shore."

* * *

Dee Dee was at Apples place, anxiously waiting for Charlie and Juice to walk through the front door. At Charlie's entrance, she hurried over to throw her arms around his neck, kissing him soundly. He was not up for grabs and she wasted no time in letting it be known.

"I have to leave around midnight." Charlie told her.

"Oh no! Does my Prince turn into a pumpkin at the stroke of midnight?" She quizzed.

"Very funny," Charlie chuckled. "No, I have some business I need to take care of."

"What kind of business?" She inquired, knowing that whatever it was, he was up to no good.

"Just business. And no, it's not another girl." Charlie grinned.

"That makes me a little happier."

"When will you be leaving to return home?"

"In a few days." Dee Dee answered. "And you?"

"My flight leaves Tampa Monday afternoon. We will have all day tomorrow and tomorrow night to spend together. That's if you want to."

Without a moment's hesitation, Dee Dee snapped. "Of course I do!" She grabbed his arm and led him to the dance floor.

It was 11:45 p.m. when Juice found Charlie on the dance floor. "We've got to go," he said.

Charlie gave Dee Dee a quick kiss and rushed from the bar behind Juice.

Within ten minutes, they were at the dock preparing to shove off. Juice started the engines while Charlie untied the ropes that secured the bow and stern to the dock. Charlie hopped aboard the Donzi, shoving the boat away from the dock. Juice put the engine in reverse, propelling the boat backwards away from the pier. The waves were two to three feet high and the wind was bone chilling cold. It was going to be a rough ride, but the Donzi cut through the waves at speeds of 30-35 miles per hour. The further out to sea, the higher the waves rose above the keel. With five feet waves Juice slowed the Donzi down to 10 to 15 miles per hour.

Several hours later floating on the choppy waves, in the distance they spotted the shrimp boat heading in their direction.

At least they hoped it was their boat. If it was the Coast Guard or Custom Officials, the Donzi would pass inspection, but the last thing they wanted was to draw any unnecessary attention to themselves. There was no fishing gear on board and they had no logical explanation for their being twelve miles out to sea. Once they were loaded they would turn their running lights off and make a bee line for the docks.

A light rain began to fall. The waves and swells began getting higher and deeper with every passing minute.

Finally, there was the signal. The shrimp boat flashed its lights twice. Juice flashed the lights of the Donzi three times, the waves now rising five and six feet high. There was no way they could risk tying the boats together in the storm. The wooden shrimp boat had higher rails and it could easily tear the fiberglass Donzi to shreds. Juice had to maneuver the Donzi close, keeping five feet between them while men on the shrimp boat tossed the kilos to Charlie, one kilo at a time.

It was Charlie's responsibility to catch the kilos, toss them inside the cabin, then go below to stack and count them. What normally took fifteen minutes to unload, stack and store, took over an hour. It would be costly to drop a single kilo into the water. By the time the two hundred kilos were accounted for, the waves had reached 8 to 10 feet, the swells sometimes dipping to twenty feet. Unless the weather changed for the better which was unlikely, there was no chance they would reach the dock before dawn.

On all of the other trips the Donzi was loaded and speeding towards the shore at speeds reaching sixty miles an hour, with its running lights off. The mere thought of hitting something floating in the water sent chills up and down Charlie's spine. He wished they could do the same thing now, but the Donzi was crawling at a snails pace. No sooner had they topped one swell, the boat fell down into another. Charlie leaned over the side and puked his guts out.

"How long before we reach the dock," he yelled into the swirling wind.

"I don't know. The compass is spinning like a top and I have no sense of direction. We have to ride out these swells with me steering directly into them."

"Fuck!" Charlie cursed, wondering how long the storm would last. He wished they had paid more attention to the news. He had never experienced weather like this, especially not five miles out to sea. Were they moving closer to shore? He wondered. Or were they heading further out to sea? More importantly, would they have enough fuel to make it through the storm and to shore?

Juice kept the running lights on, desperately needing them to see the top of the swells through the driving rain. Soon both men were drenched from head to toe.

Throughout the night, the Donzi continued to go up one swell and down another, Juice assuring Charlie that everything was going to be alright.

"I've been in rougher weather." Juice chuckled, water pouring in streams down his face. He was lying and Charlie knew it.

As dawn broke, Charlie's fears magnified by the sight of the massive swells. He swore before God that if he lived, he would live a more righteous life. Over the next twenty minutes, Charlie made a lot of promises. Sometime around 8 a.m., the sea began to calm. Juice set a course for due northeast and sped up to twenty miles per hour, then thirty, forty, fifty, and finally reaching a speed of sixty. It was one-thirty in the afternoon when the Donzi pulled up to the dock. By then Charlie had forgotten every promise he had made to God.

CHAPTER THIRTEEN
LIFE'S A BITCH

The Donzi slowed as it approached the dock, the two men sitting in a white Ford van had waited throughout the night for its arrival. The driver flipped a lit cigarette from his window, opened the door and stepped out. The second man opened the passenger door, stepped out, and opened the rear doors. Working together the two men loaded a medium sized push cart with four empty cardboard boxes. One man stood back to keep an eye on the surrounding area of the private dock while the other man pushed the cart to the end of the pier.

With the lines to the boat secured, Juice grabbed a box and tossed it to Charlie, who filled the box with fifty kilos of cocaine, then passed it back. After the four boxes were filled and loaded onto the cart they were wheeled back to the van, picked up and shoved inside. The rear doors were closed and the two men hurried into the automobile and drove away. There were never any introductions, needless conversation, or questions asked. Juice and Charlie's job was done and that was all that concerned them.

Charlie's promise to spend the day with Dee Dee was broken.

It was now 2:30 in the afternoon and Charlie was mentally and physically exhausted. From Juice's condo he called her to apologize, promising to call her when he woke up.

"I'll be waiting for your call." She said, with a sigh of disappointment.

Charlie slept the sleep of the dead until midnight. When he awoke the first thing he did was to call Dee Dee.

"Hello?" She answered.

"Hi sweetheart. I just woke up."

"I thought you weren't going to call."

"I'm sorry." Charlie smiled to himself. He was pleased that she wanted so badly to be with him. "Would you like to get something to eat? I'm starved!"

"Crystal left for the bar two hours ago. I don't have any transportation." Dee Dee replied.

"Give me the directions. I'll take a quick shower, then pick you up."

"Directions? I'm not from here," she reminded him laughing.

"How did you get home when you left here?"

"Crystal drove. Leaving the parking lot she turned left. We went about two miles and turned right at a traffic light. I'm not sure if there are any traffic lights in between, but I remember that when we turned right, there was a McDonalds restaurant on the corner. The condo is two blocks behind that. Why don't I meet you at the McDonalds?" Dee Dee suggested.

"I'll be there in twenty minutes."

"Don't fall back to sleep."

"I won't!" Charlie laughed.

Dee Dee was standing in front of the golden arches of the McDonalds when Charlie arrived. She wore a short white mini-skirt, a low cut yellow blouse with no bra, and white sandals. Her hair was curled to fall below her shoulders and her fingernails and toenails were polished a hot pink. She looked stunning! Charlie wore brown shorts, a short sleeved tan T-shirt, and brown sandals. On the front of his T-shirt there was a ships wheel with the words 'Anchor's Away'.

"You look beautiful." Charlie smiled as she climbed into the passenger seat beside him. He kissed her softly on the lips, causing her to smile with happiness. "Where's a good place to eat?"

"Remember, I'm not from around here," she laughed.

"Then we'll drive around until we find a place you like." He offered, returning her smile.

Dee Dee shook her head. She found Charlie to be incredibly amusing. "Did you get your business taken care of?"

"Yes, I did." He replied, offering nothing more.

They drove up and down the quiet early morning streets of Florida, listening to Frank Sinatra over the radio. The silence between the two of them was a comfortable silence, each of them just happy to be with the other.

"There," Dee Dee suddenly pointed. "Let's grab a bite at the Steak and Shake."

The restaurant provided curb service and were well known for their steak subs and thick milkshakes. Charlie backed the white Ford compact into a parking space, the waitress took their order, returning to place a tray on the edge of the driver's door window with their order on top of the tray.

"Turn on your headlights and I will return to take your order or pick-up the tray. Enjoy your meal." The waitress smiled.

The restaurant was a gathering place for a much younger crowd, giving them a chance to showcase their older model cars and hot rods, Charlie concluded.

After eating they went to Apples Place and partied until closing time. Dee Dee told Crystal not to wait up for her because she would be spending the night with Charlie.

* * *

After closing the Two O'clock Club, Peaches decided to stop by the Wee Hours. The place was crowded with party goers, forcing her to push her way through the packed bodies to where Gus stood behind the bar.

"Look what the cat dragged in." Gus shouted over the loud music, a grin lighting his face.

"Did you miss me?" Peaches teased.

"How am I supposed to get my nuts out of hock if you don't ever give me a chance?" Gus replied.

She laughed, knowing that Jerry Everhart, the owner of Hector's, must have told Gus about her giving him a blow job. There were only three after hour clubs in Baltimore. The Wee Hours, Susie's, and Hector's. Jerry and Gus were competitors and best friends.

"Fair exchange ain't no robbery," Gus added.

"Would you like to see some photos?"

"Of you?"

"Yes."

"With your clothes on or off?"

"On." She giggled.

"Do you have any photos of yourself naked?"

"No!"

"Would you like some?" Gus offered, grinning from ear to ear.

Peaches smiled and shook her head. Gus always made her laugh. She grabbed the Polaroid photos from her purse of her and Bulldog at Disneyworld, along with the ones taken in Georgia of her mother and sister when they were at the flower garden called 'The Willow's.

"That's my little sister." Peaches announced proudly.

"Does she fool around?"

"You just don't give up, do you?" Peaches laughed.

"Step into my office so I can show you something."

Nicole hesitated only for a brief moment before following him down the short hall towards the back office. Gus closed the door behind them, leaning back against the door. Nicole turned around to face him. He unzipped his pants and pulled out his dick.

"How can you resist this?" He asked.

Laughing, Peaches moved forward to wrap her hand around his shaft, falling to her knees and sucking him until he was fully erect. She suddenly stopped and got back to her feet.

"Me first. I've been tricked before." She giggled. "And remember, fair exchange ain't no robbery."

Pushing her back towards his desk, he cleared a space with a sweep of his hand, sending papers flying across the room. Gus quickly pulled down her jeans and black lace G-string, letting them both fall to the carpeted floor. He lifted her bare ass onto the desk top, pulling up a secretary chair behind him, and taking a position between her smooth thighs. He threw her legs over his shoulders, forcing her to lean back on her elbows, as he parted the lips of her pussy with his experienced tongue. Gus proceeded to eat her pussy better than anyone ever had in the past and it drove her nuts, making her climax again and again.

After licking her through a fourth orgasm, Gus came up for air with a big smile. "My turn!"

Peaches was glad to return the favor. She climbed down from the desk to fall to her knees. Gus placed a hand on the back of her head and ran his fingers through her hair as she sucked him deep into her mouth. It felt so good that it made him weak in the knees. It was a long time before she allowed him to finish, and when he did she stood to pull up her clothes.

"Fair exchange ain't no robbery," she smiled.

* * *

It was 4:30 a.m. by the time Peaches parked the yellow Bug next to her Mercedes. She locked the door and was walking towards the elevator when she heard a car door banging closed. Before she could turn around, she felt a knife pressed to her throat.

"Don't move bitch!" The voice instructed coldly.

"What do you want?" She asked, her heart suddenly racing a million miles a minute.

She was surprised to discover that she was not scared or nervous, her thoughts already moving ahead to plan her next steps. Would the attacker give her a chance to reach the gun in her purse, or would he separate her from her one chance of escape?

"I want some of that pussy, baby." His breath rasped in her ear, his arm tightening around her neck. "And I want the money you got stashed in your apartment."

"All of the money I have is in my purse."

"Don't fuckin' lie to me, bitch." He growled jerking her back against his big body, his beard rubbing along her neck. "I know that you've got money stashed, but I want some head before I fuck you like a rock star. If you lie to me again about the money, I'm going to fuck you in the ass with no grease. By the time I'm finished you will be begging me to kill you. Do you hear me, you sorry ass slut?"

Peaches nodded her understanding, clutching against her stomach. Slowly, her assailant removed the knife from her throat.

"If you try to run or don't fully cooperate, I will gut you like a fish. We're going to walk over to the elevator. Do you understand me, bitch?"

"Yes." Peaches replied, her voice remaining soft in an effort to keep him calm.

She never turned to look behind her. She slowly headed for the elevator some ten feet away, her hand silently opening her purse. Reaching her hand inside she grasped the handle of the .45 automatic flipping the safety off with a practiced thumb. She suddenly released her hold on the purse, the gun coming free in her right hand.

"Bitch, what th…" But it was already too late for the bearded man.

Nicole had already twisted her body slightly at the hips and pulled the trigger.

"Boom!" The gun blast echoed around the underground garage.

The bullet hit her attacker in the stomach. He screamed, staggered forward, and lurched against the concrete wall next to the elevator, collapsing on to his back.

"No… please… don't!" He pleaded as Peaches pointed the gun at his head.

Peaches stood over him with ice in her heart and death in her eyes. "Life's a bitch, ain't it." She pulled the trigger.

The gunshot echoed for a second time. She looked around to make sure no one was looking. There was no one in sight. She hurried over to the door leading to the stairway, snatched open the door and ran up the stairs as fast as her little feet could run. She unlocked the door to her apartment, stepped inside, and sat down on the kitchen floor, suddenly feeling exhausted and sick to her stomach. Her mind continued to race a hundred miles an hour. She had just killed a man.

Oddly enough her only regret was that it had happened too fast, the asshole deserved to be tortured.

She questioned whether she had overlooked anything, such as fingerprints or other evidence that could possibly implicate her. She knew she had left the two spent shell casings behind, but there would be no fingerprints on those. Per Ramrod's instructions, she had wiped them clean before loading the gun. Once the gun was disposed of, there would be no links. But there was gun powder residue on her as well as her clothes. Everything she was wearing needed to be trashed.

She thought about her attacker. He was probably in his twenties with long reddish brown hair and a full dark beard. He had been wearing jeans, a red flannel shirt, a blue winter coat, and black leather motorcycle boots. She wondered if he was a member of a rival biker gang.

Nicole pushed to her feet, walked to the kitchen, turned the cold water on, and splashed water on her face slowing her heart down to a normal beat. She toweled dry, then sat down at the kitchen table.

"Fuckin' asshole!" She cursed as she walked to a cabinet and grabbed a Hefty trash bag. She walked to the bathroom to fill the bathtub with warm water. Removing her clothes, she stuffed them into the trash bag and tied it closed. Next, she took a long bath, scrubbing herself clean with comet cleanser, using a brief shower to make sure she was completely clean.

At 5:30 a.m. a female resident on her way to work discovered the body when the elevator door opened. She screamed and another male resident rushed to see what was going on. He placed a call to the Baltimore City police. Within minutes Nicole heard sirens, the police and paramedics were soon on the scene. The unknown man was immediately pronounced dead. The ambulance was standing by, waiting for the body to be released, so they could transport the corpse to the morgue.

Detective Marks was the first to arrive on the scene from the Baltimore City Homicide Division. He was followed by Betty

Crawford, Greg, and Wyatt.

The two spent shell casings were bagged and marked as evidence. The blood splatters were marked, photographed and samples taken for the crime lab.

Detective Marks searched through the pockets of the deceased male. In his wallet, he had a Pennsylvania driver's license, with a motorcycle endorsement under the name, Ryan Porter.

"What are you doing here?" Detective Marks questioned the dead man.

* * *

It was nine o'clock in the morning. Charlie awoke to the smell of Dee Dee cooking bacon and eggs in the kitchen. She wanted to surprise Charlie and serve him breakfast in bed.

"What are you doing?" Charlie grinned, leaning against the kitchen wall wearing white shorts and a tan T-shirt. He was barefoot, his hair was ruffled, and he looked to be half asleep.

"What does it look like I'm doing?" She smiled back over her shoulder at him.

Charlie thought to himself, ask a stupid question, get a stupid answer.

"You know that I will be flying back to Maryland later this afternoon."

"Will you miss me?" Dee Dee asked.

"Of course."

"Then you will come to see me?" Dee Dee questioned with a hopeful smile.

Charlie thoughtfully countered. "I think you should come visit me at my new house."

"Is that an invitation?"

"Any time is a good time."

Dee Dee sat a plate on the table, waiting for Charlie to seat himself before asking. "Would you like a cup of coffee or orange juice?" She had already looked through the kitchen cabinets and refrigerator, so she knew what was available. Which to her was not much. It was obvious that Juice was a bachelor who prepared very few meals at home.

"I hope you have more groceries in your house," Dee Dee laughed.

"There's no food in my house yet. I just moved in a few days ago. But by the time you come to visit I promise my cabinets will be well stocked."

On Charlie's flight home to Maryland he was consumed with thoughts of Dee Dee. His heart longed to be with her.

CHAPTER FOURTEEN
ON MY HONOR

The moment Charlie turned the key to unlock the door of his house, he immediately thought how good it was to be home. It felt great having a place that belonged solely to himself and he could hardly wait to have Dee Dee see his new home. He envisioned her standing on her tip toes in the kitchen, stocking the cabinets with groceries. He thought about how he could wrap his arms around her small waist and kiss her neck. Next, he had a vision of laying her ass down on the white bear skin rug in the den and fucking her until the cows came home.

Drinking a cup of coffee in an effort to warm up after being outside, Charlie stood looking out of the kitchen window. The sky was overcast and dark. He turned on the small television sitting on a kitchen counter, the weather report calling for snow flurries. The report made Charlie realize that it was time to purchase a second vehicle, possibly a four wheel drive truck with a snow plow. His asphalt driveway was long with a gradual incline, providing ample parking with a two and a-half car garage attached to the house. The garage doors opened to the side of the house, featuring a backboard with a hoop and net above the double garage door. Charlie smiled at the thought of his playing basketball, he had never shot a day of hoops in his life.

* * *

Dorothy Dawn Carusso was delirious with happiness. She could not stop thinking about how strongly her feelings were for Charlie, almost overnight falling in love with the mysterious man. What was it that Juice nicknamed him? That's right, he had named him Peanut. The thought of Charlie with a Planter's peanut for a head made her laugh aloud. Every night since meeting him, she had prayed that he would be her knight in shining armor and take her away from her life in her father's Pennsylvania home. No man dared to look at her twice for fear of her father. Antonio Carusso was a notorious mobster. It was rumored that he was in charge of the Eastern Seaboard, from Maine to Florida.

Since the time of her birth she had been "Daddy's little girl." Whatever she wanted was hers for the asking. She was envied by every young girl, and every kid in the neighborhood looked forward to Dee Dee's birthday, all in hopes that they would be invited. It was always the event of the year, not even the school prom could compare to the spectacle that was Dee Dee's birthday party.

Dee Dee grew up in a huge red brick Mansion that set on eight acres of manicured land. It was located in a gated community that offered a fantastic view overlooking the City of Harrisburg, Pennsylvania. A private gated entrance led to the Carusso residence, the grounds kept perfect by a trained grounds-keeper, uniformed servants in the residence going quietly about the task of taking care of all household duties. Dee Dee was never required to make her own bed, wash or iron clothes, or cook. Her every wish was catered to whether she willed it or not.

At the age of five she was riding the new pink bicycle her father recently purchased for her, when out of nowhere a neighbor backed out of his driveway hitting her and crushing the bike with his automobile. Striking the bicycle the pretty pink basket attached to the handle bars went flying. Dee Dee lay in the street holding her head in her hands and screaming at the top of her lungs. It was a chilling sound that shook Antonio Carusso to his core. By the time Antonio and the ambulance arrived on the scene Dee Dee had slipped into a Coma. At the hospital she was quickly diagnosed as having a broken leg and a fractured skull. Antonio lay at his daughter's bed side day in and day out, his one and only concern being his daughter's returned good health. Two months passed before Dee Dee opened her eyes. The next door neighbor visited on several occasions to apologize, only to be told by Carusso henchmen that his presence would not be welcome at this time. A month after Dee Dee's recovery, the neighbor and his car disappeared.

It was put out that the neighbor had disappeared in fear for his life. It was also rumored that the neighbor was hacked into small pieces, fed to the fishes, and his car run through a shredder at a local junk yard. Some people claimed hearing rumors that the neighbor was buried alive in his car. Nobody knew for sure what the truth was, but no one doubted that it was linked to the accident, nor that the neighbor or his car would ever be seen again.

* * *

The Heathen clubhouse was on Orange Blossom Trail in Orlando, Florida; three miles from Jolly Roger's bar and grill. It was a cinder block building, painted a dirty yellow. The windows were boarded closed and at the entrance a solid metal door was propped open. At the rear of the building the Exit door was kept securely locked.

Inside the club, there was a bathroom with a shower, and bedroom with two bunk beds. In the common area there was a conference table with wooden chairs, as well as two card tables with chairs on each side of the room. There were two refrigerators: one for food, the other holding a pony keg of beer. There was a coffee pot on top of the counter along with plastic cups and containers of sugar and cream.

Big Moose called the meeting to order. Nasty, the other scooter tramps, and the Prospects stepped outside while the patched brothers gathered at the conference table to discuss business. They were moving one hundred and twenty kilos of cocaine every month, their distribution network reaching as far north as Jacksonville. It was the new product called 'Crystal Meth' that they were hoping to bring to the table. They all agreed that it would be a lucrative venture and voted unanimously to investigate the opportunity further.

* * *

Detective Marks called everyone into the conference room. "This is one Hell of a way to start out the New Year. Not one, but two unsolved murders in January! Has there been any new developments on the Pickett murder?"

There was no response. Nothing from Ronnie, Greg, Wyatt, or Betty.

"Well, what do we have on the Ryan Porter murder?" Marks asked in frustration.

"Sir, Porter has an extensive arrest record. As a juvenile, he stole a car, burglarized a house, and beat a man with a baseball bat. His adult criminal history includes burglary, extortion, kidnapping, and four assaults." Betty Crawford reported.

"Has he ever been to prison?"

"No, Sir. The majority of charges were dismissed because the witnesses refused to testify. He's a member of the Argot motorcycle gang. The authorities in Harrisburg informed me that he is better known to them as, Dollar."

"Do we know what he was doing in the underground parking lot at Regency Towers at such an early hour?"

"No, sir." Betty answered.

"All we know is that the casings are from a forty-five automatic. There were no fingerprints on the casings." Detective Wyatt added.

"Forensics said the blood splatters indicate that he was shot at close range, the head wound indicating an execution style murder." Detective Greg offered.

"Do we have any leads? Did he have any enemies? Why would someone shoot him in the stomach and then the head? It doesn't make sense. Why not simply shoot him in the back of the head?" Detective Marks wondered, verbalizing his thoughts.

"There was a knife found by his body, but there's no fingerprints on the knife or any indication that it was in any way connected to the murder." Betty Crawford added.

* * *

Nicole was sitting on the couch in the living room with her feet propped up on the coffee table, watching to see what the eleven o'clock news had to report about the murder of her mysterious assailant. The a.m. news reported that an unidentified male member of the Argot motorcycle gang was found murdered, execution style, in the underground parking garage at the Regency Towers. The name was being withheld pending notification of his next of kin.

"Shit!" She cursed. "Those son of a bitches set me up!"

She was sure of one thing, Bulldog could not have been told of their plan. There was no doubt in her mind that he loved her. She picked up the phone and called the cabin. "Hello." The Prospect answered.

"I need to talk to Bulldog," she said coldly.

"He's sleeping," the Prospect complained.

"Don't fuck with me. Do we really have to go through this again?"

A long time passed before Bulldog's voice came over the line. "Hello?"

"I need to see you now!" Peaches explained, placing emphasis on the 'now'.

"Is this a booty call?" Bulldog growled.

"Keep your dick in your pants, asshole. I need to see you now!" This time the emphasis was on the word 'need'.

Even in his half awake slumber Bulldog's instincts told him that something was terribly wrong. Peaches had never called him an asshole before.

"I will be there in two hours." He said, already calculating the time it would take him to get ready.

"No, not here. I'll meet you at the White Coffee Pot in Glen Burnie. Make sure you come alone, and don't tell anyone where you're going." The last thing she needed was for another Argot to be seen at Regency Towers, especially with her.

"That's fine. I'll see you there."

Nicole grabbed a gym bag from the hall closet, emptied it, placing the Hefty trash bag inside containing the clothes she had worn during the murder. She tossed the .45 automatic on top and zipped the bag closed, dreading the thought of her having to walk through the underground parking garage carrying the gym bag filled with incriminating evidence, but she had no choice.

She stepped out of the elevator to a scene from a movie. To the left of the elevator lay a white chalk outline around an area saturated with dried blood. Yellow crime scene tape sectioned off the space where the body had lain. No one had cleaned the cement floor, and she could easily imagine how the police had swarmed around the underground garage in search of some clue to the man's murder. It had not happened yet, but she was sure they would get around to questioning the building's occupants.

Nicole quickened her step, unlocked the door to the yellow Bug. She tossed the blue gym bag on the floorboard behind the passenger seat, climbed behind the wheel and started the engine, driving out of the parking lot as if it was just another day. A police cruiser suddenly appeared in front of her, passing the entrance to the garage at a slow roll. She made eye contact with the uniformed officer in the passenger seat, returning his brief smile with one of her own, glad that he couldn't tell how fast her heart was beating. As she pulled out onto the street, she sighed a sense of relief, and the butterflies in her stomach slowly fluttered away.

Nicole parked near the front entrance of the White Coffee Pot, locked the doors, and was walking towards the restaurant when she heard a horn honk several times. A blue Ford Maverick sped up next to her, and the smiling driver rolled down his window.

"Hi, Nicole."

"Hi, yourself." She replied, managing a smile for Detective Hill.

A year earlier, he was the officer in charge of investigating her daughter's death. They had a brief affair, ending after a single night. Actually, she would call it a one-night stand. She awoke from a terrible nightmare to find herself alone in his bed. She left a note on the door of his refrigerator that simply read, "Fuck you!"

"How have you been?" He asked smiling.

"Okay."

"You look good. I like what you did with your hair."

"Thank you," she spoke softly.

"Can I call you sometime?" he asked hopefully.

"No, I'm married." She lied, hoping he would leave before Bulllog arrived.

"I'm not sure what I did that upset you that night, but I'm truly sorry that things ended so badly. I've thought about you often and I've always wished you well."

"Good luck to you." She said, turning away, not bothering to watch him drive away with a sad look on his face. He must have recognized my car, she thought. She was sure that he was clueless about the path her life had taken over the past year. Oddly enough, all things considered, she felt he was a decent guy.

Nicole walked into the restaurant, seating herself in a back booth to wait for Bulldog's arrival. He pulled up driving an older red Ford truck. He parked and came inside the eatery to join her, taking a seat in the booth across from her. The elderly waitress brought them both a cup of black coffee.

"What's up?" He demanded.

A single tear fell from Nicole's eye, and Bulldog knew that whatever the problem was, it was serious. He asked a second time. "What's up?"

When she still did not respond, he said. "Baby, there's nothing that we can't work out."

"Ramrod set me up." She wiped at the tear angrily.

"What?" He demanded, sitting up and fully alert now. His eyes turning as hard as stones.

"The asshole set me up." She repeated, then began to ramble. "It all happened so quick. I didn't know what to do. I just reacted!"

"Slow down! Slow Down! What exactly happened?" He said in a whisper, looking around the almost totally deserted restaurant.

"You don't know?" She leaned over the table to whisper back.

"Know what?"

"One of your brothers tried to rape and rob me, and I killed him."

"Killed who?" Bulldog said, trying to make sense out of what she was saying.

"I don't know. All I know is I shot the mutha fucker twice. Once in the stomach, then once in the head."

"Who? Who did you shoot?" he hissed. "When and where did this happen? Are you sure the guy you shot was a member of the club? Tell me exactly what happened!"

Nicole took a deep breath before beginning to explain in a very quiet voice. "After work last night I stopped by the Wee Hours so I got home around four-thirty in the morning. I was on my way to the elevator when I heard a car door close behind me. Before I could turn around some asshole put a knife to my throat. He tells me that he's going to rape and rob me. Calls me a slut and demands I give him the money in my apartment.

I shot him in the stomach. He begged me not to shoot him a second time, but I shot the bastard right between the eyes. He deserved it. He was going to kill me, I'm sure of it."

"Who in the fuck did you shoot?"

"I didn't stop to ask his fuckin' name." Peaches snapped.

"How do you know he was a brother Argot?"

"It was reported on the news. His name was being withheld pending notification of his next of kin. I called you right away."

"Did anyone see you?"

"No!"

"Are you sure of that?"

"Yes."

"Can you describe the guy?"

"Late twenties. Wavy brown hair and medium built. He was wearing jeans, a red plaid shirt, a blue jacket, and black leather biker boots."

"That sounds like Dollar. He joined the club a year ago. We need to go to the cabin now and address this before the news reaches the other members."

They left without finishing their coffee. Nicole stopped at the Bug, unlocked the door, and grabbed the gym bag from the rear floorboard. She locked the door before walking over to join Bulldog in the truck. They headed for the cabin located in the Pennsylvania hills.

"I'm sorry." She sighed as they hit the highway.

"You didn't do anything wrong to be sorry for. Everything is going to be okay." He put his arm around her and pulled her closer.

It was two hours later that they pulled up and parked in front of the cabin.

Bulldog looked at Peaches. "Are you ready?"

She nodded, grabbed the gym bag and followed him inside the cabin.

Ramrod was standing at the kitchen counter preparing a sandwich. A loaf of bread and a package of bologna sat on the counter. Other members of the club lounged around the open area, enjoying the warmth from the large fireplace. They greeted Bulldog and Peaches as they entered the cabin.

"We need to talk to you in private." Bulldog directed his request to Ramrod.

Ramrod looked at Peaches, then the gym bag, his first thought was that they needed to see him on business. He tossed two slices of bologna between two slices of bread, and walked into his bedroom. Nicole brought up the rear, closing the door behind them. When Ramrod turned around he found himself looking down the barrel of the chrome .45 automatic he had given Peaches for protection. His eyes suddenly narrowed, his blood turning ice cold.

"You better tell this crazy bitch to get that fuckin' gun outta my face before someone gets hurt!" Ramrod growled in bewildered anger.

"What in the fuck is wrong with you!" Bulldog asked in shock, stepping in between them.

"He set me up!" She cursed, feeling betrayed.

"I set who up? What the fuck is this crazy bitch talking about?"

"Has anyone seen Dollar this morning?"

"Not that I'm aware of. Why? Would one of you tell me why Peaches is pointing a fuckin gun at me? Let me in on what's going on."

"Someone tried to rape and rob Peaches last night. She shot him twice and he's dead. The news reported that he was a member of the Argot motorcycle gang. His name was withheld pending notifying his next of kin. By Peaches' description, it was, more than likely, Dollar."

"Where did this happen?" Ramrod demanded, his face a hard mask of rage.

"In the underground parking garage where she lives."

Ramrod looked at Peaches, the gun now starting to waver uncertainly in her hand. "And you think that I sent him there to rape and rob you?"

"Did you," she asked, looking in his eyes for any signs of deceit.

"No!" he stated, letting her see the truth reflected in his eyes. "That's not how we do business. I had nothing to do with what happened to you. We protect our own, and you're one of us. You did the right thing by killing the son of a bitch. If he tried to rape and rob you, then he was never one of us."

"Do you believe him?" Bulldog demanded of her.

She handed Bulldog the gun, then hurried forward to throw her arms tearfully around Ramrod. She trembled against him and his arms tightened around her protectively. He stood there holding her, looking over her shoulder at Bulldog with a sad little smile.

"I'm sorry for pointing a gun at you." Peaches sniffled against Ramrod's chest.

"It's okay this time," he stroked the back of her head. "My concern is for you. Did anyone see what happened?"

Peaches collected herself, stepping back to wipe at her tears with the heel of her hands. "There were no witnesses. I'm sure of that! I rushed to my apartment, showered, and I scrubbed my hands with comet cleanser trying to get rid of any powder residue. The clothes that I was wearing are inside the gym bag. I did leave two shell casings at the scene, but I wiped them clean when I loaded the gun."

Ramrod grabbed the gym bag, and said, "Let's go!"

He lead the way outside, dropping the gym bag into a fifty gallon drum. Ramrod doused the bag with gasoline, then set it on fire, Next, he took them to a shed out back where he ran a drill bit down the barrel, then he cut the barrel into three pieces, disassembled the gun, and told Bulldog to scatter and bury the parts in the woods. The only thing he saved was the pearl handles.

"Would I be correct in assuming that you, Bulldog, and myself are the only three people who know about this?"

"Yes." Peaches promised.

"Swear to me that you will never tell another living soul about this."

"I swear!" Peaches said, looking Ramrod in his eyes.

"Bulldog, tomorrow I want you to offer a fifty thousand dollar reward for the person who murdered Dollar. If we don't take action, the police will assume that we either know who committed the murder, or that it was the club."

"That makes sense." Bulldog agreed.

"Are you upset with me?" Peaches wanted to know.

"Not at all. I'm fuckin' proud of your scrawny little ass. Girl, you've got more balls than the law allows!" he grinned.

Peaches smiled. This was her family. It was where she belonged, and she was damn proud to call Ramrod her big brother and Leader. The Argot colors suddenly took on a more important meaning for her.

CHAPTER FIFTEEN
FEAST OR FAMINE

Peaches spent the night at the cabin, waking up early to a ground covered in snow. The fireplace in the common area was stoked and burning brightly, both of the bedroom doors were left open in the hopes of letting the heat circulate throughout the entire cabin. They had space heaters, but they were used sparingly due to fuel consumption. Ramrod was already up and moving around in the small kitchen.

"Good morning." Ramrod grinned, pouring a cup of coffee and offering it to Peaches.

"Good morning!" She accepted the cup with a bright smile.

"Would you like for me to make you some breakfast?"

Ramrod grinned. "Thanks, but I've already had breakfast. The peanut butter and jelly is still on the counter if you want to make yourself a sandwich."

Peaches looked over at the offered food and shook her head. She knew that Bulldog must have complained to Ramrod about her not being able to cook. Her idea of breakfast was two slices of toast.

She opened the refrigerator, saw there was nothing edible to eat, and laughed. "Where's the bread?"

At that moment, Bulldog stumbled from the bedroom, squinting and rubbing his eyes.

Ramrod smiled, reporting. "I held church yesterday. Since you were the one who presented the proposition of our selling crystal meth to the Heathens, I didn't feel that your presence was necessary. The vote was unanimous, it's a go!"

Suddenly, they heard the roar of a Harley engine, a loud clang, followed by ranting, raging, and a string of obscenities. The three of them rushed to the front door of the cabin. Being the first to arrive, Ramrod snatched the door open. Peaches burst into uncontrollable laughter, followed closely by Bulldog and Ramrod.

"I don't know what's so fucking funny!" Rooster barked. He was laying on his back, covered from head to toe in snow. His Harley lay next to him, the rear tire spinning wildly. With each rotation of the tire there was a loud clanking noise. It was the funniest sight they had ever seen. Rooster had fitted the tire with a snow chain of his own invention. He reasoned that if cars and trucks could have snow tires, why not motorcycles? No one had ever taken him serious. On his first trial run, the chain broke and they were on hand to witness the results.

"I'm tellin' ya, it's gonna work!" Rooster yelled, climbing to his feet and brushing the snow off.

* * *

Bulldog drove Peaches back to Maryland and dropped her off at her car at the White Coffee Pot. The little Bug was completely covered in snow the vinyl seats freezing cold. If there was anything she disliked about the little car, it would be that there was no heat until the engine warmed up, which meant no defroster either. After scraping the windshield she wiped the inside glass with her glove. She returned to her apartment at Regency Towers, showered, and made a cup of hot chocolate with marshmallows.

Two hours later, Charlie knocked on the door. In his right hand he carried a blue gym bag. She did not need to ask what was in the bag, she knew.

She unlocked and opened the door, Charlie stepped inside and sat the gym bag on the table.

"Wanna do a line," he offered.

"Of course." Nicole laughed.

Charlie made four lines of cocaine on top of the table, pulled a plastic straw from his shirt pocket, and offered it to Nicole.

"Ladies before gentlemen," he grinned.

"Carrying your own straw now?"

"It's disposable. We could probably market it and make a fortune."

Nicole nearly choked. She laughed aloud while snorting a line.

"They are already on the market, Charlie. Where do you think you got this straw?" She finished snorting her lines, tilted her head sniffed hard, and passed the straw to Charlie.

"I met a girl in Florida this past weekend. Her name is Dee Dee and she lives in Harrisburg, Pennsylvania, She's drop dead gorgeous and I can hardly wait for you to meet her."

"Why would I want to meet any of your girlfriends?" Nicole snapped, somewhat confused by her feelings.

"I don't know. I just…"

"Well, stop thinking." She suggested angrily.

Charlie quickly changed the subject. "I've been warned that if I don't start moving more kilos per month, my source is going to start looking for someone who can."

"What?" Nicole spat in disbelief.

"What the fuck, Charlie! Who is this greedy bastard that you're working for?"

"I can't tell you that! I was told bluntly that we need to step up our game. Would you like for me to try to sell some?"

"Fuck no!" Nicole said coldly, remembering the last time Charlie sold some cocaine. She couldn't trust him to not fuck things up. "I'll think of something."

Who was Charlie's source, she wondered. Just how many kilos was Charlie expected to sell in a month's time?

There were so many unanswered questions, but she had no time to worry about that now.

"I've got to go, Charlie. We need to talk more about this later."

"I've got to do something." Charlie reminded her.

"I'll take care of it!" Nicole replied flatly.

"Thanks!" Charlie sighed, as he walked out the door.

On Wednesday, Harold made his routine pick up and delivery. Nicole placed the money in a brown paper bag and then sat it on the floor in the hall closet. After Harold left, Nicole prepared to go see Manny. It was 3 p.m. when Nicole pulled into Marsha's driveway and parked. She walked to the front door, opened it, and stepped inside.

"Mommy, I'm home." She yelled.

"I'm in the bedroom." Marsha shouted.

Nicole stepped lively down the hall, turning left and walking into Marsha's bedroom.

"You're one sexy looking bitch." Nicole smiled, admiring Marsha's outfit. She was wearing a light blue mini-skirt, a white frilled blouse, nylons, and white high-heels. She was beautiful, Nicole thought. But dressed more for summer and was going to freeze her ass off.

"It's been a long time since anyone has called me a bitch." Marsha laughed softly. "But coming from you, I'll take that as a complement. How was your trip?"

"Fantastic. Have you ever been to Disneyworld?"

"No."

"Maybe next year we can talk Manny into taking us and the kids. I don't even know where to begin. We spent two days there and didn't get to see everything. But I took some photos." Nicole said, reaching into her purse. "But I forgot to bring them with me," she frowned.

"Now why doesn't that surprise me?" Marsha smiled. She stood up from her vanity, giving Peaches a warm embrace. "I missed you."

"I missed you too."

"I bet Manny really missed us." Marsha smiled.

A year earlier, Manny had taken Nicole, Marsha, and her five children to Honolulu, Hawaii for Christmas. This past year he took them to the other side of the world, Australia. Every year he promised a new adventure and the girls looked forward to it.

They were an hour later than usual arriving at Manny's apartment. To their surprise, the door was answered by a butler. "Ladies, may I take your coats?"

Manny stood behind the butler grinning. He hugged the girls as the butler took their coats.

"I thought we would do things a little different tonight. If that's alright with you ladies?"

Nicole and Marsha looked at each other and smiled, wondering what was coming next. A sweet aroma from the kitchen filled the air.

"I hired a chef to prepare a meal for the three us tonight. I hope you both like seafood. We have lobster, oysters, clams, and shrimp salad. I took the liberty of selecting tonight's menu. Now, if you would join me in the living room for a glass of champagne while dinner is being prepared."

"I would've been fine with McDonald's," Nicole laughed.

"My two favorite foods are pink salmon and lobster." Marsha smiled broadly.

"So how is your mother and sister?" Manny asked, pouring three glasses of champagne.

"Mom is doing well, and Charlotte Lynn has turned into a beautiful young woman. I had a terrific visit. I rented a car and took them to the Willow's. The Willow's has a nice restaurant and acres of beautiful gardens."

"Tell Manny about the fish pond, bridge and butterflies."

Manny and the girls chatted, drank two bottles of champagne, and enjoyed a romantic candle-lit dinner.

"I have another surprise for you girls." Manny grinned as the butler grabbed their coats.

"You've already surprised the Hell out of me," Nicole said.

As the elevator made its way down to the foyer, Manny stood behind the girls making adjustments to his gray wool coat with matching hat.

Marsha looked at him and reported that he reminded her of a gangster from the roaring twenties, which seemed to please him immensely. Nicole fell into deep thought, only half hearing their exchange. She was thinking about all of the things she had done that Marsha and Manny knew nothing about. Charlie and the cocaine, the Argots, and the murder. She had never planned on a lot of things throughout her young life, but she faced them head on. Ramrod was right about her having brass balls, but she had to have them in order to survive in a male dominated world.

Parked at the curb, there was a long stretch limousine with dark tinted windows. As they walked from the building the uniformed driver stepped lively to open the rear doors for them. Marsha and Nicole sat across the seat making themselves comfortable. Manny climbed into the back of the spacious automobile, taking a seat across from them.

"Where are we going?" Marsha asked.

"For a long ride," Manny answered. He pressed a button that closed the dark tinted window separating them from the driver. "I've never had sex in a limousine. Have you?" Manny grinned, looking at the two women hopefully.

"I haven't." Peaches answered eagerly.

"Neither have I." Marsha giggled.

Manny popped the cork on another bottle of champagne, pouring everyone a glass. "Whenever you girls are ready."

Nicole was wearing jeans, a gray pullover sweater with no bra, a white leather coat with brown fur lining, and zip-up black leather boots. Nicole moved to sit directly across from Marsha, slid her hands up Marsha's thigh to slide her red g-string panties off from under her mini-skirt, then pulled her to the edge of the seat, exposing her fur lined pussy. Nicole buried her head in Marsha's pussy and went to kissing and licking her moistness. She paused from eating pussy just long enough to produce a small vibrator from her purse. It was a chrome battery operated vibrator with three speeds. She caressed Marsha's breast while working the vibrator around her clitoris.

Marsha wiggled, moaned, and in a matter of seconds had an incredible orgasm.

Marsha unzipped Nicole's blouse and pulled it over her head. She unbuttoned her jeans, and slid them to the floor. Nicole removed her feet from them, revealing that she was not wearing any panties. Marsha kissed Nicole, sucked on both of her hard nipples, and ran her hand between her legs to feel the warmth of her pussy. She licked her clitoris, inserted the vibrator, and moved it rapidly back and forth.

Nicole looked out of the window. They were stopped at a red light in downtown Baltimore, and people were crossing the street in front of them. The sight turned her on. She reached over beside her to unzip Manny's trousers, pulling his dick out of the confines of his pants, and dropped her head to take him inside her mouth. She slid it back and forth in her mouth while she sucked, making him match his moan to her own. She sucked and sucked until he exploded in her mouth.

Seconds later, Marsha sucked her to an orgasm, causing her to grip the seat with both hands, her knuckles turning white, and her lips parting in a cry of sheer ecstasy.

Manny chuckled, taking the time out to pass glasses of champagne to each girl. Nicole's butt was naked and Marsha sat with her mini-skirt on with nothing underneath. They rode around the city aimlessly for a couple of hours before the limousine dropped them off. The women kissed Manny goodnight, then walked to Marsha's Mustang.

The next day at 4 p.m., Nicole stopped by Charlie's new house to drop off his money, making inquiries about his Trust Fund. She had three quarters of a million dollars saved, stashed under her bed. Since the attempted robbery, she had thought about getting a safe deposit box. If something happened to her, what would happen to the money? She needed to know that if anything happened to her, Charlotte Lynn would be taken care of. Charlie explained how his Trust Fund worked, adding that he received a monthly check from it. Technically the house belonged to the Trust, but since he was the owner of the Trust Fund it was actually his property. Nicole was impressed. The thought of the authorities never knowing who owned what appealed to her, so she decided to contact Harold Glazer to inquire about setting something up similar for herself, concluding that it was much better than a safe deposit box.

The following week, when Harold arrived at Nicole's apartment to make the exchange, she invited him in. Offering a cup of coffee, she inquired about a Trust Fund. He assured her that if she wanted to name her sister as the beneficiary in the event of her death, it could be done. And if she ever wanted to withdraw a large sun of money there were ways to make that happen. She set up an appointment to meet him at his office at seven o'clock the following morning.

"I'm going to bring five hundred thousand dollars to start the Trust Fund."

The following morning, Nicole showed up at his office with a suitcase of One Hundred dollar bills. "I got all of these from you?" She smiled. As a second thought, she added. "I want my suitcase back, it's a matching set."

"I promise to return it on Wednesday," he grinned.

"It seems as though it's been feast or famine most of my life. I'm not sure what normal is anymore."

"It appears to me that you've done very well for yourself." Harold nodded at the money in the suitcase.

Nicole wondered at what cost.

* * *

Three weeks later, after closing the Two O'clock Club, Peaches stopped by the Wee Hours. It was packed elbow to elbow. Rose was at the front counter serving alcohol to the regulars while Gus hung around in the back shooting darts for a hundred dollars a game.

Whenever there was going to be a bust, Gus was always given ample warning by the authorities. It was routine for the police to raid the club, find a couple of drinks of alcohol and run everybody downtown. Gus always bailed everyone out and paid their fines, the amount paid never being too large.

When it was time for the owner to make a court appearance, Gus always wore his full length black leather coat to court. Harold Glazer would be there to stand by his side. The Judge would impose a small fine and that would be the end of it. The newspapers would report the raid making the police look good, giving the appearance they were protecting the community. This occurred two to three times a year.

Peaches had a couple of drinks, talked to Rose, then yelled goodnight to Gus.

The phone was ringing when Peaches stepped into her apartment. It was 5 a.m. Bone tired, she answered the phone wondering who would be calling at this time of the morning.

"Hello."

"Nicky, Mama's dead!" Charlotte's hysterical voice came over the line.

"Oh my God!" Peaches legs wobbled beneath her. She grabbed hold of a chair and sat down. She was stunned speechless as tears begin falling from her eyes.

"Nicky?" Charlotte cried out.

"Yes, I'm here baby." Nicole collected herself, knowing that she had to be strong for her sister. "When did it happen? What happened? Where are you?"

"Mama was perfectly fine. She hadn't complained of being sick at all. I found her out by the pond yesterday afternoon. She was sitting in a chair feeding the ducks. The next time I looked out she was laying on the ground. The paramedics tried for twenty minutes to revive her."

Charlotte Lynn's voice sounded to be in a panic. "I don't know what I'm supposed to do now, Nicky?"

"Where are you?"

"At the trailer. I don't have anywhere else to go."

"I'm going to call Bulldog. As soon as he can get here, we'll be on our way. We will drive straight through. I promise."

"Okay." Charlotte's sniffles came over the line.

Peaches hung up the phone and immediately called the cabin. Ramrod answered.

"It's an emergency. Wake Bulldog up!" She said tearfully.

Several minutes later, Bulldog answered. "Peaches?" He questioned, wiping sleep from his eyes.

"Mama died yesterday." She broke all the way down, tears and sobs raking her small body. "I need… you… to go to Georgia… with me."

"Calm down, baby. Take a deep breath." He instructed her in a calming voice. "I need to know when?"

Nicole took several deep breaths, fighting for the control she needed. "As soon as you can get here. Charlotte Lynn is there all by herself. She's alone and scared."

"Let me pack a bag."

"Just come!" If we need clothes I'll buy them new."

It was normally a two hour drive from the cabin, but one hour and thirty minutes later, Bulldog knocked on the door to Nicole's apartment.

"Let's go!" She said, not allowing herself to fall into his arms and give in to the tears that were almost choking her to death. She had to get to Charlotte Lynn.

She led the way out into the hallway, letting him secure the door behind her. They took the elevator to the underground parking garage in silence, Bulldog choosing to let his presence be the support she needed. The door chimed open, and as they stepped out Bulldog saw the dried blood on the concrete floor. There were a number of residents already coming and going to work.

Nicole pressed the button on her key chain to turn the alarm on her Mercedes off. Bulldog pulled the protective cover off, and within minutes they drove out of the garage, completely unaware of the pair of eyes following their every move.

CHAPTER SIXTEEN
BOUND BY LOVE

The first thing every morning when she arrived for work, Betty Crawford made a fresh pot of coffee. This morning was no different. She looked at the clock on the wall, noting the time was 7:55 a.m. She had not taken a day from work since joining the Baltimore Homicide Division. From the first day, she knew that if she wanted their respect, she would have to earn it. It was a man's world and her God given womanly duty was to make the damn coffee. The mere thought riled her, but she always made the coffee.

When the phone rang, she walked across the room to her desk to answer it, while Greg and Wyatt sat at their desks reading the morning newspaper.

"Baltimore City Homicide Division, Betty Crawford speaking, How may I help you?"

"About a month ago a man belonging to the Argot motorcycle gang was found dead in our underground parking garage. As I was leaving for work this morning a man with long brown hair wearing a black leather jacket, with the name 'Argots' boldly written across the back was in the underground parking lot. He got into a silver Mercedes Benz."

"Can you describe him?"

"He was about six-two, two hundred and sixty pounds, with a full beard. And he was with a woman who wasn't very tall. She had platinum blonde hair and was very attractive. I'm not sure if there's a connection or not, but I thought I should report it and let the police do their jobs." The female caller said.

"Have you ever seen the Mercedes or the girl there before?"

"The Mercedes is generally parked in the same space. It's normally covered up. The girl obviously lives in the building."

"Aren't the parking spaces designated?" Betty asked.

"Yes. As a matter of fact they are. See, that's why I wouldn't make a very good detective. Something as simple as that and I would never think of it."

"Thank you for calling. We appreciate your help and concern."

"You're most welcome." The caller sounded pleased as she clicked off.

"Shit!" Betty cursed. The very first thing she was taught in training was to ask for the callers name and phone number. In her excitement she had done neither. A blunder like that was surely going to land her in hot water with Detective Marks. She had also failed to ask the caller if she thought she could identify the biker if she saw him again.

As expected, Detective Marks read Betty the riot act for her failing to ask for the caller's name and phone number.

* * *

Bulldog and Nicole drove throughout the night, stopping only for gas and restroom breaks. Whenever they stopped, Nicole called Charlotte from a pay phone. Three times Nicole broke down and cried. Bulldog tried to console her, but only God could comfort matters of the heart. Nicole could not understand how a perfectly healthy woman could just suddenly die like she had. On the third call, Charlotte Lynn explained how her mother's heart had just stopped beating. It was then that Nicole cried the hardest, knowing that her mother had only been waiting to see her one more time. Her mother had never stopped missing and loving her late husband and she must have decided that it was finally time she join him.

"Your mother is at peace now." Bulldog said, trying to ease her pain for the hundredth time.

"It's not Mama that I'm worried about. Charlotte is sitting in the trailer all by herself. I cannot imagine what she's going through, Mama was her whole world and this has to be awful for her. Do you understand?"

"Absolutely!" Bulldog replied, which was far from the truth.

Nicole was the only person he had ever loved wholeheartedly, loving her with all of his heart and soul.

At eight o' clock in the evening, the Mercedes pulled into the driveway. Nicole sprang from the car and ran inside the trailer, finding Charlotte asleep on the small couch in the living room, curled up like a little girl. With new tears filling her eyes, Nicole knelt down on her knees beside her sister and softly rubbed her back.

"Charlotte Lynn?" She whispered, gently stroking her hair.

"Nicky! Oh Nicky!" Charlotte came awake, throwing her arms around her sister's neck.

"I'm here, everything is going to be okay." Nicole promised, holding her sister tight.

Bulldog entered the trailer to find the two women crying in each others arms. He closed the door behind him, and leaned against a wall with his hands in his pockets. He had never felt so helpless in his life. For once, there was nothing that he could say or do.

Within minutes, the sound of raindrops hitting the tin roof could be heard. The windows soon became fogged over with heavy raindrops, and the wind picked up to the point of a deep howl. Bulldog started a fire in the pot bellied stove, rolled a joint and lit it, while the girls left to be alone in Charlotte's bedroom. The rain and storm raged throughout the night, as if the heavens were shedding its own tears.

The breaking of dawn brought the sun rising over the horizon, bringing with it the warmth and birth of a new day. Nicole had fallen asleep on the bed next to Charlotte, while Bulldog slept on the couch. Red eyed and feeling better after a night of comforting one another, the sisters were able to laugh at the sight of Bulldog's bare feet sticking out a foot beyond the couch. His boots and socks were laying on the floor.

Charlotte Lynn immediately started cooking a huge breakfast, finding joy being in the small kitchen where her and her mother had spent so many days. Neither of the girls had much of an appetite, But they felt an obligation to take care of Bulldog. Each woman, in her own way, depending on him for his strength.

"Mama wanted to be cremated and have her ashes spread down by the pond."

"Whatever she wanted." Nicole agreed, then asked, "Would you like to come live with me?"

Charlotte Lynn eyes went wide. "Are you sure, Nicky? I have always dreamed of leaving here, but not like this. Nor do I want to be a burden."

Nicole smiled at the hope she saw lighting her sister's face. "You're my little sister. You could never be a burden! I have always loved you and I always will. Through thick and thin, no matter what."

Bulldog came out of the bathroom to join them at the table.

"My, aren't you two cute?" he grinned, seating himself at the kitchen table.

"Good morning! We were just making you breakfast. Would you care for a cup of coffee?" Charlotte Lynn offered.

"Yes, thank you."

"You two keep each other company. I've got to make some calls." Nicole smiled.

Nicole called Marsha, Manny, Charlie, and Blaze. She promised everyone that she would return as soon as possible. Next, she phoned her mother's church to set-up time for a eulogy.

She called the funeral home and made arrangements to have her mother cremated, ordering the most expensive urn and two gold pendants with some of her mother's ashes in them. A neighbor agreed to purchase the trailer for forty thousand dollars and she donated the furnishings to her mother's church. After the eulogy, Charlotte Lynn and Nicole spread their mother's ashes by the pond, bowed their heads and silently prayed.

Nicole rented a U-Haul van loading it with Charlotte Lynn's bedroom outfit, clothes, and a few keepsakes she wanted to keep to remember her mother by. Nicole only asked for two things for herself. She kept her mother's wedding rings and a quilt her mother had hand stitched. She wanted Charlotte to have everything else, along with the forty thousand dollars.

Bulldog drove the U-Haul van following Peaches and Charlotte Lynn in the silver Mercedes-Benz. Charlotte was exhausted, excited, and very much afraid of what the future might bring. Everything was going to be new and different, forcing her to learn about a world she knew very little about.

* * *

Detective Marks parked his white Cadillac Deville, lit a cigar, and listened to the morning news. There was nothing new he needed to concern himself with. Exiting the car, he walked to the office, immediately going to make himself a cup of coffee and calling a meeting in the conference room.

"Any new developments on the Pickett murder?"

No one had anything to offer.

"Anything new on the Porter murder?" Again, no response.

"Well, does anyone know who the silver Mercedes belongs to?"

"Yes, sir." Betty Crawford replied. "The vehicle is registered to a Nicole Redman. She lives at the Regency Towers. The license plate was special ordered with the name 'Peaches' on it. She's twenty-seven and she also owns a yellow Volkswagen. She hasn't been seen for at least 70 days. The tenants say she is very quiet, keeping mostly to herself. My sources say she performs burlesque at the Two O'clock Club."

"Good work." Marks nodded his approval. "Anything else?"

Greg, Wyatt, and Ronnie looked at each other before shaking their heads in the negative.

"So the name Nicole Redman means nothing to any of you?" Detective Marks asked.

The detectives looked at each other dumbfounded.

"What a bunch of morons!" Detective Marks shouted. "A year

ago when Domenic Coroza was blown up in his car in Essex, Nicole Redman was found inside his house in an upstairs bedroom tied up. She claimed not to recall anything. Roger Pickett was busted for possession of cocaine. He agreed to wear a wire and set up her ex-husband, Charlie Redman. Roger Pickett was murdered. Charlie retained Harold Glazer as his attorney. Ryan Porter, a known member of the Argot motorcycle gang, was murdered in the underground parking garage of Regency Towers where Nicole Redman lives. Is it just me, or does anyone think there's something terribly wrong with this picture?"

"I think you're on to something." Detective Wyatt blurted out, immediately wishing he had kept his big mouth shut.

Detective Marks ignored him. "I want to know where Nicole Redman was on the night Ryan Porter was killed. And, I want to know who was with her wearing Argot colors in the underground parking garage."

"Yes, Sir," they replied in unison filing out of the conference room one by one.

* * *

When Bulldog stopped for gas in Virginia, he called the cabin and told the Prospect to meet them at Regency Towers at noon. Ramrod and Rooster offered their help to unload the van.

Bulldog, Nicole, and Charlotte arrived in Maryland at ten o'clock in the morning, stopping at the White Coffee Pot in Glen Burnie to grab a bite to eat.

"It's cold up here!" Charlotte complained, rubbing her shoulders. Better get used to it, girl. Winter is a bitch here." Bulldog chuckled.

"I don't have any clothes for this kind of weather."

"Tomorrow we will go shopping." Nicole promised.

"I also want to get my driver's license, and buy a car. Maybe I'll buy a Mercedes-Benz like yours."

"I also have a cute yellow Volkswagen that's fun to drive and gets great gas mileage."

"I don't think that's what she wants." Bulldog chuckled. "What she wants and what she gets may be two different things, I don't want her to blow her money and have nothing to show for it."

"All I want is something to eat." Bulldog growled,

After breakfast, they headed for Baltimore. Nicole followed Bulldog in her Mercedes to Regency Towers where the expected brothers waited. Ramrod opened the passenger door of the van and hopped into the front seat while the Prospect and Rooster jumped onto the running boards grasping the door handles. Bulldog drove into the underground parking garage and backed the van up to the freight elevator.

Nicole and Charlotte covered up the Mercedes, then walked to the van. Ramrod and Charlotte Lynn's eyes locked. Nicole looked at Ramrod, then her little sister. The way they were looking at one another could spell trouble with a capital 'T'.

"Who is the guy with the brown curly hair?" Charlotte whispered behind her hand at Nicole.

"Why do you want to know?"

"I'm just curious."

"Curiosity killed the cat." Peaches looked at her sternly.

"Is he married?"

"No, he isn't. His name is Ramrod. He's the president of the club. I will introduce you to him later, so he'll know to stay away from you."

Charlotte rolled her eyes in response. As Nicole and Charlotte headed for the elevator, Charlotte glanced back over her shoulder. Ramrod was watching her every movement, sending a tingling sensation racing up her spine.

"That must be Peaches' little sister." Ramrod said to Bulldog grinning.

"She's not so little. She's a looker and the girl can cook!"

"What else can little sister do?" Ramrod smiled.

"I think Peaches just might shoot your ass if you mess with Charlotte Lynn. I don't think she's ever had a man, the highlight of her week was going to church on Sundays."

"You're shitting me!" Ramrod said in disbelief, a thoughtful look in his eyes.

Having unloaded the truck and putting Charlotte Lynn's bed together, they were all gathered around the kitchen table drinking coffee and snorting lines of cocaine. Charlotte recalled the feeling of euphoria she got from snorting crystal meth. When the straw was passed to her, she dared not look towards Nicole for her approval, she snorted only half lines up each nostril, tilting her head back and sniffing hard, just as she had watched everyone else do.

Nicole introduced Charlotte to Ramrod. The two had not stopped gawking at each other since their eyes first met. Out of respect for Peaches, Ramrod had been on his best behavior.

There was an unexpected knock at the door. Nicole looked through the peephole, It was a woman wearing a suit. She placed the chain on the door, opened it slightly, and asked. "May I help you?"

"I'm with the Baltimore City Homicide Division." Betty Crawford flashed her badge. "And I would like to speak with you in regards to the murder of Ryan Porter."

"I'm sorry, but I don't know a Ryan Porter." Nicole replied flatly.

"He was a member of the Argot motorcycle gang. You were seen earlier this week in the underground parking garage with another member of the club. May I come inside and talk with you?"

"It's not a good time. I just returned from my mother's funeral. I have company and I'm exhausted from the trip. If you would like to leave a card, I will give you a call at a better time."

Betty Crawford handed Nicole a card and left, her womanly instincts telling her that Nicole knew more than she would ever be willing to volunteer.

Ramrod and Bulldog overheard the entire conversation, and so did

Charlotte and the other two club brothers. Realizing they had made a huge mistake showing up at the apartment, Bulldog and Ramrod looked at each other and shook their heads. Charlotte sensed that there was something terribly wrong.

When Nicole returned to the table, Charlotte asked, "What was that all about?"

"It's nothing." Peaches smiled. "Some guy was shot in the underground parking garage a few weeks ago and the police are still interviewing the tenants."

"Why was he shot?" Charlotte's curiosity piqued .

"I have no idea." Peaches shrugged her shoulders. "My guess is it was probably a robbery."

CHAPTER SEVENTEEN
LUCKY DEVIL

Detective Crawford lived in a small, white, two bedroom, stucco home in a rural section of Baltimore City. Her front and backyard was not much bigger than a postage stamp. She lived alone, her only companions being two miniature poodles, Cha Cha and Pierre, who were as different as night and day. Cha Cha was white, cuddly, and very affectionate. Pierre was black, hated to be picked up, and had a nasty temperament.

It was eight o'clock in the evening as Betty stood over the kitchen sink washing dishes, reflecting on her conversation with Detective Marks earlier in the day. When he arrived for work she had presented him with a cup of freshly brewed coffee, then briefed him on the short exchange between her and Nicole Redman. He had stood in one spot, twisting that damn cigar in his mouth, waiting patiently for her to finish her report.

"And?" He asked, urging her to give him more.

"She wouldn't talk to me. She said that she just returned from her mother's funeral. She had company and she was exhausted. I left my card behind. But guess what else I discovered." She smiled, pleased with herself.

"Oh boy! Now we're playing guessing games." Marks said, being the perfect bastard. "How many guesses do I get? Does Nicole Redman have a forty-five caliber pistol registered in her name. And, you got a search warrant and found it."

"No, Sir. She may have one, but I never thought to check that. But I did find out that Nicole and Charlie Redman are divorced. From the marriage they had a daughter named, Charlotte. When Charlotte was six years old she was killed by a hit and run driver. The car that hit her was stolen and believed to have been used in an assault. The victim of the assault ended up in a coma and later died."

"What a tangled web we weave," he said with a thoughtful smile, accepting the photo of Nicole that Betty handed over to him. Twisting the cigar in his mouth, he stared down at the picture of the very attractive woman, already ignoring Crawford's presence. There was no 'thank you' for the coffee, nor a 'that a girl', certainly not a pat on the back for her good work.

She had stood motionless looking like a fool, deciding there on the spot that from now on he could get his own damn coffee. The white dog at her feet barked several times.

"What do you want Cha Cha? Do you want to go outside?"

* * *

"I really need to go to work tonight." Nicole announced, "But I don't want to leave my sister here by herself."

"We'll stay and keep her entertained." Ramrod volunteered.

"Where do you work?" Charlotte asked.

"The Two O'clock Club. I already told you I dance burlesque."

"She's a stripper." Ramrod laughed.

"I am not!" Peaches snapped, then asked her sister. "Have you ever seen girls dance provocatively to music while taking their clothes off? They still keep all of their privates covered. They only strip down to their panties, g-strings, or bikinis. They always have tassels covering their nipples?"

"Oh. I've watched that on television." Charlotte Lynn replied, not at all shocked or surprised.

"Maybe little sister isn't quite as innocent as you think she is." Ramrod grinned, staring at Charlotte Lynn hungrily.

"You guys had better not take advantage of my little sister while I'm at work!" She told Bulldog and Ramrod. The Prospect and Rooster had long since left for the cabin.

"We'll be good." Bulldog chuckled, then turned to Charlotte. "Do you know how to play strip poker?"

Peaches could not stop herself from laughing. "I'm warning you.

You better take care of her."

"Yes, Mama." Ramrod laughed.

Nicole grabbed her sister by the hand and took her into her bedroom, closing the door behind them. In the large walk in closet Charlotte saw the variety of costumes.

"Are those what you wear on stage," she asked.

"Sometimes. These are the ones I bought myself. I wear them only at the beginning of the performance. Now listen carefully." She faced her sister, a serious expression covering her face.

"I'm not setting a very good example for you. I'm not a role model and I don't want you following in my footsteps. I want you to go to college. Someday get married, have a house full of kids and live a normal life. I want you to take advantage of the opportunities I can give you. I know I can't live your life, but I want you to be safe and happy."

"Nicky, remember we're sisters through thick and thin. For better or worse. I know you love me, but it's time I made my own decisions. I love you and you love me, and that's how it's always going to be!"

* * *

Charlie was stoking the fire when he heard the sound of the phone ringing. He walked into the kitchen, lifted up the receiver and said.

"Redman's morgue. You stab em, we slab em."

"Charlie?" Came Dee Dee's uncertain voice, but tinged with just a touch of laughter.

"Dee Dee." He said excitedly, feeling his pulse quicken. "It's me."

"I've missed you. How have you been?"

"Lonely. I thought you were going to call me?" She complained.

"You're not going to believe what happened."

"Let me guess, the dog ate the paper my phone number was on. Happens to me all the time." Dee Dee said with a voice filled with laughter.

"No, smart ass. I don't have a dog. I washed it when I did my laundry. I've been going crazy thinking about you. I stocked the kitchen with groceries. Why don't you spend the weekend and I'll serve you breakfast in bed."

"Why don't you have me for breakfast?" She offered in a seductive voice.

"I like that even better," Charlie chuckled. "I checked the map and it's only a couple hours drive from Harrisburg."

"Give me your address. I will be there Friday night before six in the evening."

"Fantastic. I'll see you then."

"Ugh, don't you want my number?"

"I'm definitely not the sharpest tack in the box, am I?"

Charlie wrote Dee Dee's phone number in his rolodex director sitting next to the phone in the kitchen, determined not to ever lose it again.

* * *

Returning from work, Peaches stepped from the elevator to the sound of loud music coming from her apartment. It sounded like a party was going on behind the closed doors. She opened the door to find Charlotte dressed in skimpy shorts, a tank-top, and nothing else. She was giving Ramrod a lap dance, his hands running up and down her long bare legs.

"Charlotte Lynn!" Nicole snapped, banging the door closed. Charlotte jumped away from Ramrod as if she had been burnt, and Bulldog quickly switched off the loud music from the radio. He was smoking a stick of marijuana and smiling stupidly.

"I told them you would freak." Bulldog chuckled.

Nicole glared at him, then turned on Charlotte. "Your new name should be trouble!" She snapped, then turned accusing eyes on Ramrod. "I thought you were going to look after her?"

"I am. Nobody has taken advantage of her. She hasn't left the apartment or the front room. All we're doing is having a little fun."

Nicole could see there was no regret in his eyes. She could clearly see that if Charlotte was willing, Ramrod was determined to have her. She thought about taking Charlotte and running as far away as possible. Instead, she gave a sigh of defeat, knowing that she could not control or live her sister's life for her. If Ramrod was able to make her happy, so be it. But she would keep a close eye on how he treated her. Giving them one last stern look, she snorted two lines of cocaine, deciding to teach her sister how to dance.

"Roll your hip like this," she instructed.

Charlotte rolled her hips in perfect imitation of her sister's movements, her firm breasts and semi-hard nipples showing through her bra and tank top.

"Ramrod gave me a nickname. It's Sugar."

"It fits you." Nicole smiled.

Bulldog turned the radio on, the music at a much lower volume. For the next fifteen minutes, Nicole taught her sister a series of dance moves, knowing that their provocative movements were turning on the two men.

"Enough!" Ramrod groaned, not being able to watch the movements of Charlotte's sexy body a second longer. Nicole and Bulldog laughed at his discomfort, while Charlotte blushed a bright red.

"This weekend we're having a bonfire and pig roast for the club members and their families. I hope you will come, Sugar." Ramrod suggested.

"She'll be there." Nicole spoke for her sister. "I need to discuss some business with you, so don't get too drunk before we get there."

"Sounds good to me." Ramrod looked back to Charlotte.

"Next week I will be sitting in on Billy King's trial. She was a dancer at the Two O' Clock Club until she shot and killed her boyfriend for cheating on her. Blaze, and all of the girls are attending the trial to support her. Since you've got a hundred acres, would you mind teaching my sister how to drive, so she can get her driver's license? I would appreciate the help."

Ramrod grinned broadly at the still blushing Charlotte. "It will be my pleasure." As much as he lusted after Charlotte Lynn, Ramrod was not the type of man that would take advantage of a girl's virtue.

* * *

"Hey, boss." Betty Crawford called to Detective Marks as he entered the squad room, removing his coat.

"Hey what? This had better be good, I haven't had time to make a cup of coffee yet." He growled.

"This is good." Betty smiled . "Nicole Redman lived in Blossom Hills at 108 Dupont Avenue. About a year ago her daughter was killed by a hit and run driver. The police found a stolen car that matched the description abandoned in the parking lot of an IGA grocery store on Fort Smallwood road. Jeff Miles lived in an adjacent neighborhood, Sharonville. As he was leaving for work he was attacked by someone swinging a baseball bat.

He collapsed into a coma, eventually dying, The pol..."

Marks cut her off. "I hope there's a point to this story."

"There is. The police traced phone calls from Jeff Miles' residence to Harold Bennett's. It turns out that Marsha Bennett, Harold's wife, was a call-girl and Jeff was paying for her services."

"I'm not impressed." Detective Marks interrupted her a second time.

"Harold Bennett received a phone call from a bar on Howard street called the Blue Onion. He tells his wife that he's going out to help a friend move some furniture and..."

"That's not illegal." Marks shook his head, still not following where the other detective was leading him.

"...and that night." Betty ignored him, continuing her flow of words. "Harold is discovered on a country road in Baltimore County, laying next to his car in a pool of blood with five forty-five caliber bullets riddling his body."

"I'm sure there's a reason for this story."

"There is. Tony Bedsoe was the manager of the Blue Onion. He's blown up in an explosion at his house, and killed. Guess who was a dancer at the Blue Onion?"

"Nicole Redman!" Marks guessed correctly. "This Peaches gets around."

"Yes, she does." Betty smiled. "Domonic Coroza was blown up in his car and she was found tied to a bed inside his house. It appears like the Black Widow has nothing on our little girl, Nicole."

"Have you checked with ballistics to see if the forty-five caliber slugs found in Harold Bennett match those found in Ryan Porter." Detective Marks asked.

"It's being done as we speak. Ballistics has already matched the .45 bullets that killed Harold Bennett to the .45 automatic found in the glove compartment of Tony's Bedsoe's car."

"Joyce 'Stormy' Winland also danced at the Blue Onion. She and Nicole were best friends. Stormy was found floating in the harbor. She was killed by a single gunshot."

* * *

Friday afternoon Nicole and Charlotte were in the kitchen hanging out and making lunch when the phone rang. They had been arguing about Charlotte's demands that she be called only Sugar from now on.

"Hello?" Sugar answered, hoping it was Ramrod.

"Nicole?"

"No. This is her sister, Sugar. Just a minute." She passed Nicole the phone.

"Hello, Nicole?"

"Hi Harold." Peaches said, recognizing his voice.

"I need to see you in my office immediately. How soon can you be here?"

"Twenty minutes." She said, hearing the urgency in his voice.

Nicole left Charlie at the apartment, rushing over to Harold's office in the yellow Bug. When she entered, he motioned her past his receptionist. "We've got a problem," he said, closing the door of his office for privacy . "Over the weekend I played golf, and I heard through the grapevine that the Baltimore City Homicide Division is investigating you for a string of unsolved murders. Do the names Jeff Miles, Harold Bennett, Tony Bedsoe, Joyce Winland, Domonic Coroza, Roger Pickett, or Ryan Porter mean anything to you? In one way or another, they have all been linked to you."

Nicole was frozen in place, her head bowed, and she said nothing.

"Right this minute, Ballistics is comparing casings and slugs from the Bedsoe murder with the Porter murder. Please tell me they aren't going to match."

"They aren't going to match!" Nicole raised her head.

"Well, we have to make some new arrangements. I can't continue making pickups and deliveries from your apartment. It's too much of a risk."

"I will make other arrangements. Just take twenty thousand dollars from the money before you drop it off and deposit it in my Trust Fund. I will call you from a pay phone with the new address later this afternoon."

"Be careful." Harold cautioned.

* * *

Saturday afternoon, Peaches and Sugar drove to the cabin. Nicole wore her black leather jacket with the Argot's colors, her name, and her property patch.

"The property patch means that I'm his old lady." She explained to Sugar. "In the biker world sometimes that's as close as a girl ever gets to being married. But nobody messes with a chick wearing a property patch unless they are prepared to suffer the consequences."

Bulldog and Ramrod were standing on the porch of the cabin when the girls drove up. Bikers and their tramps were already hanging out and acting in a festive mood. Smiling, the two men greeted the girls with warm hugs, Nicole noting how willingly Charlotte went into Ramrod's arms.

"Welcome to my world." Ramrod told Sugar.

"I love it!" She said, taking in the sights.

Once inside the cabin, Sugar felt right at home. She was quite the Susie homemaker. Charlotte Lynn's mother had taught her to sew, cook, and can fruits and vegetables while Nicole's father taught her how to trap, fish, and shoot a gun.

"I think we should talk before we start partying." Nicole suggested to Ramrod.

Ramrod and Peaches stepped into the bedroom and closed the door. She told him about her conversation with Harold Glazer. Other arrangements had to be made. She suggested the pickup and delivery be made at her ex-husband Charlie's house. She asked for his word that he would never try to cross her out. He gave it to her.

"I want to meet your former husband. Today, if possible." Nicole called Charlie to inform him that she needed to introduce him to someone today, the emphasis being on 'today'. It was urgent, and it could not wait.

"I've got company." Charlie replied.

"It's only going to require ten minutes of your time."

"Okay." Charlie reluctantly agreed. "See you when you get here."

Bulldog, Nicole, Ramrod, and Sugar got into Ramrod's car, heading for Charlie's house in Millerville, Maryland.

Charlie's 1965 blue Corvette Stingray was parked in the driveway. Behind it, a white Mercedes convertible with a Pennsylvania license plate that read Dee Dee.

"Holy fuck!" Ramrod shouted, driving past the house.

"What's the problem?" Peaches asked.

At the corner there was a small shopping center with a donut shop. Ramrod told Peaches to call her ex and have him meet them at the donut shop. "And tell him to come by himself!"

Peaches called from a pay phone.

Bulldog and Sugar went inside the donut shop, ordering coffee and donuts. They sat down at a table to talk.

After calling Charlie from the pay phone, he showed up two minutes later. Nicole introduced him to Ramrod and they sat down in the car to talk.

"I thought you were coming inside?"

"We were until I saw who your company was." Ramrod chuckled.

"You know who my visitor is?" Charlie asked in surprise.

"I know who her father is. He's the mob boss for the entire Eastern Seaboard. I don't want him to know I'm doing business with you."

"You sure do know how to pick them, Charlie." Nicole laughed.

Ramrod explained. "We've got a problem. There's too much heat on Peaches for the moment. So, we need to have the pickups and deliveries made at your house around two p.m. every Wednesday. Harold Glazer will drop the money off and pick up the gym bag of cocaine."

"The Attorney." Charlie grinned.

Ramrod handed Charlie a card with the cabin's phone number. "If you ever have a problem or need our help we are just a phone call away. But never, and I mean never, discuss business over the phone."

"One more thing." Nicole said to Ramrod. "We've got to start moving more product or we may lose the connection."

"I will bring it up at the next club meeting." Ramrod promised.

Charlie returned to his house. When they returned to the cabin the party was in high gear.

Ramrod looked at Sugar, grinned and said. "If only you weren't a virgin."

"Who said that I am?" She giggled. "I did go to my senior prom."

Peaches overheard Ramrod and her sister's conversation and

laughed so hard she nearly tossed her cookies.

The members of the club drank, snorted lines, laughed, and enjoyed themselves until the early morning hours. It was sometime after two in the morning when Bulldog picked Peaches up and carried her into his bedroom, closing the door behind them.

The next morning, when Peaches stumbled into the kitchen Ramrod was making a sandwich and singing. "Sugar in the morning. Sugar in the evening. Sugar at supper time. Be my little Sugar and love me all the time."

Sugar stood in the doorway to his bedroom wrapped in a blanket wearing a pleased smile. Bulldog came out of his bedroom, saw Sugar and grinned. "You lucky devil." He told Ramrod. Peaches smiled, shook her head, and poured herself a cup of coffee.

Later that day, Ramrod presented Sugar with a black leather jacket with the Argot colors, her name, and a property patch reading PROPERTY OF RAMROD.

CHAPTER EIGHTEEN
SOUTHERN COMFORT

Monday morning, the trial of Billy Natasha King began. It was a trial by jury, consisting of seven women and five men, who were selected from a pool of twenty-four, with a female alternate. If convicted, the jury would also decide whether or not to invoke the death penalty.

Blaze, along with all the girls from the Two O' clock Club were seated in the second row behind Natasha . As the deputies escorted her into the courtroom, they exchanged smiles and waves.

On the opposite side of the aisle, the seats were taken by family of the deceased. The witnesses during the trial would be dominated by the prosecution's witnesses. There would be detectives, experts, the clerk from the motel, a man returning to his room carrying a bucket of ice, and the cheating woman who was with Tommy Brown during the shooting. Billy would have killed her too, if she had not ran out of bullets.

Betty Crawford and Detective Marks were both seated in the rear of the courtroom.

"That's her." Betty was saying in a low voice, her gaze zooming in on Nicole.

"That's who?" Detective Marks asked, turning his head to follow the direction of her gaze.

"The platinum blonde in the first row. That's Nicole Redman. Peaches."

On the second day of trial, during recess, Betty Crawford and Detective Marks approached Nicole in the hallway. She was standing next to Blaze and several other girls. They were talking in low tones, so not to let there voices carry.

"Excuse me." Betty cut in. "I left you my card and I haven't heard from you. Do you need another card?"

"I don't know the guy. I told you that. I have nothing else to add."

Nicole smiled smugly.

"Do you know Jeff Miles, Harold Bennett, Tony Bedsoe, Roger Pickett, Ryan Porter, Domonic Coroza, or Joyce Winland?" Detective Marks ran off the long list of names, a cold look in his eyes.

"They all have two things in common." Betty Crawford added.

"They all knew you, and they're all dead."

"Let's save us both a lot of time and trouble. If you have something to talk to me about, call my attorney."

"Who would that be?" Betty Crawford asked.

"Let me guess." Detective Marks interjected. "Harold Glazer."

Nicole smiled.

As the detectives turned to walk away, Betty looked over at Marks. "Either you're getting better at the guessing game, or you're a mind reader."

After the detectives were out of ear shot, Blaze pulled Nicole away from the other gossipy women. "Would you like to tell me what in the Hell that was all about," she asked.

"Not really." Nicole answered smiling.

"I don't want to be attending another trial anytime soon."

"Neither do I." Nicole countered.

"If you need me for anything you know I'll be there for you."

"Thanks."

After a four day trial, the jury was given instructions and sent to deliberate. Forty-five minutes later they returned with a verdict. GUILTY! The Baltimore Sun reported later that evening.

On the penalty phase, the jury showed compassion and sentenced her to serve life in prison. She was sent to a women's prison in Jessup, Maryland.

* * *

Friday night, Nicole stopped by Charlie's house unannounced only to discover the same white Mercedes-Benz parked behind his

Corvette as the last time. The license plate still read 'Dee Dee'.

Normally, if the front door was unlocked, she would have simply walked in. But since Charlie had company, she rang the doorbell.

"Can I help you?" Dee Dee asked, answering the door.

Nicole's first thought was that Dee Dee looked like a Barbie Doll. Her auburn hair was wrapped in a bun on top of her head. Her brown eyes were captivating, and she had pearly white teeth.

Not only was she beautiful, she was dressed to the tens. Dee Dee was wearing an elegant blue strapless evening gown with diamond earrings and matching necklace. On her left wrist she wore a white gold Rolex watch, and on her right a white gold diamond tennis bracelet. A white fur coat was hung from a hanging tree just inside the doors of the front entrance.

"You must be Dee Dee," Nicole smiled introducing herself. "I'm Nicole, Charlie's ex-wife."

"What can I do for you?"

"For starters, you could invite me inside."

"I'm sorry, but I don't know you. Let me get Charlie, he's just getting out of the shower." Dee Dee replied, shutting the door in her face.

Nicole stood at the front door, waiting in the cold, for what seemed like a very long time. Finally, Charlie opened the door and invited her inside introducing her to Dee Dee who now lounged on the sofa.

"We've met!" Nicole snapped. "You better tell this bitch that the next time I knock on the door she better let me in."

Dee Dee jumped to her feet, kicking off her high heels. "Bitch? Who are you calling a bitch? I'll kick your ass, you whore!"

"Whore?" Nicole screamed. "Bring it bitch!"

"That's enough!" Charlie shouted, stepping between the two, apologizing to Nicole, explaining Dee Dee did not know who she was. He also made it clear that Dee Dee had done the right thing. It was not intended to be disrespectful.

"I was respectful. Instead of just walking in I rang the doorbell."

"I'm sorry. I didn't know what I was supposed to do." Dee Dee replied, in a much calmer tone.

"I'm sorry too." Nicole said, then laughed. "We sure got off on the wrong foot. And, it would have been unforgivable to mess up such a beautiful gown."

Dee Dee laughed, not taking offense. "Thank you." She smiled.

"I need to discuss something with Charlie in private. It won't take more than a couple of minutes." Nicole explained to Dee Dee.

"That's fine. I'm not the jealous type." Dee Dee smiled.

"Me neither." Nicole replied.

Charlie escorted Nicole to the garage, shut the door, and asked. "What's up?"

"If you could sell a large amount of cocaine in Florida, how difficult would it be for you to have it shipped there?"

"No problem. I could have it delivered within twenty-four hours."

"That's all I need to know. Have a nice evening. By the way, where are you and Dee Dee going dressed like that?" She questioned taking in his silk bathrobe.

"We're going to the Opera." Charlie grinned. "If you had waited for ten more minutes you would have seen me in a tuxedo.

"I wish I had brought my camera." Nicole laughed.

* * *

The cabin was packed with Argot brothers when Peaches and Sugar arrived. The girls were dressed alike in jeans, matching yellow blouses, and black zip-up boots with two inch heels. Over this they wore their Argot leather jackets. The moment they stepped through the door, Bulldog and Ramrod claimed their property.

"I missed you, baby." Ramrod grabbed Sugar in his arms.

"I missed you too, Boo."

"Boo?" Bulldog laughed, putting his arm around Peaches. He pulled her close for a quick kiss, then asked Sugar. "Did your sister tell you how I earned my red wings?" Bulldog grinned from ear to ear.

"Shut up!" Peaches shouted. "I'm warning you."

"Warning me?" Bulldog chuckled. "I ate her pussy while she was on the rag. I did it in front of the brothers."

"No, you didn't." Sugar laughed.

"The Hell I didn't! I ate her on the picnic table in front of the cabin. There's two hundred witnesses to prove it."

Peaches was livid. She threw his arm off her shoulder, walking to the kitchen where she had left her purse. Turning around with her back to the room, she pulled out a stack of photos sorting through them until she found the one she wanted. By this time a number of brothers had followed her trying to see what she was up to. She went over to a wall covered in club pictures and pinned up a single photo. At the sight of the photo, the club members broke into hilarious laughter. It was a picture of Bulldog at Disneyland wearing a pair of Mickey Mouse ears. Bulldog forced his way through the crowd of brothers to tear down the photo. Nicole stood out of sight, hiding behind several club members by the front door.

"Where are you, bitch?" he growled, looking around for her.

"All's fair in love and war." Ramrod laughed.

"The bitch has declared war." Bulldog spat.

Peaches laughed and streaked out of the front door of the cabin with Bulldog in hot pursuit. She did not stand a chance of outrunning him through the thick snow in high heel boots. He caught her in a few long strides, tackling her in a cloud of powdery snow. He pinned her legs, holding her arms to her side, allowing snow to get in her face and hair.

"Who's your Daddy?" he demanded.

Peaches laughed. While spitting snow out of her mouth, she spat, "Who's your Mama?" Then she hollered, "Ramrod!" knowing that he always took her side in the uneven contest.

"Let her go, bro." Ramrod yelled from where a crowd had gathered at the front of the cabin. Sugar stood at his side laughing her head off.

The brothers laughed as Bulldog rolled off of her defeated. They began to chant. "Peaches! Peaches! Peaches!" Bulldog had heard it all before. It was their chant for whenever she bested him. The last time he heard the brothers chant was when he was eating her pussy on top of the picnic table.

"You bitch!" he cursed, giving her a quick kiss before jumping to his feet.

Nicole stood, brushing herself off. "I need to talk some business with you and Ramrod before things get too carried away." She laughed.

The threesome walked inside the cabin and into Ramrod's bedroom, closing the door for privacy.

"I have an idea." Nicole began. "First, I checked to make sure that I could guarantee delivery, and it can be made within twenty-four hours. I think it's time for the club to expand. How do you feel about opening a Chapter in Orlando, Florida? I picked Orlando because it's central with easy access to Miami, Fort Lauderdale, and Daytona. Interstate 75 and I-4 are also easily accessible."

Bulldog gave Ramrod a shoulder shrug. "Bro, we're already selling the Heathens meth. We could set up a local lab." Bulldog suggested.

"I can present the idea and take a vote on it at church. Give me a week."

"Let's get this party started." Opening the door, she yelled into the living room. "It's party time!"

The brothers cheered, clanged beer bottles, and started laying out lines of crystal meth and cocaine, Peaches and Sugar joined the party, leading the other biker tramps into the midst of the bikers.

Within an hour, Sugar whispered in Ramrod's ear and they walked into his bedroom, closing the door behind them. Sugar undressed him, sat down on the bed, and took his manhood in her mouth until he was rock hard. It was the trick that he had taught her the day before, amazing her with her ability to arouse him so easily. She took off her clothes, pushed him down on the bed mounting him, and rode him hard. He grabbed her firm round breasts, teasing her nipples and groaning his pleasure. Before now, he never realized what being pussy whipped felt like. Her warmth felt so good it took his breath away, making him wish he could live inside her forever.

It was two in the morning when Bulldog and Peaches retired to his bedroom. Bulldog undressed, walked into the bathroom and stepped into the shower. He turned the water on full blast, letting the hot water cascade down over him. Peaches waited a few seconds before undressing and joining him. They kissed for what seemed like an eternity taking turns soaping each others bodies, Nicole slid down the powerful muscles of his wet body, taking his raging hard-on deep into her mouth. For five long minutes she sucked him until he could not stand the pleasure another second. Bulldog pulled her away and spun her around. She placed her palms flat against the shower wall, arching her back as he cupped her hot pussy with one hand and guided his dick deep inside her cunt with the other. Peaches moaned with pleasure as he rammed her with a quickening pace, deeper and deeper as the steaming water pour down over their naked bodies.

They stopped only long enough to slowly dry off and retire to the bed. Peaches mounted him, riding his powerful body until she was having one orgasm after another. They both lay in the aftermath panting with racing hearts. Bulldog pulled the sheet up over their naked bodies and they both slid into a deep sleep.

Sunday afternoon, Ramrod called a church meeting. All of the board members voting unanimously to start a new Chapter in Florida, not limiting the location to Orlando.

"It's a go." Ramrod informed Peaches as he exited the cabin after the meeting.

"Why don't the four of us fly to Orlando next Thursday night. We can rent a car, spend the weekend, and fly back Sunday night. All we need to find is a house to rent in the right location. A base, a place to operate the new Chapter from."

"Sounds like a good idea. Do you have any objections if Sugar stays with me for a few days? You said she needs to learn how to drive. She can drive around the property and practice all she wants, and I'll help her study for the test."

"You'll help her alright. You'll help yourself." Peaches laughed.

"It's up to you." Peaches told her sister.

"Would you get upset with me if I did?"

"It's kind of too late for that." Peaches laughed, making her sister blush.

"I'll stay!" Sugar decided, throwing her arms around Ramrod's neck. They kissed passionately.

Nicole shook her head, but secretly pleased that her sister had someone to make her happy. Now she could barely wait until Thursday. She would have left sooner, except she did not want to disappoint Marsha and Manny. She never wanted them to think, not even for a second, that they were not important to her. She loved them both dearly.

* * *

Charlie rented a limousine for the trip to the Opera. He did not have much appreciation for the fine arts, but Dee Dee enjoyed them immensely, much of her young life having been spent at charities supporting the arts, all on behalf of her father. Her enjoyment was all that mattered to Charlie. When he asked what type of work her father did, she explained that he was a contractor; building foundations for high-rise buildings.

He learned that Dee Dee was an only child and very much a daddy's girl, her father spoiling her rotten. Charlie learned a great deal about her childhood. When she was twelve, her father bought her a brown spotted pony that she affectionately named Freckles, due to its white spots. In the backyard, she had a huge swing set, an Olympic swimming pool, and a tennis court.

Returning from the Opera, Charlie stood in the living room stoking the fire in the large fireplace. He was consumed with the memory of Dee Dee wearing a pink negligee with no bra, her well rounded breasts welcoming his caress. Just the thought of her sexy little ass gave him an instant erection. Dee Dee had driven herself, home after the Opera and he could hardly wait until the weekend. Friday night, she would return and it could not come quick enough.

* * *

Thursday afternoon, Ramrod and Sugar, Bulldog and Peaches boarded TWA flight 723 for Orlando. Nicole's thoughts were of warm, sunny days, sandy beaches, and a little southern comfort.

Charlotte Lynn had a different thought. She had never been on an airplane before, and she wanted to find out what Ramrod meant by their joining the mile high club.

Ramrod and Bulldog were both thinking about the new Chapter, and wondering what their next move would be.

"Are you ready?" Ramrod grinned, looking at Charlotte Lynn. She giggled, and when he stood up, she followed him. Not a passenger flinched as they entered the small bathroom together, locking the door behind them.

CHAPTER NINETEEN
THE PROSPECT

First Ramrod and Sugar, then Bulldog and Peaches, took turns going to the bathroom to have close hot sex, becoming faithful members of the mile high club. They also took turns snorting lines of cocaine, becoming high to the point of disregarding the sneers of their fellow passengers. One of the perks of being an Argot was they gave less than a fuck about what anyone else thought. If any of the passengers had dared to voice an opinion, there would've been consequences for their doing such a stupid thing. The brotherhood ran deep, and their colors were earned the hard way. If an Argot ran from a fight, he lost his patch and was banned from the club forever. Tattoos bearing the club's name had to be blacked out, burned, or cut off. If an Argot committed the cardinal sin and snitched, it would be unforgivable. For snitching he would lose his life.

At the moment, the four of them were seated, with Peaches and Bulldog in front of Ramrod and Sugar.

"If everything goes well, I'm thinking about patching the Prospect into the club. Conditional on his relocating to Orlando to help start the Florida Chapter." Ramrod said.

"I think that's a good idea." Bulldog agreed.

"The club is his only family. He's loyal, and I think that would be a very wise decision." Peaches added.

"What's a Prospect?" Charlotte Lynn asked. Everyone laughed.

Ramrod ordered another round of drinks. Jack Daniel's in miniature bottles, and four glasses of Coca-Cola. Then, he explained to Sugar what a 'Prospect' was.

It was a smooth flight, landing on time at Orlando International Airport. Ramrod stopped at Hertz Rent-A-Car and rented a brand new white Cadillac Coupe Deville with red interior. It was fully loaded, and still had that new car smell. They were traveling light with only carry-on luggage, Nicole had brought five thousand dollars in cash.

Ramrod brought credit cards because Nicole didn't have any.

After they placed their prized possessions in the trunk, Ramrod handed the keys to the Cadillac to Sugar. "She got her driver's license yesterday." He announced, grinning.

As Bulldog and Peaches seated themselves in the rear seat, Peaches declared. "Oh, my God. We're all going to die."

"Stop that!" Sugar laughed. "I'm a good driver."

"The only experience you've had is driving around the cabin for three days." Peaches snapped.

Sugar started the car. She placed her foot on the brake, put the car in drive, and pressed on the gas pedal. The car jerked forward, then stopped abruptly.

"You might want to fasten your seatbelts." Ramrod suggested, laughing.

"Might Hell!" Bulldog growled.

"If I'm killed, I want to be cremated." Peaches announced.

"Shut up, y'all is making me nervous." Sugar cried.

"I'm making you nervous." Nicole said in disbelief. "I'm scared to death."

On her second try, Sugar backed the car out of the parking space driving only as far as the street before stopping and placing the car in park. She looked over her shoulder at Nicole. "I scared you, didn't I?" She said, already in the process of switching seats with Ramrod. From the passenger seat she opened her purse and removed her license. "But I did get my driver's license yesterday." She proudly showed her license to Nicole and Bulldog. "There's no way I would drive in traffic like that," she pointed to the four lanes of heavy traffic with people driving recklessly. Vehicles changed lanes without using signals, some of them speeding up to cut in front of oncoming cars.

The day was still early, the clock on the dashboard reading 11:40 a.m. The sun was bright and the sky a baby blue with scattered white powder puffs. It was 78 degrees, the weather forecast predicted the high eighties by mid afternoon.

"If we can squeeze it in, I would like to take my sister to Disneyworld. Have you been there, Ramrod?"

"I've seen a photo of it." Ramrod chuckled, pulling into the fast lane of traffic.

"Fuck you!" Bulldog snapped.

They laughed at him, realizing that he was still pretty sore about that one.

The Heathens' club house was on the south side of Orlando, so they decided to look for a place far north of Orlando.

Ramrod stopped in front of a shopping center and purchased a newspaper from a rack. They stopped at Buddy's bar and grill, took seats at the counter, and ordered drinks and sandwiches. Bulldog chatted with the barmaid while Ramrod thumbed through the Classified Section of the Orlando Sentinel. As he flipped past the Help Wanted section an ad caught his eye: "Shangrilla Nightclub... strippers wanted."

"Well, I've found work for you girls. It's a place called the Shangrilla." He chuckled.

"Not there, you didn't." the barmaid chimed in, looking over his shoulder as she sat a plate with a sandwich and chips in front of him. "That's the sleaziest club in town. As a matter of fact, there aren't any nice clubs."

It was as though someone flipped on a light inside of Peaches' head. The lights came on, and her mind was whirling in high gear. She suddenly saw a business opportunity for herself and Sugar. But for now she needed to keep her thoughts to herself.

"We're looking for a house to rent somewhere north of Orlando that's not very populated. Any suggestions?" Bulldog asked the barmaid.

"Here's a three bedroom house for rent on a Lake in Fern Park for three hundred and fifty a month." Ramrod read from the newspaper.

"That's a very nice quiet area," the barmaid offered.

"How far is it from here?" Ramrod asked her.

"Maybe twenty miles. Take a left when you leave here. That's 17-92 in front of the bar. Take a left, and just keep going. If you reach Altamonte Springs, turn around, you've gone too far."

"Do you have a phone that I can use?"

"Sure, baby." The barmaid sat a phone on top of the counter. Ramrod looked at the newspaper and dialed the number, speaking to the owner for a long five minutes, making sure he had the directions down pat. "Let's go for a ride, boys and girls."

There were only two houses on Pot lake and they were spaced well apart. The rental house was a white stucco ranch with an attached carport, outside utility room, and screened rear porch. It had three bedrooms, one a-half baths, large kitchen, dining room, with central air-conditioning. The yard was huge! In the backyard there was a dock and a patio with a surrounding railing standing beside a huge oak tree. The lake was spring fed by a steady supply of fresh spring water.

"This is beautiful." Sugar exclaimed.

"I don't think the Prospect would complain about living here." Peaches giggled.

Ramrod took the short walk down the street to introduce himself to the neighbors next door who also lived on the lake. The neighbor was outside pulling weeds from around a flag pole, the American flag proudly waved in the wind. Below the flag flew the flag honoring the missing P.O.W.'s.

"Hi friend." Ramrod extended his hand in friendship. "I was looking at the possibility of renting the house next door when I saw that you fly two flags."

"The name's Johnny Nash." The neighbor grinned, shaking Ramrod's hand. He looked at the P.O.W. flag, sighed and said. "We left a lot of brothers behind."

"That we did." Ramrod declared, with a deep sigh of his own regret.

Like himself, Johnny Nash was a Vietnam veteran. Johnny was six feet tall, a hundred and ninety pounds, with brown hair and a beard, both well groomed. He was shirtless, barefooted, wearing nothing more than cut-off jeans. For a man in his late forties, Johnny was in great physical condition, other than a noticeable limp which Ramrod assumed was a reminder of Vietnam. Johnny was married with two teenage girls who were in school. His wife, Christy, was at work. Two trucks were parked on the property: an older Ford pick-up and an older Ford stake bed. They were matching green.

"Christy drives a new yellow Mustang convertible. You know how women are, they have to keep up with the Joneses."

"Well, unless she decides to buy a brand new pink Harley, I think you're pretty safe." Ramrod chuckled.

Johnny assured Ramrod the club would be welcome. The lake was small, spring fed, and extremely cold. Johnny boasted the lake was well stocked with bass if he enjoyed fishing. As a welcoming gesture, he offered Ramrod the use of his Ford state bed if he needed to move anything.

Returning to the rental house, Ramrod signed a six month lease. Peaches and Sugar took the Cadillac and went shopping for curtains, pots and pans, dishes, glasses, and groceries.

Ramrod borrowed Johnny's state bed truck, and he and Bulldog went shopping for furniture. Ramrod bought a dining room set, a complete living-room group, and two bedroom outfits. He furnished the kitchen with tables and chairs, and purchased a used washer and dryer. When the girls returned they had to go back out to buy sheets, pillows, and towels.

By ten o'clock that night, the house was furnished and they were sitting in lawn chairs in the backyard drinking cold Budweisers while Ramrod cooked steaks on a grill left behind by a previous tenant.

As the night slipped away, butterflies appeared.

"Look!" Peaches pointed. "Lightning bugs." Every star in the sky shined brightly. The air was warm and a cool breeze occasionally came blowing in off the Lake. Bulldog rolled a joint and passed it around. Everyone was lost in their own thoughts and Peaches was fixated on the barmaid saying there were no nice clubs in Orlando.

* * *

"That little bitch thinks she's so smart." Detective Marks was mumbling to himself.

"Sir." Betty asked, unsure of what he said.

"Nothing. I was just thinking out loud. Did you get anything from ballistics?"

"Yes, Sir, the report is on your desk. There was no match."

"Why doesn't that surprise me?" He grumbled.

* * *

Saturday morning Sugar prepared a hefty breakfast. It was the first time Ramrod would be tasting her country cooking. The dining room table was covered with platters of bacon, eggs, pancakes, fresh homemade biscuits, and sausage gravy.

As they devoured the food, Bulldog grinned. "Peaches may shoot me, but if Sugar gets upset with you, you're going to die a painful death. She will poison your ass."

"But he's not an asshole." Peaches said in Ramrod's defense.

Daytona was only fifty miles away, straight down Interstate 4. They decided to spend a day at the beach frolicking in the ocean. In the evening they would go to Disneyworld. Ramrod laid out lines of crystal meth.

"It's time to party," he grinned.

On the way to Daytona they stopped and bought blankets, beach towels, suntan lotion, and an ice-chest that they quickly filled with ice and beer.

"There's a bar in Daytona called the Landing, It's where I met Big Moose and the Heathen's during bike week." Bulldog explained to Ramrod.

"Our business with the Heathen's is done. This is when we get to spend some quality time with our girls." Ramrod grinned and smiled at Sugar.

Hearing this brought huge smiles to the girl's faces.

They drove onto the sandy beach, backed the Cadillac up facing the ocean, and parked. The girls spread blankets on the sand, then took turns putting on their bathing suits inside the car. A full fledged celebration was happening on the beach. Children, mothers, fathers, grandparents, and people of all ages were enjoying the sand, sun, and water. Laughing and shouting their pleasure, Bulldog and Peaches were team-mates against Ramrod and Sugar in a game of water polo, the women straddling the shoulders of the men. Then they lay on the blankets and opened cold bottles of Budweiser.

"Pop a top again." Ramrod sang, rubbing suntan lotion on Sugar's back.

Bulldog rented two large beach umbrellas from a vender and stuck them in the sand. They offered some much needed shade and protection from the scorching sun.

"I bet you could fry an egg on the hood of the car." Bulldog declared, jerking the palm of his hand away from the scorching hot hood.

By mid afternoon the heat became too much so they started packing up to leave. On their returned trip home, Ramrod pulled over and told Sugar to take the wheel.

"Oh God, we're all going to die." Peaches cried.

"Shut up!" Sugar giggled, sliding behind the wheel.

"We're on the friggin' Interstate. She's got to get some experience." Ramrod said flatly.

Sugar had no problem driving. She stayed in her lane at a steady fifty miles a hour. After riding along for thirty miles Peaches and Bulldog were nice enough to complement her on how well she was doing. When it was time for them to exit the Interstate, she pulled to the side of the road and Ramrod drove the rest of the way home.

Arriving back at the rental house they showered, changed clothes, and quickly hopped back into the car, their destination Disneyworld.

At 8 p.m., they walked up to the booth and purchased tickets. The tram was the fastest way into the Magical Kingdom, so they hopped aboard. Sugar was overwhelmed by the sight of Cinderella's Castle. She had never seen anything like it before, making her feel as though she was living a fantasy world.

They went to see the attractions as quickly as possible. The Haunted Mansion; It's a Small World, The Tiki Hut, The Hall of Presidents, and the Mickey Mouse Revue. As they neared A Thousand Leagues Under The Sea, Nicole announced she was not getting into a submarine and going underwater. Everyone laughed .

At the souvenir shop, Bulldog did his best to put a pair of Mickey Mouse ears on Ramrod and have Nicole snap a Polaroid photo, but Ramrod would have no part of it, hiding behind Sugar.

Ramrod promised Sugar that someday he would bring her back, and they would stay at the Polynesian motel.

Sunday morning, Peaches took some photos of the house, the furnishings, and the lake. She wanted to show them to the Prospect. J.D. would be happy living in Florida, she thought.

At 10 a.m., they boarded a returning flight to Baltimore.

* * *

Sunday night, Ramrod shared the photos taken of the house with the Prospect, then he called the members informing them that he would be holding church Monday at one p.m. and they needed to be in attendance.

"How do you like the house?" Ramrod asked the Prospect.

"It looks very nice. Sure beats the hell out of this cold ass cabin."

"It's hot in Florida. We went swimming in the ocean."

"Damn."

At the moment, the Prospect slept on the couch or curled up in a blanket on a rug next to the fire. He had been sleeping like this for over more than a year without complaining.

Monday afternoon Ramrod held church. Only patched members were allowed inside meetings.

For this reason, the Prospect was surprised when he was called to church. He became apprehensive, his first thought being that he was in trouble. But for what he didn't know. When he entered the small log cabin, he was instructed by Rooster to face Ramrod within the circle of brothers.

"Are you loyal to the brotherhood?" Ramrod asked bluntly.

"Yes!" The Prospect answered.

One by one the brothers lowered their heads as if they doubted him.

"I am!" The Prospect repeated, looking around the room for a sign that someone believed him, but no one budged. Ramrod stepped forward, ripping the 'Prospect' patch from J.D.'s black leather jacket. Then, he grinned pouring a beer over J.D.'s head.

"You're one of us now." Bulldog announced with a big smile. Ramrod handed J. D. his Argot rocker. "This comes with a lot of responsibility. Are you prepared for that?"

"Anything." J.D. nodded.

"The house in Orlando is going to be the start of a new Chapter. You are going to live there, recruit new members, and if any members want to transfer to the Florida Chapter they are welcome to do so. You will answer only to me. It takes twelve members to become a Chapter. You can elect new members until there's twelve. Give preference to the Vietnam veterans. Recruit new members based on their qualifications and experience. Newly elected members who are not veterans are solely your responsibility. Once a Chapter has twelve members, all new members will be Prospects. That includes veterans. Our purpose for opening the new Chapter is to extend distribution and increase our sales in crystal meth and cocaine. So you think you can handle it?"

"I'll do my best." J.D. promised.

From that day forward, J. D. would no longer be labeled a Prospect. He was a patched member who now out ranked everyone in the new Chapter. It was a rare promotion, but one the members thought to be wise.

"There's food and everything else that you will need already at the house. The utilities were transferred into my name this morning. The telephone company is installing a phone this afternoon. The neighbor's name is Johnny Nash. Like myself, he's a Vietnam veteran. Johnny is a nice guy. Introduce yourself, and should you need anything I'm sure he will lend you a hand. I will fly down periodically to check on you. Concentrate on moving kilos of cocaine for twenty-seven thousand. Cash only."

"When will I be leaving?"

"Whenever you're ready. You can ride or take the train and I will ship your Harley."

"I'll ride. I don't want to be without my Harley, not even for a day."

"When you're ready to leave, I will give you two thousand dollars. Whatever extra you make from selling kilos will be yours to keep."

"If it doesn't snow tonight, I'll leave in the morning."

"Remember, when you have twelve members, I will start the Chapter and you will fly the Florida rocker . And, I will also open a clubhouse for the members."

"Sounds good." J.D. smiled his pleasure.

CHAPTER TWENTY
THE PINK PUSSYCAT

It took J.D. three days to ride his Harley to Orlando. The first two days he road through rain and snow, stopping every few hours to warm his freezing hands and toes. He stopped at cheap motels along the way, just to escape the bitter cold at night.

As he moved closer to Georgia the weather warmed up and when he crossed the state line he was riding in sunshine and wonderful heat. By the time he reached the house in Fern Park, J .D. had stripped down to a lightweight shirt and his black leather jacket, boldly displaying the Argot patch with the Pennsylvania rocker. The upper rocker displaying the state, the lower rocker showing the Chapter.

At the house he parked the motorcycle under the carport, shutting off the engine and sliding down the kickstand. He stepped from under the carport to the side of the house pausing to gaze upon the small lake. Taking a deep breath of the summer air, J. D. walked up onto the porch and let himself inside the front door. He immediately went to the telephone resting on a small table at the hall entrance and called the cabin to let Ramrod know he had arrived. The phone rang several times, then J.D. heard a familiar voice answer "Hello'.

"Hello." J.D. responded.

"How was your trip?" Ramrod asked, without hesitation.

"Rough as Hell!"

"How do you like the house?"

"I just walked in, but from what I've seen I love it. Is it alright if I take the master bedroom for myself?"

"Of course! It's your home, your Chapter. Just never forget it's my Charter. It's your responsibility to make things happen in Orlando. Are you up to the challenge?"

"I think so." J.D. replied. But deep down he wished some of the brothers had joined him. Being by himself would certainly get lonely, and the past had taught him that it was a terrible feeling to have.

"I shipped your things by U.P.S. this morning. They should be there by noon tomorrow."

After they ended their conversation J.D. walked out to the dock, stripped down to his shorts and dove in. "Aye!" He cried as his head popped out of the water. It was freezing. No one had told him that the lake was spring fed. He swam around in the lake for another ten minutes, wondering at the follies of man. When he was in the cold of Pennsylvania he was constantly trying to get warm. Now that he was in the heat of Florida, he was working to cool off. Returning to the house, the phone was ringing as he entered.

"Hello?" he answered.

"How are you, Sweetie? I left you a present in the top corner of the kitchen cabinet."

"Peaches?" J.D. laughed.

"I thought you might be lonesome?"

"I just went for a swim. I wish someone had told me the lake was spring fed. My balls shriveled up like two peas in a pod."

Peaches laughed.

"Hold on!" J.D. ran into the kitchen and found an ounce of marijuana and an ounce of cocaine in the kitchen cabinet. He picked up the phone extension in the kitchen. "Good looking out." He told Peaches happily. "I didn't bring any drugs with me because I thought there was a good possibility of my being pulled over and harassed along the way."

"I need a favor."

"Anything." J.D. promised.

"I need for you to keep this just between the two of us, okay."

"Sure."

"During your travels, I want you to keep your eyes out for a vacant building, or a bar that's closing. Something that could be made into a first class club. It must be very close to the city."

"I'll keep my eyes and ears open. How do I reach you if I find something?"

Peaches gave J.D. the phone number to her apartment.

* * *

J .D. left the house early Saturday morning and rode his Harley to South Beach. It was his first time being in Miami. As a matter of fact, it was his first time being in any parts of Florida and he enjoyed taking in the sights. He stopped at Mango's on Ocean drive, entered, and seated himself at the bar.

Chris Delgado, a young entrepreneur was passing by when he stopped to look at the patch on the back of J.D.'s leather jacket with the Argot colors.

"Pennsylvania? You're a little out of your territory, aren't you?" Chris asked, then told the barmaid to give his new friend a drink on him.

"Thanks." J.D. replied, sizing Chris up. He was young and well dressed. Maybe five foot eight, a hundred and seventy pounds. His dark hair was cut short and well groomed. His features appearing to be Hispanic.

"Kinda hot in that leather, aren't you? What brings you to this part of the country?" Chris asked, noticing that the biker was not much older than himself.

"I'm here to open a new Chapter in Orlando."

"That's cool. My name is Chris. Chris Delgado." Chris extended his hand in friendship.

"J.D." Came the reply with a firm handshake.

Soon they were matching drinks. One of them bought a round, then the other. Chris introduced J.D. to every girl they walked by, even those he had never met before. Chris appeared to be very outgoing with a friendly personality.

"Hey, come here." He called to random women. "This is my friend J. D. What's your name?" Chris grinned, offering an introduction. Within a few hours they were at Chris' condo on 7th Street, naked in a hot tub with four girls. Chris was laying out lines of cocaine and J.D. was matching him. Chris' cocaine was cut so much that they were blown away by the purity of J.D.'s. It was not long before everyone was snorting only J.D.'s cocaine. They stepped away from the women and hot tub to discuss business.

"Would you like to buy some?" J.D. offered.

"I don't buy ounces." Chris laughed. "I'm way out of your class my friend. I purchase kilos."

"What are you paying for a kilo?"

"Thirty to thirty-five thousand, depending on how many I buy." My brother usually pitches in, allowing me to get a better price."

"How many kilos a month do you think you could move if I were to sell you uncut kilos for twenty-eight thousand five hundred each?"

"Fifty." Chris replied quickly, doubting seriously if J.D. could handle that amount.

J.D. was skeptical as well, and he wondered if Chris could deliver on his end of the bargain.

"I'll start you out with ten kilos. When you place an order, you can expect delivery within twenty-four hours. But, you will have to come to Orlando to pick them up."

"Not a problem." Chris grinned, jumping back into the hot tub with the girls. One of the girls quickly dove under the water taking his dick into her mouth.

J.D. spent the night at Chris' house partying.

Chris drove a brand new red Corvette convertible and lived in a two hundred thousand dollar condo. He dressed nice and there was no shortage of women in his life. He obviously had something going on. If he could deliver on the cocaine deal, J.D. felt he could be in hog heaven with the club.

J.D. took the scenic route on his way back to Orlando. The white sandy beaches reminded him of grains of sugar. Girls wearing string bikinis were in abundance, and a warm breeze blew through his hair. Life just could not get much better than this, he thought, gunning the motorcycle down the paved street.

They agreed that the code for a kilo of cocaine would be 'a chainsaw', just in case their phones were being monitored. To eliminate the possibility of a problem on his end, Chris would call from a pay phone.

* * *

Three days later, Chris called the house, wanting to buy ten chainsaws, promising he would be there Saturday afternoon to pick them up. J.D. gave him the address.

"I live on a lake, so bring your swimming trunks and plan on staying the night. We'll have a little celebration."

"Sounds good."

"You are coming by yourself?" J.D. asked.

"Of course."

"Great, I'll see you then."

Within an hour J.D. phoned Ramrod.

"How are you doing Pros... I'm mean, brother?" Ramrod caught himself before he called J. D. a Prospect. For so long he had referred to him as a Prospect that it was difficult not to now, but he recognized J. D. as a member and brother that he would willingly die for.

"I need ten of those this weekend." J. D. said, wishing that he and Ramrod had thought to make a code of some sort.

"No problem." Ramrod assured him.

After hanging up, Ramrod called Charlie and placed the order.

Friday afternoon at three o'clock, two packages were delivered to Jack Boyd at the house on Pot Lake. J. D. opened the packages, each contained ten kilos. They were individually wrapped in light brown plastic and sprinkled with foot powder to mask the overpowering smell.

When Chris arrived, he did not bother asking about the cocaine. Instead he asked. "Where's the girls?"

"I just moved in a few days ago. I don't know any girls yet."

"Why would I spend the night if there's no girls?"

"We can go to the bar, pick some up and bring them back." J.D. suggested.

"I have a better idea. I have a friend who lives in Orlando. How about if I call him and ask him to bring some girls over for a party?"

"That's cool, but first let's take care of our business."

"No problem. Do you have the merchandise?"

"Of course."

Chris walked outside to his Corvette, pressed a button that released a hidden compartment, and returned with a bag of cash. Two hundred and eighty-five thousand dollars in fifty and one hundred dollar bills, counted and wrapped.

J.D. placed the ten kilos on the kitchen table and Chris sat the bag of money on top of the table.

Chris pulled a pen knife from his pocket along with a small testing kit for checking the levels of opiates in drugs. He randomly selected a kilo and tested it. It was ninety-two percent pure. J.D. thumbed through the wrapped bills.

"All good?" J.D. asked.

"I'm good." Chris reported with a grin. He walked outside and quickly packed the kilos into the secret compartment while J.D. hid the cash in the attic of the house.

With their business completed, J.D. laid out lines of cocaine. It was time to party.

Chris called his good friend Ulises Alverado, and asked if he knew any girls that liked to party.

"They all like to party." Ulises laughed.

"I'm visiting another friend in Orlando. He lives on a lake and he's new to the area. How about bringing some girls over for a party?"

"Give me the address. I'll be there within the hour."

"Tell the girls to bring their bikinis."

"Fuck that. They've got their birthday suits under their clothes."

Ulises chuckled.

As promised, one hour later Ulises Alverado pulled into the driveway in a new two-tone metallic gold Lincoln Towncar. The doors opened and beautiful girls began to exit the car. They stepped out wearing everything from string bikinis and cut-off jeans to skimpy skirts. There were brunettes, redheads, and blondes. Both tall, and short. There was even a Chinese girl who could speak absolutely no English. They all had one thing in common, they were all drop dead gorgeous.

Chris was the first to dive into the lake. When his head popped up, he laughingly said. "It's as cold as a polar bear's balls."

J.D. laughed. "I forgot to tell you that the lake is spring fed."

"Son of a bitch!" Chris yelled, shivering as he climbed the ladder and stepped back onto the dock.

"Where's the booze?" Ulises asked.

"I don't have any." J.D. replied.

"What kinda party doesn't have booze?"

"I don't have a car. I ride a Harley."

"Fuck all that. You've got money, don't you? I'll make a phone call and have the booze delivered."

"That's fine. I've got the money." J.D. laughed.

Ulises made a call, ordering enough liquor to stock a good sized bar, all at J.D.'s expense.

Stripping down to their birthday suits, the women held hands before jumping into the lake with wild screams. Some cried out at the coldness of the water while others quickly climbed the ladder attached to the pier wrapping themselves in towels. For those brave enough to stay in the water, after a few minutes the water became soothing and fun.

When the booze arrived, J.D. paid for it while Chris and Ulises made drinks. As the trio walked into the kitchen, Chris asked Ulises how much he was paying for a kilo of cocaine?

"I've been paying between thirty and thirty-two thousand a kilo.

Since when did you start calling me Ulises?" Nuni asked Chris. For years he had been calling his friend 'Big Nuni'. Sometimes just 'Nuni', depending on his mood.

"I've been paying thirty thousand dollars a kilo, sometimes more. What if I could sell you uncut kilos for twenty-nine thousand five hundred each?"

J.D. watched and listened with a small smile parting his lips.

"I would buy twenty tomorrow." Nuni grinned.

"Cash." Chris added.

"I never knew there was any other way." Nuni chuckled, venturing outside with a drink in each hand.

Chris whispered in J.D.'s ear. "Order me twenty kilos."

"No problem." J. D. replied, trying hard not to laugh. He was amused and happy to make the deal.

They went outside to join the party.

"Most of these girls were dancers at the Starlite Lounge. It went out of business last month." Nuni told Chris.

J.D.'s ears perked up at the conversation. He asked where the lounge was located? Was it in a nice area? Why did it close? Most important of all, what kind of condition was it in?

"It's located in downtown Orlando. It was remodeled before it opened two years ago, and there's plenty of room for parking. I think it closed due to poor management." Nuni explained.

"Is the building for sale, or rent?"

"I'm not sure, but there's a sign in the front window."

"Would you do me a favor? I don't have a car or know my way around. Would you mind picking me up tomorrow and taking me to see the club?"

"Sure. If you want me to, but do you mind me asking why?"

"I have a friend whose interested in opening a club. Would you be interested in managing one?" J.D. asked.

"Do I look like I need a job?" Big Nuni countered with a laugh.

The party lasted until the early morning hours. J.D. took the

Chinese girl, along with another girl to his bedroom and fucked them both. Big Nuni took a girl into the bathroom to let her give him head. Chris grabbed the two freakiest girls, took them to the spare bedroom and locked the door behind them.

The following morning, Chris drove back to Miami, and Nuni took the girls home. J.D. called Ramrod at the cabin and ordered twenty more kilos.

At 2 p.m, Big Nuni returned to pick up J.D. and drove him to the closed Starlite lounge. From the outside it appeared well kept. The sign in the window read 'for sale'.

"It's even nicer on the inside." Big Nuni promised. Later that afternoon, J.D. called Peaches with the news.

"Make arrangements for me to inspect the club this Saturday. I want to see it inside and out. I'll catch an early bird flight and fly back that evening. No one will miss me for a day."

The next day two packages were delivered to Jack Boyd at the rental house.

J.D. called Chris and he drove back to Orlando, picked up the twenty kilos and left to deliver them to Nuni. An hour later, he returned with the cash to pay off J.D. "Twenty thousand isn't bad for a days work." Chris smiled broadly.

Big Nuni offered to drive J.D. to the airport to pick up his friend and drive them to the Starlite lounge. He had no idea that J.D.'s friend was a beautiful woman. From the moment he laid eyes on her, Ulises was head over heels in love.

J.D. introduced Peaches to 'Big Nuni' and they were soon in his Lincoln, cruising down the highway on their way to the Starlite lounge. Peaches was very much aware of her effect on Nuni, and found herself amused by his desire to get his hands on her.

"If I buy this place, you will have to help find someone to manage it." She told J.D.

"I have experience. If you need someone, I'll be happy to help with that." Big Nuni quickly volunteered.

"I thought you said you weren't interested?" J.D. chuckled.

"I didn't say that!" Big Nuni countered. "I asked if I looked like I needed a job."

The owner of the lounge was asking two hundred and fifty thousand dollars for the liquor license, business, and property. After inspecting the inside, Peaches offered two hundred thousand dollars in cash and he accepted the offer without a moment's hesitation.

"What are you going to name the club?" Big Nuni asked.

"The Pink Pussycat."

"I like that."

"Would you mind if I just call you Nuni?"

"Can I call you Peaches?"

"Of course, but my name is Nicole. Nicole Redman."

"And mine is Ulises Alverado."

"So how have you been doing, J.D.?"

"Great! So far I have done exceptionally well."

When they arrived at the house Peaches laid out lines of crystal meth. It was the first time Nuni tried the drug. As he watched Peaches moving around he got a boner that would not go away. Peaches did not notice it, but J.D. did, and he could not help the chuckle that escaped from his lips.

CHAPTER TWENTY-ONE
TROUBLE IN PARADISE

Monday morning, Peaches called Harold Glazer and made arrangements for her Trust Fund to purchase the closed lounge in Orlando, which would also give her the liquor license, furnishings, and property. She wanted to close the deal within thirty days. She explained to Ramrod and Bulldog that she was purchasing the lounge as an investment with no intentions of moving to Florida to live.

"How did this opportunity come about?" Bulldog inquired.

"When did this happen?" Ramrod added.

"It's none of your business, but if you must know, I mentioned to J.D. that I was interested in buying a club in Orlando. If you recall, the barmaid in Orlando said there wasn't any nice clubs in Orlando. J.D. was told about a club that had been remodeled two years ago. It was closed due to poor management. I flew down and back in one day. I looked at the place, liked what I saw, and made an offer. The owner accepted it right away." Peaches looked at Ramrod, and asked. "Why should you care about that?"

"I don't! Very few things surprise, but you surprised the hell out of me." Ramrod said, looking at Bulldog.

"Don't look at me, bro. It surprised the hell out of me too!" Bulldog grinned.

"You guys have issues. It's just business!" I saw an opportunity to buy a club and I took advantage of it. That's all there is to it." Peaches declared.

"You could have told me." Bulldog replied.

"I intended to, but there's been too much going on."

Bulldog shrugged his shoulders. There was nothing else to say and he saw no reason to provoke an argument.

* * *

In Orlando, J.D. decided to offer any new Prospects kilos for twenty-seven thousand dollars each. If they sold the kilos for more, the profit would be theirs. He reasoned that everyone had bills to pay. Some would have families to support and J.D. wanted to be fair minded. When they finally became a Chapter, the club president would be voted in by the twelve new members. Until then, the Prospects would not be patched in. The work expected of him was mind numbing, he had a lot of work ahead of him and no one there to help.

"Can I go to the Two O'clock Club with you tonight? Please! I just want to watch you perform." Charlotte Lynn pleaded with her big sister.

Nicole called Blaze to ask if she minded her bringing her little sister to work. Blaze laughingly said she did not mind, and looked forward to meeting her little sister.

"You had better be on your best behavior." Peaches warned.

Charlotte giggled and started singing. "Sugar in the morning… Sugar in the evening… Sugar at supper time. Be my little Sugar… "

"And be good all the time." Nicole cut in. They both laughed. It was a song Ramrod loved singing to Charlotte at the top of his lungs.

On the drive down Baltimore Street, Charlotte marveled at the neon lights, bright colored flashing lights, adult book stores, and prostitutes standing on street corners yelling at potential customers as they drove past. Drunken sailors stumbled down the street, trying to find their way back to their ships in port, the docks being only three blocks away. It was fast paced, lots of action.

"There's the Two O' Clock Club on the left." Nicole pointed.

The sign was neon blue, double doors opening to the entrance, and a sign at the front door in bold black letters reading 'NO COLORS'.

Nicole parked the yellow Bug near the front doors, the doorman acknowledging Peaches as she walked into the club with her sister in tow. Blaze was sitting at her place at the bar.

She turned on the barstool to greet them with a smile.

"My goodness." she beamed. "This must be Charlotte Lynn. She's gorgeous! When you said that you were bringing your little sister with you to work I had a much younger girl in mind."

Charlotte blushed her pleasure at Blaze's praise. "Thank you so much. I'm glad to meet you, my nickname is Sugar. That's probably easier to remember."

"Well Sugar, sit down and take a load off. Would you care for something to drink?"

"A White Russian, please."

"Are you old enough to drink?" Blaze asked.

"Yes, I am. I'm twenty-one."

Blaze gave Peaches a questioning look, and she nodded her head to confirm that her sister was indeed twenty-one. Peaches looked at her sister wondering where she had gotten that from, a White Russian? A few weeks with Ramrod and she seemed to be well educated. What other surprises would be forthcoming, she wondered.

After a few drinks, and watching her sister perform, Sugar asked Blaze if she could go on stage to perform. Blaze wondered if she might have the same talent as her big sister. With that hope in mind, she said, "Sure, why not?"

Blaze quickly escorted Sugar to her dressing room and told her to pick out any outfit or costumes she felt comfortable wearing. The liquor coursing through her system had Sugar feeling loose and excited, her entire body warm with anticipation. As Peaches was coming off the stage, Sugar walked right past her wearing a big smile and dressed like a giant Peacock.

Sugar took the stage by storm, shedding her feathers to reveal lush curves and long legs. The crowd went crazy at the sight of her firm young breast, the nipples covered by the brief tassels. She was a natural. But then again, it was like throwing fresh meat to a bunch of hungry wolves. Sugar was moved by the crowd's cheers. Just like her sister, she loved being in the limelight, the center of attention. Twirling and swinging her hips in the moves taught to her by her sister, Sugar danced until the crowd was at a fevered pitch, then danced her way off the stage, leaving them wanting more. It made her feel powerful and she laughed her pleasure.

"Sugar! Sugar! Sugar!" The crowd chanted after her. Peaches was there waiting when her sister exited the stage.

"I knew that bringing you here was a bad idea." Peaches frowned her displeasure.

Peaches practically dragged her sister into her dressing room.

"What's next?" Sugar asked.

Peaches looked at her glowing sister and shook her head. Maybe it was time for her to stop trying to shelter her sister and just guard her back. With Ramrod helping to guard her back she was sure that Charlotte Lynn would be well taken care of. She locked the door to her dressing room and laid out lines of cocaine.

"After closing we can go to an after-hour club. I'll introduce you to Gus at the Wee Hours." She snorted a line up each nostril. "But promise me that you won't go into the back office with him. Gus is a dirty old man!"

"I promise." Sugar giggled, pausing to snort a small line of cocaine up each nostril.

A half hour later, Peaches and Sugar were inside the crowded after-hour club, and Peaches escorted her sister straight to the bar where Gus stood watching the club's action. She introduced her sister to Gus.

"My pleasure, Sugar." Gus took her hand, his eyes roaming hungrily over her jean clad hips and nipples showing clearly through the white tee-shirt she wore. "Let me give you the fifty cent tour. My office is down...."

Peaches interceded, grabbing her sister's hand. "Oh no, you don't!"

"What?" Gus grinned, shaking his heard, acting as if he had no ill intentions.

Peaches knew better. "He's like a kid in a candy store. He wants every girl he sees. And, he's very good at seducing girls," she laughed.

"Fair exchange ain't no robbery." Gus grinned.

"Gus has two rules," Peaches explained to her sister, "He hates drugs! If he catches you buying, selling, or using in his club you are banned for life. If a girl takes a trick out of the club, she pays him fifteen dollars in advance."

At that moment, Jerry Evarhart, the owner of Hector's, pushed his way up to the bar.

"Peaches?" he smiled at the sight of her. "What? You don't like my club anymore?"

Peaches returned his hug. "I love your club, Jerry. I've been very busy lately. Let me introduce you to my baby sister, Sugar."

"My pleasure!" Jerry smiled broadly, giving her the once over.

"How have things been with you?" Peaches said, drawing his attention away from her sister. Jerry was a pimp and Ramrod would destroy him if he fooled around with Charlotte Lynn.

"Slow. I thought I'd come visit Gus and steal some of his customers. No one has danced on the stripper pole since you and Stormy."

"It's been quite awhile, hasn't it?"

"Every time I look at that pole I think of you and Stormy."

Peaches eyes teared. "She was a good girl."

"Yes, she was."

"What happened to her?" Sugar asked.

"That's a story for another time." Peaches said flatly.

"Promise you will stop by soon." Jerry asked.

"I promise." Peaches replied, forcing a smile. Thoughts of Stormy made her heart fill with sadness.

They hung out at the after-hour club for another hour, laughing and joking with Gus and Jerry, letting both men flirt outrageously. It was on their way home to the apartment that Charlotte surprised her with a question out of the blue.

"Where do you go every Wednesday afternoon?"

Caught completely off guard and unsure of how to respond, Peaches answered her question with a question. "Have you ever been curious or wondered what it would be like to be with another girl?"

"You've got a girlfriend?" Charlotte asked in disbelief, then, for some reason she found it funny and giggled.

"Not exactly." Nicole smiled, glad to see that her sister was not freaking out on her. "About two years ago, after Charlotte was killed, I met a woman, her name is Marsha Bennett and she's a call girl"

"A prostitute?" Charlottes eyes went wide.

"No! Prostitutes work the streets. Marsha only sees men by appointment. She has more class than a prostitute. Anyway, Marsha invited me to go along with her to a client's condo. The client's name is Manny." At this point in the story, Nicole smiled broadly. "Manny is an older man, a real sweetheart, and the retired owner of Bethlehem Steel. He paid Marsha and I five hundred dollars each to have sex while he watched!"

"You had sex with her in front of him?" Sugar asked, her eyes going wide.

"Yes, I did. And, every Wednesday since. Manny bought me the Mercedes. One year, he took me, Marsha, and her five kids to Hawaii. The following year, Australia."

"You've got a sugar daddy!" Charlotte declared, giggling.

"It's not like that." Peaches corrected her sister. "Marsha and Manny are my family. There's nothing that I wouldn't do for them, and vice-versa."

"Does Bulldog know about that?"

"Hell no." Peaches laughed.

* * *

The Bottoms Up was a small neighborhood bar less than two miles from where J.D. was now living. For this reason he began patronizing the bar whenever he had free time. A regulation pool table was centered in the room between the bar and the wall. The front door was propped open, letting in some much needed fresh air. J.D. was playing a game of pool against another patron for a dollar a game. The patron missed his shot at the eight-ball. J.D. sat his long neck bottle of Budweiser on the edge of the pool table, took aim at the eight-ball, and pocketed it. Game over. The unmistakable roar of approaching Harleys suddenly cut through the quiet noise of the bar. Within minutes three burley bikers wearing black leather Heathen colors walked through the door, and bellied up to the bar. They ordered shots of whiskey and beers to chase them with.

The biggest biker placed a quarter on the edge of the pool table to challenge the winner. The bikers lounged around while J.D. beat the nervous looking patron for a second time and he quickly moved away from the table.

"Whatcha playing for?" the biker asked.

"One dollar." J.D. replied looking at the other man calmly. The biker racked the balls, telling J.D. to break them.

J.D. broke the balls with a loud smack, sending balls spinning across the green felt in all directions. The three ball and the thirteen ball dropped into pockets.

"What's your name partner?" the biker asked.

"The names J.D."

"Mine is Bones. Long way from home, ain't ya?"

J.D. looked at Bones' jacket. He had both silver and red wing patches. J.D. leaned over to pocket the yellow one ball, choosing the solid balls. He decided to play it cool.

"It was a long, cold ride." J.D. admitted.

"Well, I'm here to tell ya, this ain't bike week! Your colors aren't exactly a welcome sight."

"I'm not looking for any trouble." J.D. stood there holding the pool stick, ready for any trouble that might come his way. The Argots were fearless and he planned on representing the club if necessary.

"Me neither." Bones expressed with a knowing smile. "Give my new friend a drink on me." He yelled across the room to the barmaid.

"Thanks." J.D. said flatly.

"The first one's on me. I don't expect to be buying you another drink anytime soon. If you get my drift?"

Without finishing the game, Bones gave J.D. a slap on the back, chugged his beer, and he and his brothers walked out of the bar. A few minutes later, the other patrons sighed their relief as they heard the Harleys roar to life.

Later that night, J. D. phoned Ramrod to tell him about the run in with the Heathens. Ramrod immediately ordered Bulldog and Jammer to go to the house in Florida and look after J.D.

Bulldog called Peaches to let her know that he had to go to the house in Florida to help with the new Chapter, explaining that he would be gone for a while.

"Don't worry, I'll be seeing you soon. I have to fly down to close on the club."

Before leaving, Bulldog and Jammer made sure they grabbed some warm weather clothes. They left for Orlando early the following morning.

* * *

Thursday night, Peaches and Sugar boarded Flight 721 for Orlando, Florida. When the airplane touched down, Nuni was standing at the gate waiting for the girls to walk down the ramp. His eyes going from one passenger to the next in anticipation.

"Peaches!" He yelled at the sight of her, waving his hand in the air to attract her attention.

Nicole heard her name being called and went to join him.

"Do you got any luggage?" Nuni asked smiling broadly.

"Just carry on. Nuni this is my little sister, Charlotte Lynn."

"She doesn't look so little to me." Nuni chuckled.

"I seem to hear that a lot," Charlotte replied, then added "Please, call me Sugar."

"Nuni is going to manage the club." Peaches told her sister as they walked to the waiting Lincoln Towncar.

The trio sat in the front seat, with Peaches in the middle. Nuni felt the warmth of her leg pressing against his, and he glanced in the rearview mirror at the face of an angel with platinum blonde hair. No woman had ever affected him in such a way. He constantly dreamed of making love to her.

"I've got some ideas for the club." Peaches announced.

"Oh Yeah?" Nuni replied, as if he was truly interested.

"If you can pick me up around noon tomorrow, we can go to the club and discuss it."

"It's a date!" Nuni beamed.

Bulldog was under the carport working on his Harley when they arrived. As Sugar opened the car door and stepped out, Peaches ran around her racing over to jump into Bulldog's arms. She wrapped her legs around his waist, kissing him passionately.

Nuni sat in the car, wishing he hadn't seen Nicole in another man's arms. From that day forward, he disliked Bulldog. In his mind, Peaches was his woman, she just didn't know it yet. But she would, that he was sure of.

CHAPTER TWENTY-TWO
YAHOO

When Nuni arrived to pick Nicole up the following day, he was surprised to see that Sugar, J.D., Jammer, and Bulldog were tagging along. Sugar and J.D. hopped in the front seat, while Jammer, Peaches, and Bulldog rode in the back.

Peaches introduced Nuni as her club manager. Nuni begrudgingly gave Bulldog a handshake, pissed because he was hugging Peaches against his side. He swore that things between them were going to change. When it did, Nuni would have no problem with Bulldog not liking him. As a matter of fact, he would prefer it that way. He started the car and soon they were on the Interstate heading for the club.

Much later, Peaches stood outside the lounge making her visions for the club's future known.

"I want the outside of the club painted a very light pink, with pink and blue neon lights in the shape of a girl displayed in the windows. I want her in different poses! Maybe a girl on her back kicking her legs in the air. Another girl standing with her hand on her hip, Sexy images in pink and blue neon tubing.

"I like that." Nuni agreed.

"And, I want a girl larger than life in pink neon tubing on the roof. I want large neon lights that read The Pink Pussycat in big capital letters."

"I like that too!" Nuni smiled.

"Inside I want a giant horseshoe bar. I want it with the stage in the center of the bar."

"I like that too." Nuni nodded, still smiling.

"It seems you like everything she says." Bulldog grumbled under his breath, watching the other man closely.

"Maybe you should take a page from his book." Peaches laughed.

Nuni grinned, thinking to himself. "Yeah, bitch ass mothafucka, take that."

Peaches finished with her instructions, then signed the papers to have the title and liquor license transferred to her Trust. She asked Nuni if he had any questions, and if he understood what she wanted.

"I gotcha! I'll take care of everything," he smiled.

One month later, Peaches and Sugar flew to Orlando for the Grand opening of 'THE PINK PUSSYCAT'.

A huge crowd gathered in front of the club waiting for the doors to open. Sugar was excited about performing. She and Peaches flipped a coin to see which of them would perform first. Sugar called the flip of the coin in the air.

"Tails."

"Tails it is." Nuni announced.

The bar was fully stocked, providing plenty of serving alcohol for the four bartenders, four barmaids, four waitresses, and five dancers. Behind the bar there were two large ice machines. Nuni had thoughtfully purchased a second ice machine to use as a backup in the event the other broke down. The interior of the lounge was enormous, leaving plenty of room for the crowd outside to fit inside.

There were two dressing rooms. Peaches and Sugar shared one, the other five dancers sharing a much larger one.

Nuni had a Manager's Office next to an Executive Office for Peaches, complete with an executive desk with a high back black leather chair that swiveled and a black leather couch. Seeing her office Peaches gave Nuni a big hug.

"Yes!" Nuni thought to himself. He was finally making progress with his lady.

Sugar took the stage, causing the crowd to go wild with excitement. She was wearing a Fireman's outfit and carrying a small fire extinguisher.

"That little bitch is wearing my outfit!" Peaches laughed at her sister's devious actions.

"You can put out my fire anytime," a customer yelled. Sugar pointed the fire-extinguisher in his direction, pulled the trigger and did just that, spraying a brief flood of water in his face. She put his fire out amidst loud catcalls and cheers. The rowdy crowd had the bartenders and waitresses scrambling to serve liquor. Sugar was in her glory, loving the attention.

Nuni had hired four bouncers and instructed them to throw anyone out of the club if they behaved badly. Touching the beautiful barmaids, dancers, or waitresses would not be allowed. Unnecessary rudeness would not be tolerated, and there would be no threats of violence at any time.

Nuni was mesmerized the second Peaches stepped on the stage. He could not take his eyes off of her, not even for a second. With her every move, another piece of clothing hit the floor. She was wearing a black wrap around skirt, a black fur coat, nylon mesh stockings, a black g-string, four inch high heels and a pair of Mickey Mouse ears. My God, she's beautiful, Nuni thought. She striped down to the g-string, black tassels covering her nipples, the mesh nylon stockings, four inch high heels, and the Mickey Mouse ears stuck in her platinum blonde hair.

Out of nowhere a customer tried to reach across the bar to grab her ass, and before the bouncers could react, Big Nuni had the guy hemmed up.

"It's not nice to touch the ladies." Nuni said, turning the guy over to the bouncers.

Peaches glanced down at him from up on the stage with a smile. She was sure that she had hired the right man for the job. If she felt a sense of security with Nuni, so would the other girls. At closing, she called him into her office. "One more thing," she told Nuni as he walked through the large oak door.

"What's that?"

"I want a large sign at the front door that reads No Colors."

"I like that!" Nuni replied, and he meant it. Since bikers wear their colors wherever they go, Bulldog would be barred from entering. And if he was barred, it would give Nuni more alone time with Peaches.

The thought made him smile.

Six months later, the Orlando Chapter of the Argot's got its Charter. New members were patched in and they voted unanimously to elect Jack 'J.D.' Boyd as their club president. "You've come a long way in a short time. We're all proud of you, brother." Ramrod toasted him.

Ramrod rented an abandoned store on highway 17-92 in Altamonte Springs. The brothers gutted the inside, covered the windows with plywood, and replaced the wood entrance and exit doors with steel doors. Inside, they built a bar with a counter top. They purchased six bar stools, a pool table, and four tables and chairs. They built a bathroom, installed a shower, and bought two sets of bunk beds.

The Florida Chapter was moving more than a hundred kilos of cocaine a month throughout central Florida, and as far north as Blue Ridge Mountains.

Including Pennsylvania, Charlie was moving nearly two hundred kilos of cocaine monthly. At two thousand a kilo, Peaches was earning some serious cash. Chris Delgato was moving eighty kilos a month.

Nuni could have made more connections in the club and expanded his cocaine customers, but he made it a rule and strictly enforced it that no drugs would be sold in the club. If a patron was caught in possession of drugs while in the club, they were barred for life.

Nuni called Chris. "You've got to come see this club. It's something else. But I want you to come when Peaches is in town. Man, the woman is beautiful."

Due to the relationship with J.D., Chris and Nuni were frequent visitors to the new clubhouse, but neither were interested in the females that hung out there. They were some nasty bitches.

Shortly after the new Chapter opened, Ramrod, Jammer, and Bulldog returned to the cabin in Pennsylvania. The weather was warmer and the ride enjoyable.

* * *

"Please, daddy!" Dee Dee tearfully pleaded.

"You've been lying to me for six months. I had to hire a private investigator to find out where you've been going every weekend. Imagine how I felt when I found out that you've been shacking up with some low life drug dealer?"

"I love Charlie, daddy. He's not a low life." Dee Dee shouted.

"Charlie Redman is a drug dealer."

"He took me to the Opera. I have photos of him wearing a tuxedo and our getting out of a limousine." She protested, trying to show that he was not a street drug dealer.

"You can put lipstick on a pig, but it's still a pig." Antonio Caruso shouted angrily.

Caruso was a big man. Six feet two and nearly three hundred pounds. He wore expensive hand tailored Italian suits. Today he had selected a charcoal striped suit from his huge walk-in closet. His coal black hair was slicked back, his brown eyes piercing. His only daughter was on her knees pleading with tears streaming down her cheeks. His heart was breaking, but he felt that he knew what was best for her. In this kind of situation he had to be decisive.

"Please daddy." She begged.

"I forbid you from ever seeing him again. And that's final!"

* * *

J.D. was riding his Harley down highway 17-92 on his way to the clubhouse when three Heathens fell in behind him. One raced up beside him whipping out a metal pipe quickly shoving it into his rear wheel before he had time to react.

"Yahoo!" The Heathen laughed, racing away down the highway, followed closely by his two buddies.

The rear wheel on J.D.'s motorcycle locked, causing him to burn rubber before the front wheel jack knifed. The Harley spun out of control, spinning wildly into oncoming traffic. J.D.'s skull was immediately crushed by the bumper of an oncoming automobile. Several vehicles swerved to a stop, rushing to the aid of the fallen biker. The sight of his crushed skull and the shower of blood and gore, letting them know that they were too late. Much later the coroner's wagon arrived to carry away his lifeless body to the morgue.

Witnesses gave the police an account of what they saw. Three bikers, all wearing Heathen colors, were responsible, one of them sticking a metal rod into the rear wheel of Jack Boyd's Harley, causing him to spin out of control.

Later that evening, Ramrod got the full report surrounding J.D.'s death. He immediately called a church meeting. All two hundred members of the Pennsylvania Chapter of Argots were ordered to attend the funeral of their fallen brother in Orlando. Only then would they worry about avenging the tragic death of their brother Argot.

Peaches, Sugar, Chris, and Nuni all attended the funeral. All of the Argots were assembled at the lake house after the funeral, Ramrod assured everyone that business would be uninterrupted, but strongly urged them to lay low for a couple weeks.

"Stay away from the clubhouse! We won't be returning to Pennsylvania without settling the score." Ramrod swore.

On the way home from the funeral, Chris explained to Nuni that he would still be getting his cocaine through him.

"Oh, no problem." Nuni nodded, understanding clearly that a biker war had been started and the bullets were about to fly.

Ramrod ordered four Argot brothers to go down to Daytona in the middle of the night and steal two Ford vans. They needed to be a solid color, preferably white. He wanted nothing out of the ordinary that would stand out.

Alex hand selected twenty Argot brothers and divided them into two groups for the mission ahead.

Six Harleys were parked in front of the Jolley Rogers bar, the front door propped open allowing clouds of cigarette smoke to escape. None of the bikers inside noticed the white van pull up to the right side of the building, or the side door of the van swing open. Argots rushed inside the bar swinging chains, baseball bats, and iron bars. The bikers inside were taken completely by surprise and beaten within an inch of their lives.

A second van pulled up to the Heathens clubhouse, emptying Argots out onto the pavement. They rushed inside carrying weapons and guns in their waistbands. They beat the Heathens unmercifully, then cut off their patches and set the clubhouse on fire.

Ramrod dragged a screaming and defiant Big Moose to the rear of the stolen van. "An eye for an eye!" He told the big man coldly.

A rope was wrapped around Big Moose's legs and tied in knots. Ramrod attached the other end of the rope to the trailer hitch on the bumper of the ragged white Ford van. Big Moose was dragged from the parking lot down Orange Blossom Trail, his body twisting and bouncing violently until he drew his last breath.

The Orlando Sentinel reported: OUTLAW BIKER GANGS AT WAR OVER DRUG TURF. The murders and publicity brought in the F.B.I. and the D.E.A.

As word reached Norman's Bay, John Leder wondered why the Argot motorcycle club from Pennsylvania would want to start a Chapter in Orlando. He also wondered where the Argots were getting their drugs. He supplied the Heathens.

He thought of Charlie's recent surge in drug sells. Could his actions be responsible for this war? John Leder thought that he had made it clear that he needed someone he could trust to sell kilos of cocaine on the East Coast. Florida was not Charlie's territory!

Ramrod and the brothers from Pennsylvania returned to the cabin, leaving behind a nest of angry Heathens. The Orlando Chapter of the Heathens called the other Chapters throughout Florida. There were Chapters in Daytona, Miami, Fort Lauderdale, Tampa, and Jacksonville.

* * *

As Peaches took the stage at the Pink Pussycat, Chris Delgado watched with Nuni.

"This bitch is something else!" Nuni beamed.

"I'd like to watch her and her sister get it on. That's what I'd like to see."

"You're a sick puppy!" Nuni snapped angrily. Chris laughed.

* * *

Juice walked into his condo to the sound of the phone ringing.

"Hello?" He answered.

"Hello, Juice?"

"Yeah, who's calling?"

"Who in the fuck do you think it is!" John Leder demanded.

"Hey, Johnny Boy."

"Have you been watching the fuckin' news?"

"Yeah, why."

"You see there's a war going on between the Argots and Heathens."

"What about it?"

"I want to know what the fuck Argots from Pennsylvania are doing in Orlando. I also want to know if your friend Charlie has anything to do with it?"

"I hope not."

"I hope not too, because I've got the damn F.B.I. and D.E.A. crawling up my ass."

Juice called Charlie. Charlie explained that his ex-wife Nicole has a boyfriend that's a member of the Argot motorcycle club. And yes, she sells to them through him. Her stage name is Peaches and she owns a club in Orlando called The Pink Pussycat.

"Charlie, you were given the East Coast. Your bitch has started a fucking war in Orlando that has brought in the F.B.I. and D.E.A. I don't know what the fuck to do here!" Juice yelled into the phone, then slammed the receiver down hard.

Juice called John Leder and reported his findings.

"Fuckin' cunt!" John Leder cursed. He hung up the phone, then ordered his men. "Bring that bitch to me."

* * *

One week later Ramrod failed to reach Charlie to fill an order for Orlando. Nicole, who was back in Pennsylvania, drove over to his house. His Corvette was not parked in the driveway. She peeked into the windows of the garage, finding the garage empty. She talked to his neighbors, and they both said they had not seen Charlie or his Corvette parked in the driveway for about five days.

* * *

While the Orlando Chapter of the Argots were holding church, the Heathens raided their clubhouse. They were heavily armed, this time with automatic assault rifles. They shot and killed the entire Chapter, then ruthlessly beheaded the corpses. They set fire to the clubhouse, stacked their Harleys on top of each other and burnt them.

The Orlando Sentinel reported: WORST MASSACRE IN FLORIDA'S HISTORY.

"Son of a bitch!" John Leder screamed reading the headlines.

Ramrod, Bulldog, and the entire Pennsylvania Chapter rode throughout the night, stopping only for gas. They were returning to bury their fallen brothers and to avenge their deaths. They would show no mercy.

"I'm flying to Orlando to attend the funeral. I want you to stay at the apartment until I return." Peaches told her sister.

"Fuck that! I wear the colors too. I'm an Argot, and I'm going to support my brothers!"

Nicole did not want to argue. Nuni picked them up at the airport.

"It's bad. It's real bad down here." Nuni reported. "You girls have gotta stay at my place."

"I'll sleep on the couch at the club. Charlotte Lynn will stay at your place." Peaches said flatly.

Nuni knew there was no point in arguing with Peaches. A person could argue all they wanted, but when her mind was made up, there was no changing it.

Shortly after closing, there was a knock at the back door. Assuming Nuni had taken the garbage out and the door accidentally closed behind him Nicole hurried to the rear of the club. When she unlocked the rear door, two men pushed their way inside, quickly covering her mouth with a powerful hand to silence her. They moved swiftly tying her hands behind her back and gagging her using a cloth and tape they had brought with them. They hustled her outside into the back alley, forcing her into a waiting car. Nicole fought her racing heart, remaining calm as the car headed in the direction of Miami. She was unsure of what they wanted, but she was certain that if they had wanted to kill her she would already be dead. The men acted like they had accomplished this task many times, and they also seemed to know exactly who she was. Upon reaching a dock in Miami, they loaded her onto a high performance boat and raced across the choppy water.

Nuni and Sugar had left the club to go pick up something to eat from a fast food restaurant. They were only gone for fifteen minutes, returning with hamburgers, potato chips, and soft drinks. When they discovered the rear door left open and Peaches missing, Nuni felt a sickness in the pit of his stomach. His first thought was the Heathens had taken her, and he swore. "If anyone harms a hair on her head I'll kill every last one of those motha fuckers!"

In tears, Sugar called Ramrod at the house on Pot Lake. Unable to talk, she passed the phone to Nuni. He explained exactly what had happened, adding they were gone for less than fifteen minutes.

"Can you get your hands on any guns?" Ramrod asked.

"Whatever in the fuck you want." Nuni spat. He was more than upset. Nuni had never been so enraged.

At dawn the F.B.I. and D.E.A. raided the rental house on Pot Lake, the cabin in Pennsylvania, and every Heathen clubhouse throughout Florida.

* * *

Peaches struggled and kicked sand as her kidnappers drug her from the beach to a small bungalow. It was a grass shack with a thatched roof and very few comforts.

Nicole found herself standing before a slender man weighing no more than a hundred and seventy pounds and standing about five foot eight inches tall. His skin was a dark olive hue, and he looked like he had not shaved in several days. The man had brown hair, brown eyes, and he was dressed in blue Bermuda shorts and a light blue tropical short-sleeve shirt, the front partially unbuttoned. On his feet, he wore a pair of well worn brown sandals.

"So, this is the bitch that has cost me my empire? Are you happy?" He demanded of her.

"Who in the fuck are you?" Peaches replied.

"Me? Right now I'm your worst fucking nightmare." He grinned sadistically. "My name is John Leder, and this is my island, Norman's Cay."

"What do you want?" She asked, a note of fear creeping into her voice.

"You don't know what you've done." He asked in disbelief.

"No, tell me."

"I gave your ex-husband Charlie the East Coast to sell cocaine. But you wanted to sell drugs in Florida. It wasn't his territory! You are responsible for the war between the Heathens and Argots. A lot of people have died because of you. Now, you are responsible for the F.B.I. and D.E.A. crawling up my ass."

"I'm sorry about your problems. Nobody told…"

"Shut up!" Leder screamed in rage. "Nothing else matters. Cage this bitch and send her to search for Davy Jones' locker."

Hollering and screaming Peaches was dragged from the room. She was wrapped in chicken wire, causing the skin on her arms to split and bleed, then dumped on the same boat that had brought them to the small island, her head slamming hard on the bottom of the boat.

"You look like a hot tamale," one of her kidnappers laughed, as he pushed the boat away from the island into deeper water. He hopped into the boat, as the second man started the engines. The boat sped away from the island, slowing to a stop three miles out to sea.

Peaches was stood upright on the back of the Donzi and two cinder blocks were tied to her feet.

As the kidnappers prepared to shove her off the rear of the boat, she began to speak desperately. "I will give you both five hundred thousand dollars, just set me free!"

The two men looked at each other, and grinned. She looked into their eyes, examining them closely. They were poorly dressed in faded jeans that were ragged and patched, their short sleeve shirts unbuttoned and stained. They smelled badly and looked as if they hadn't shaved in days.

She knew they doubted her sincerity. In hindsight, she wished that she had made a more realistic offer. But the men hesitated which she saw was a positive sign.

"I have money! I own the nightclub where you kidnapped me from!" She pleaded with her eyes.

A rogue wave hit the side of the boat, rocking it side to side causing the wire cage to slide closer to the end of the boat and sending shivers up Nicole's spine.

Her kidnappers appeared to be Cuban and much younger than she had first thought. Without saying a word, they grabbed the wires around her body, one on each side, looked at each other, and grinned.

"Fuck you motha fuckers!" Peaches shouted.

Twinkle twinkle little star
how I wonder where you are
up above the world so high
like a diamond in the sky
Star light, star bright
first star I see tonight
I wish I may, I wish I might;
have the wish I wish tonight...

DON'T MISS!

THE WEE HOURS PART III: FLORIDA SNOW

BY W. D. BURNS

CHAPTER ONE
THE LOCAL NEWS

"Good morning Miami. Susan Lichtman of WTVJ reporting. Early this morning F.B.I. and D.E.A. agents raided the Heathen's clubhouses throughout central Florida arresting more than two hundred outlaw bikers. In Altamonte Springs, a house was raided and automatic weapons and hand grenades seized. Johnny Rowe and Richard Allen Doyle, members of the Argot outlaw biker gang were charged with federal firearms violations, murder, attempted murder, and conspiracy to commit murder. A gold Lincoln Towncar was seen leaving the residence a half hour before the pre-dawn raid. Let's go to Richard Bower, reporting live from the scene in Altamonte Springs. Richard, what can you tell us?"

"Susan, the raids stem from and ongoing war between the two biker gangs that have left thirteen dead. State and Federal agencies have joined forces to end the mayhem. Agencies throughout Florida have been told to arrest any biker wearing the Heathen's or Argot's patch."

"Thank you, Richard. WTVJ will continue updates as information is received. On the other side of the news, powerboat designer Don Aronow, the winner of the 1969 Bahamas 500, announced his company Apache Performance has reached an agreement to build powerful Catamarans for the U.S. Customs Service. The Dade County weather service reports blue skies today and tomorrow. Sunny, in the high 80's with possible showers towards late evening. It's a great day to spend at the beach. Pitch your umbrella in the sand and relax. Have a great day Miami. Susan Lichtman for WTVJ, Channel 4."

* * *

"We are forming a task force. I want anyone who is remotely associated with this investigation here to answer questions. That means every agency. The Argot motorcycle gang is believed to be responsible for several murders occurring in the State of Maryland. I want detectives from Maryland and Pennsylvania in the conference room at nine o'clock in the morning." Special Agent H. Thomas Moore barked.

Moore had been with the F.B.I. for 15 years, and he was a seasoned investigator graduating with honors after his 18-months of rigorous training at Quantico, Virginia. Every morning before breakfast, Moore dressed in a jogging suit or shorts and began his day with a five mile run. He stood six feet one, weighing a firm 185 pounds. He was clean cut and well groomed, his hair graying slightly around the ears.

"Yes, Sir!" F.B.I. Agent John Sweeny snapped. Always quick to please, Sweeny had been Moore's sidekick for the past five years. His attitude made up for his short stature.

"Also invite D.E.A. Agent Pete Elliot to the meeting." Moore added.

The first call was made to Detective Daniel Marks of the Baltimore City Homicide Division. Marks supplied the names of two known associates of the Argot motorcycle gang, Charlie and Nicole Redman. Charlie's current address was in Millersville, Maryland which was in the jurisdiction of the Anne Arundel County Sheriff's Department

The second call was placed to Detective Sergeant Hill of the Anne Arundel County Sheriff's Department.

A third call was placed to Detective Ralph Criswell of the City of Harrisburg, Pennsylvnia's Police Department.

The final call was to D.E.A. Agent Pete Elliot. Since he was assigned to the Orlando Office, there would be no need to do more than notify him of the meeting and request his participation.

F.B.I. Agent Sweeny made reservations at the Hilton Hotel in downtown Orlando, with separate rooms for Detectives Marks, Betty Crawford, Sergeant Hill, and Criswell. Within an hour, Special Agent Sweeny called to give them their flight itinerary, and reservations, They were already keenly aware of the meeting to be held at the F.B.I. Headquarters at 9 a.m. The detectives were in a quandary wondering why they were being to called the meeting.

* * *

After spending several hours in the drunk tank at the Orlando County Jail, Ramrod was banging on the steel bars shouting. "I know my Rights. I'm entitled to a phone call!"

One hour later, the jailer allowed him to make a five minute call. Ramrod called attorney Harold Glazer.

"You boys are making a lot of noise down there." Harold reported. The news of the biker wars had gone nationwide.

"The feds raided the house where we were staying early this morning. Bulldog and myself are charged with federal firearms violations, murder, attempted murder, and conspiracy to commit murder. We are scheduled to appear before a magistrate for a bond hearing at ten o'clock tomorrow morning. Is it possible for you to be there?"

"My license doesn't allow me to practice law outside of the state of Maryland. However, if you retain local counsel, the law allows me to act as co-counsel."

"I don't know any local attorneys and I'm only permitted one five minute call."

"Are you authorizing me to act on your behalf?"

"Of course."

"Good, I thought you might, so I've already made inquiries. I was referred to a local attorney, Harry Swogel. As we speak, my secretary is placing a call to his office."

"That's why you're the best, Harold. You are always thinking ahead. I'll see you in the morning."

"I'll be there." Harold promised.

Bulldog used his five minutes to call The Pink Pussycat. Charlotte answered on the first ring. "Hello."

"Hi Sugar. Your man used his five minute call to call an attorney." Bulldog grinned, looking at Ramrod for a reaction.

"Are you guys okay?" she asked. "Nobody has heard from Nicole. And, Charlie is still missing. I don't know what to do. When are visiting hours?"

"We're fine. Harold Glazer will be here in the morning for our bond hearing at ten o'clock along with a local attorney. This shit is driving me nuts. You will have to call the jail to find out what the visiting hours are. If you hear from Nicole, tell her that I love her."

"How sweet." Ramrod chuckled.

"Tell Ramrod that I said he's an asshole."

"C'mon guys." The jailer interrupted. "Playtime is over. You're being moved upstairs. Grab a blanket. Rolled up inside the blanket are linens, a bar of soap, and a towel. When the gates break at four o'clock, the showers are at the end of the hall. After you shower, you will be issued a fresh pair of coveralls and a clean towel. Any questions?"

"I specifically asked for a room with a view." Bulldog joked.

The cell-block housed twenty men, mostly black. There were two vacant bunks, at opposite ends of the cell-block. Ramrod and Bulldog made their beds, then sat off to themselves to discuss their situation.

"Did Harold mention a possibility of our being granted bail?" Bulldog asked in a whisper.

"Nope, but there's always a possibility." Ramrod grinned, thinking there was a better chance of eight inches of snow in Florida.

Both men were looking forward to a hot shower and a meal. When the gate opened, Ramrod and Bulldog followed the other men. As Bulldog lathered, a huge black man patted him on the ass and whispered in his ear, "Nice butt."

Bulldog grinned, then whispered in the big man's ear. "You would have a nice one too, if you kept the dicks out of it."

It was the start of a vicious brawl. It was pretty much a free for all, two against ten ending with a few black eyes and missing teeth, the floor of the shower covered in a spray of blood.

"Well, I guess there went any chance of our getting a bond." Ramrod snarled, as they were handcuffed and dragged off to the hole. Seeing the small glass window in the door, Ramrod chuckled. "But you're getting a room with a view."

ABOUT THE AUTHOR

William Daniel Burns was born in Lakeland, Florida. His family, and those who knew him in his early years called him "Danny." At an early age, he discovered his gift for conning people to get whatever he wanted. At the age of five, he convinced his best friend that two rusty nails and a piece of wood were from George 'Washington's rocking chair and they would someday be worth a whole lot more then his old shiny silver dollar.

When he was seven, his father moved the family to Baltimore, MD. It was a much tougher neighborhood. Danny learned to fight, and hustle. His parents divorced when he was twelve. His younger sister and older brother chose to stay with his mother. Danny chose to live with his father. They returned to live in Florida., and Danny changed his name to "Bill." His father remarried when he was thirteen. Bill quit school, and left home when he was fifteen. He married, and had two beautiful daughters by the age of seventeen - Tina Marie, and Kerri Ann. He was ill-prepared to handle the responsibility, and moved back to the mean streets of Baltimore, where he turned to crime as a means to support his family. The police made a game of that by telling him they rode around in marked cars and wore uniforms, then asked what does a criminal look like. Bill purchased a yellow panel truck and wrote THIEF WAGON across the back and sides in big black bold letters. The game ended with Bill being sent to prison.

Released from prison, he found his wife remarried and his daughters calling another man "daddy." Bill felt that he had nothing left to lose and devoted his life to crime!

Bill returned to federal prison twice. He furthered his education by obtaining his G.E.D., a degree in Commercial Art, and he has the equivalent of a two-year college Associates Degree. Bill has owned a number of successful businesses.

In 1988, Bill worked as an independent contractor for O's Auto Sales in Walbridge, Ohio. In 1991, while the owner vacationed in Florida, Bill was left in charge of the business. Several other guys also used the license, but they weren't registered to buy or sell vehicles at the auctions.

On May 29, 1991 Bill left with his girlfriend on a Florida vacation, returning June 8, 1991. A fire occurred at Adrian Auto Auction May 31, 1991, and a murder occurred in Northwood, OH on June 7, 1991. When questioned in regard to the murder, Bill accounted for his whereabouts for the entire vacation.

In 1993 Bill was charged with stolen vehicles in Monroe and Adrian, Michigan.

On the advice of two attorneys Bill pled guilty. At sentencing, he told the judge there was nothing anyone could do when they are signed, sealed, and delivered. That just because he signed the titles, it did not necessarily mean the vehicles were his!

Bill served his sentence, and in 1998, he was transferred to the halfway House in Monroe, Michigan. Ten days before his release, he was charged for the arson of Adrian Auto Auction. The prosecutor contended that his motive for the arson was to destroy incriminating evidence, the titles to the stolen vehicles. Bill filed three formal motions for discovery - none were complied with! He refused plea offers of 10 years, 5 years, and 2 years with credit for six months served. Bill was convicted, and sentenced to serve LIFE. He still maintains his innocence.

Bill is a strong supporter of prison reform. He wants to let the youth of today know that crime, drugs, and violence is not a "game." Bill thanks God for his love, insight, and guidance as he journeys through life. For more information on him, please contact him via www.jpay.com. He is inmate number #189577.

ORDER THE ENTIRE BAD ASS OUTLAW PUBLICATIONS LINEUP!

Bad Ass OutlawPublications

Mail:

Bad Ass Outlaw Publications
4216 Riverviwe Lane
Lorian, OH 44055

Name: _____

Address:_____

City/State:_____

Zip:_____

Quantity	Titles	Price	Total
_____	The Wee Hours	$12.95	_____
_____	The Wee Hours II: Peaches	$12.95	_____
_____	The Wee Hours III: Florida Snow	$12.95	_____

Add $3.95 for shipping and handling (Via Priority Mail) for
1 book, $5.95 for 2 books , $8.95 for 3-4 books, add $1.95
for each additional book.

Total: $_____
FORMS OF ACCEPTED PAYMENT: Certified or government
issued checks and Money Order, all mail in order takes 7-10
Business Days to be delivered.
Or, just order online at http://www.badassoutlawpublications.com!

www.ingramcontent.com/pod-product-compliance
Lightning Source LLC
Chambersburg PA
CBHW072229170626
46813CB00003B/1145